Death Spiral

Books by Janie Chodosh

The Faith Flores Science Mysteries
Death Spiral

Death Spiral

A Faith Flores Science Mystery

Janie Chodosh

An imprint of Poisoned Pen Press

Copyright © 2014 by

First Edition 2014

10 9 8 7 6 5 4 3 2 1

Library of Congress Catalog Card Number: 2014930262

ISBN: 9781929345007   Trade Paperback
      9781929345014   E-book

The Poisoned Pencil
An imprint of Poisoned Pen Press
6962 E. First Ave., Ste. 103
Scottsdale, AZ 85251
www.thepoisonedpencil.com
info@thepoisonedpencil.com

Printed in the United States of America

*In memory of Dorothy Kirschner, my grandmother,
a true Philadelphia fighter and activist*

Acknowledgments

I owe the deepest thanks to many people who have supported my writing of this book throughout its long and exciting journey. Thank you to Jennifer Owings Dewey with whom it all began many years ago on a Friday afternoon by a fire in an adobe house. I'd also like to thank the following talented writers, some of whom were sitting by that fire: Debra Auten, Jillian Brasch, Hope Cahill, Catherine Coulter, Nadine Donovan, Lizzie Foley, Karen Kraemer, Barbara Mayfield, Susan Rathjen, and Lyn Searfoss.

There are many people who read and consulted on this manuscript along the way and for whose valuable comments I am grateful: Eileen Robinson, Harold Underdown, Barbara Rogan, DP Lyle, Martha Alderson, Jamie Figueroa, Geron Spray, Susanna Space, Katharine Peters, and Carolyn Meyer.

Thank you especially to my wonderful editor, Ellen Larson. Her insightful comments, keen editorial eye, and answers to my every email and endless questions continue to be a gift. She has earned my deepest respect and admiration.

Additionally, I'd like to thank all the fine people at the Poisoned Pen Press who turned my manuscript into a real live book and who have made me feel so welcome as a new author.

Thank you also to the Genetics Science Learning Center at the University of Utah whose genetics web site fueled much of my research.

I'd like to truly thank Callum Bell, my wonderful husband, who helped create the time to actually write this book. Thank you also to Callum for sharing his wealth of experience as a scientist and for whittling down complex genetics into bite-sized chunks. I also owe a warm thank you to Isabella Berman-Chodosh whose endless enthusiasm continues to keep me smiling even when I stare at a blank page for far too long. And thank you to Liam Bell, my stepson, for believing in me as a writer.

Finally, my parents, Joan and Richard Chodosh, deserve special thanks. No matter what new adventure I've pursued or what dream I've had, they've supported my effort in every possible way.

The only good junkie is a dead junkie. They're at the bottom of everything. Down there with hookers and drunks. When a junkie dies, no one investigates. They call it an overdose and close the book.

I should know. My mom was one.

The day after my sixteenth birthday there she was, my mother, dead on the bathroom floor. Just out of the shower. Her hair still wet. I remember that. Thinking if her hair was wet, she couldn't be dead.

But she was dead, and just like that, the only thing left of my mother was her stuff. I called Aunt Theresa, then the cops. An officer poked around our apartment and scribbled a few notes. Heroin overdose was listed as the official cause of death. Of course. Mom was a junkie. What else would she die of? Everyone bought the story.

Everyone except me.

One

Six weeks since she died. Forty-two days since I left our cockroach-friendly walkup in West Philly and moved out to the Main Line with Aunt T. One thousand and eight hours since my thoughts were taken hostage, all available gray matter held at gunpoint by that day. By what really happened.

Sometimes for like ten seconds, twenty on a good day, I forget. For those few winks I'm like "Hey, life isn't so bad. I have my own room. Munchies in the fridge. TV." But then the thing is back. And I pick it open again. Let it bleed.

I'm in my new school, picking the scab, replaying the events of Mom's last day for the bazillionth time, nowhere near to occupying the same planet as the rest of the Haverford student body, the planet of perky blondes and brunettes where I'm the only girl slipping through the halls in combat boots and a thrift-store dress, when someone taps my shoulder.

"Hel-lo! Earth to Faith!"

I whirl around as if expecting, what—the Kensington strangler? It's just Anj of course, my one and only friend in this place, maybe in any place. She stands outside of the biology

3

room, her hazel eyes wide, a honey-colored ringlet sprung loose from her ponytail.

"Ohmigod," Anj pants. "New boy. Fresh meat. Just showed up today." She waggles her eyebrows. "You've been here four weeks now. Maybe you can offer to show him the ropes."

Before I can protest, she drags me through the door to sixth-period Bio and tilts her head toward the second row where a shaggy blond in serious need of a haircut is hunched over his desk listening to an iPod. I pass down the aisle and steal a quick peek at New Boy: t-shirt, jeans, skater-dude-slacker kind of vibe.

"Well?" Anj asks, nudging me in the ribs. "What do you think?"

I sink into my seat and let out the breath I didn't know I'd been holding. "Not interested," I murmur.

Anj smacks my shoulder, the one she practically dislocated when we met last August at a Judo class at the Y and got assigned as sparring partners. "Come on, Sweetpea, a little action would be good for you. You know—take your mind off stuff."

The bell rings. Mrs. Lopez, who's been teaching longer than I've been alive, steps to the front of the class holding a lipstick-stained Styrofoam coffee cup. "Class is starting!" she calls out over the noise, saving me from having to respond.

I try to rally the synaptic troops, try to bully my brain off Mom and focus instead on Biology, my favorite class.

"Okay," Mrs. Lopez says, setting her cup on a pile of books. She taps a pen against her palm and paces the room. "Today we start our end-of-term projects with a unit on genetic ethics." The use of the words *end of term* and *projects* in the same sentence provokes more than a few groans. Mrs. Lopez ignores the dissent and continues. "As you know, scientists are studying and learning about new genes all the time. This is the frontier; a scientific revolution. Who knows what will happen by the time you're my age. Designer babies? Gene therapy to change your height? Your eye color? What if I could tell you your complete genetic makeup?" Mrs. Lopez pauses and looks at Chrissy Mueller, slumped over her desk half asleep. "Chrissy, what if I could tell you that you have the Huntington's disease gene?"

"Huh?" Chrissy yawns, sitting up and rubbing her eyes.

A few kids laugh. Mrs. Lopez silences them with a look and a wave of her hand. "Carlos, what if you have the Alzheimer's gene? Jen, diabetes? Would you want to know? What if you have a gene that makes you prone to addiction, paranoia?"

My breath catches. It's not like I haven't spent half my life worrying I'm going to become a junkie like my mom, but still, the idea of an actual addiction gene that could be passed on to me as in *no refunds…all sales final* is definitely not something that's been on my radar.

"I'd want to know," I say, thinking my only hope is that if there is such a gene, maybe it's recessive and I only have one bad copy. Maybe I got a good copy from my asshole dad. He's never shown his face in my life, though, so getting anything good from him, even a gene, seems unlikely.

New Boy yanks out his earbuds, twists in his seat, and looks at me with the most ridiculously blue eyes I've ever seen. I'm thinking he might be kind of cute. But then, he speaks.

"No way, man. That's bullshit."

I wait for Mrs. Lopez to throw New Boy's ass out of class. She doesn't. Instead she says, "Okay, Jesse, save the language for the locker room, but tell us why you don't agree."

"It's obvious!" he says, thumping the table. "Haven't you ever heard of Big Brother? They're watching us, and they just want to watch us more."

Anj twirls her finger by her head, making the universal sign for crazy. Chrissy, fully awake now, snickers behind her hand. A few others stare.

New Boy doesn't notice. Either that or he doesn't care.

"Think about it," he goes on. "The wrong people get this information about you…you're screwed. Big corporate-suit types, you think they're going to give you health insurance if they know you're getting cancer? My mom couldn't get insurance because she took antidepressants. They put it on her record and called it a pre-existing condition." He snatches a pencil off the table and assaults the air with the point as he rants. "Depression's nothing. You want to talk about pre-existing conditions, try opening up your genome to a disease you don't even have yet, see what they do to you. 'Oh yeah, we'd love to hire you, but damn, looks like you're going to be getting a little nutty soon. See, it says it right here. You have the nut-case gene. We're going to hire someone else.'"

I stiffen my shoulders and narrow my eyes at New Boy. "Okay, Mr. Big-Brother's-Watching, how about this? What if by knowing you had some condition, you could avoid it? You could plan for your future. Not make so many mistakes. What if you could fix it before it even happened?"

"And what if it never happened?" he shoots back. "What if you never got the condition? You ever hear the saying 'Don't fix it if it isn't broken'?"

I thrust my hand into the pocket of my leather jacket and thumb the wheel of the empty Zippo lighter I keep hidden there. Her lighter. "What if one cigarette turns you into a nicotine addict because you have the addiction gene and you die of lung cancer?"

New Boy starts another, "What if…" but Mrs. Lopez cuts him off and asks if anyone else would like to add to the discussion. He ignores her and forges ahead with his know-it-all line of telling the world how it is. "Some things should be left alone, man. Genetically engineered plants, genetically engineered babies. That's sick stuff."

"What are you, some kind of fundamentalist?" Anj chides. "Are you on the God squad?"

Mrs. Lopez scolds Anj, tells her everyone has the right to their opinion whether or not you agree, but New Boy just shrugs, flips his hair out of his eyes, and keeps blabbering.

"It's nothing to do with religion or God. It's that I don't think we need to know everything, go about fixing all these things that work just fine. It's arrogant."

"You're arrogant," I snap. "I mean, what if you knew someone you loved was going to die? What if there was a genetic reason for it, and knowing that reason could keep them from dying? Hiding that information, now that's arrogant."

It's me and New Boy, facing off. Mrs. Lopez is saying something, but I'm not paying attention.

"So what, you live your life in fear?" he says. "What if you find out your kid's going to be retarded, or have one leg, brown eyes instead of blue? Huh? What do you do? Abort the kid until you get the right one?"

"Who's talking about abortion?" I shout.

And that's the last of the discussion for New Boy and me because Mrs. Lopez tells us to cool it, and we move on to a DVD about DNA and proteins or something. I couldn't care less.

I put my head on my desk and tune out for the rest of class.

I'm the first out of there when the bell rings, but Jerk-Off follows me to my locker. I turn to tell him to get lost, but he's got this big stupid grin on his face, like we're buds.

"You were so on in there," he says.

"Excuse me?"

"Totally awesome. You held your line, man, right in the face of fire." He makes this motion like he's shooting a gun, and now I think Anj is right. He is crazy. "Come on, lighten up. That was nothing personal back there."

"Yeah? Well, if it was nothing personal, then you should just keep your mouth shut because you don't know anything about me." I slam my locker and head down the hall.

"Hey! What's your name?" he calls after me.

I raise my middle finger and keep walking.

I can't deal with another class today, especially indoor field hockey or volleyball or whatever form of corporal punishment Mr. Griffith, our physical humiliation teacher, is planning to bestow on us for seventh period, so I blow off PE and head home to Aunt T's, my stomach in knots.

If genes are destiny, I'm screwed.

Two

When I arrive at Aunt T's place, a squat brick bungalow stubbornly planted between a pair of Dutch Colonials, I climb the steps to the front porch and wave at old Mrs. Dunnings who's out for a stroll with her lap dog, Rosy, a mutant creature that resembles an overgrown ferret. It's become a game of mine, a hobby, a suburban pastime to kill boredom and loneliness, to see if I can get Mrs. Dunnings to smile at me—or at least just say hi. As usual, Mrs. Dunnings ignores me. She calls to Rosy and shoots me the kind of look reserved for drug addicts or gangbangers or teenagers.

"Okay then, see you later. Have a nice day!" I call, prolonging my frivolous attempt at entertainment, and then turn back to the house.

It's then I see a faded paper, torn from a notebook, taped to the door. As I get closer, I see it's addressed to me. I snatch up the page and go into the house, straight to my room, where I drop onto my bed and unfold the note. My mouth goes dry when I see who it's from: Melinda Rivera, Mom's old junkie friend. I read the messy scrawl.

Faith

*I need to talk to you. It's about your mom. It's urgent.
Come see me 2750 N 5th past the liquor store.
Apartment 2E.*

Melinda

I crack my knuckles one at a time, starting with my right thumb—a nervous habit Anj says is going to give me premature arthritis. I haven't seen Melinda in what, five months? Not since she crashed at our place, stole two months' of waitress tips Mom had stashed in her underwear drawer, and vanished. I doubt she's tracking me down to apologize and pay me back. Maybe Melinda knows something. Yeah, right, I think, sliding the lighter from my pocket. More likely she's full of shit and wants money.

Great. Just what I need. Now that Melinda knows where I live, she'll be like a male dog that's found a bitch in heat. She'll stalk the place and never leave me alone. And it's not just cash she'll want. It's food, a place to crash. Aunt T will freak if some mangy stray starts showing up around here, begging for scraps.

I run my thumb over the lighter's wheel and inhale the familiar metallic smell of brass and petroleum as I reread the note. Maybe I can call Melinda and make up something to keep her away. (Contagious disease outbreak! We've been quarantined!) But there's no phone number, just an address for some dump in a part of North Philly full of abandoned rowhouses and shattered bottles of booze littering the sidewalks. Mom dragged me to those neighborhoods when she was desperate enough to go cruising for a fix. After she died, I swore I'd never go back.

I get up and flip on the light, hoping to chase away the nervous ache rooting in my gut, but my thoughts drag me into a dark tunnel. The brightest bulb couldn't illuminate what might be hiding in the gutters there. I don't know what to do with myself, so I plop onto my bed, fiddle with the lighter, and stare at the poster tacked to my wall, three guys wearing too much bling. Some hip-hop band I never heard of. Someone must've told Aunt T teenagers were into this stuff. I should get up and turn on the TV or raid the fridge or call Anj. But I just sit there, staring at the poster, listening to the clicking sound of the lighter over and over until there's a knock on my door.

"I'm home," Aunt T calls. "Can I come in?"

"One sec!" I shove the note under my pillow and grab a book. It's better for everyone if Aunt T doesn't know about Melinda. She has enough to deal with as it is, like pillaging her bank account to afford upkeep on her dead sister's teenage daughter when she was supposed to be saving up to buy a new car. How long can our cozy cohabitation last before she gets sick of dealing with another of her sister's messes and sends me packing? And then what? I lie back on my bed and pretend to be reading. "Come in!"

Aunt T walks into my room and sits at my desk. The stale smell of cigarette smoke mixed with overly sweet perfume clings to her clothes. She kicks off her clogs and massages her ankles, swollen from a long day on her feet as floor manager at the Sunrise Senior Living community. Her gold bangles jingle softly as they slide up her arm.

"Look what I found when I was cleaning out my desk at work today," she says. I sit up, and she hands me a small photograph.

I fight back tears as I study the image. Blond curls. Skin so pale you could trace the blue veins lining her temples. She's smiling and young, healthy and beautiful. Standing on a beach somewhere, toes buried in the sand, waving at the camera.

Mom hated having her picture taken. Except for the black-and-white strip taken of us in the photo booth at the mall, I hardly have any photos of her, but it's my mother, all right. It's her eyes, lit pale blue like a cloudless summer sky. Even at the end when she got those terrible scabs and lost all that weight, those eyes could pierce the night.

One thing I can say for certain—I did not inherit my mother's looks. Compared to her blue eyes and pale skin, I'm dark and loamy, built of earth. My eyes are the color of mud. My chestnut hair hangs limp and straight around my shoulders. And then there's my skin: I'm too brown to be white and too white to be brown. Sometimes I like to think I have Indian blood, that my father was Mayan or Cherokee. Iroquois, maybe. I can believe whatever I want since I never met him and I never want to.

Daddy dearest. Sperm donor, more like it. Married mom, knocked her up, then ditched. End of story. Not even a card or a note on my birthday. I gave up asking Mom about him around third grade because whenever I brought up the idea of a flesh-and-blood father, she'd get that faraway look, then go silent and reach for the bottle. Still, I've never stopped wondering if she exchanged her maiden name, Archer, for his name, Flores, because she loved the prick, or because she wanted to shed her identity and become someone new. I guess I'll never know.

I glance again at Mom's image. This time it's not sadness I feel, but anger. Fine by me. I'll take anger over sadness any day. Sadness is like when you're a kid and you think you can dig a hole to China, but once you start to dig you realize there's no end to the hole. It just goes deeper and deeper.

I hand back the picture.

Aunt T coaxes a blond wisp back into the mess of curls pinned to the top of her head and sighs. "Before things went bad."

Things going bad is my aunt's euphemism for *before your mother became a heroin addict.*

I turn to the bling trio and ball my hands into fists. "It's hard to remember how she looked before all those nasty scabs and that wheezing cough," I say, as if it's Aunt T's fault I can't remember. "She weighed what, like ninety pounds at the end?"

Aunt T scoffs. "Heroin will make you sick."

"But what if she didn't die of an overdose?" I turn back to Aunt T, desperate for her to at least admit to the possibility that Mom didn't fry her own brains, take her life, and leave me behind.

Aunt T lets the foot she'd been kneading drop to the floor and looks at me with weary green eyes. "We just saw the official death certificate two days ago. It said the cause of death was a heroin overdose, right?"

My heart squeezes, but I harden my face to stone and stare at the wall. "Yeah, well it's not like they do some detailed medical investigation on a person like her. Someone with a police record. Track marks on her arms. The cops couldn't give a shit." I close my eyes and remember that night. The sheet draped over Mom's body when the paramedic took her away. Some lower officer from the police station yawning as he wrote out his report. He already had his story. Nothing I could say would change his mind about the circumstances of her death. To the cops, my mother was just another dead junkie. I open my eyes again. "So what if there was something else?"

"They tested her blood and found morphine," she reminds me. "Not to mention the heroin in the bathroom. I know you think she was clean, but heroin addicts relapse. You know how she was."

I feel my aunt's tired frustration with my persistence, but I swallow back the lump in my throat and push on. "There might've been heroin, but there weren't any needles or spoons or any of that crap at home. She was acting totally normal. She wasn't getting high anymore."

An image breaks into my thoughts and I stop talking. I don't want to think about him, but just like every time he crashes my mental party, there he is, lurking in my mind's eye—the guy who came to our apartment the afternoon of Mom's death. I try to boot him from my thoughts, but the words he told her whisper in my ear: *You have a debt to pay.* What debt was he talking about? Was it about the heroin in the bathroom? I've seen my share of drug dealers, and I have to admit, this guy had the strung-out-emaciated-dealer vibe going. So does that mean Aunt T's right, and Mom was still using?

I force away this line of reasoning and keep talking. "She'd even started with her foreign stamps again. She'd just gotten one of the Eiffel Tower. She thought maybe we could go to Paris. She never thought about the future when she was getting high."

Aunt T's face clouds over. She crosses her foot back into her lap and starts kneading again, harder this time. "I understand that you don't want her death to have been her fault, but she died of an overdose. Don't go looking for problems when there aren't any."

"She was clean," I snap, but stop when I hear my voice. For an instant I wonder if it's Aunt T I'm trying to convince or myself. "It was something else that killed her. She didn't die a junkie." I flop onto my back and start flicking the lighter again.

Aunt T doesn't get all social worker and try and make me talk. She gets up to leave but hesitates at the door. "You can't bring her back, Faith, no matter how much you want to. Maybe it's time to let go of this and move forward."

Without another word, she slips out of my room.

I stare out the window into the fading light of the stark November sky, thinking sometimes you can't move forward until you look back.

Time to hunt down Melinda and see what she wants.

Three

I have no idea how long I've been lying down when I notice a brown bird on a branch of the oak outside my window. Its feathers are fluffed, its head drawn into its breast. It looks cold. Lonely.

The bird brings me right back to her. Watching birds was one of Mom's favorite things to do when she wasn't high. A week before she died we were sitting in the kitchen of our rental on a corner of West Philly ranked number eight in the *Philadelphia Weekly's* list of top-ten recreational drug spots in the city. We were gazing out the window past the loading platform of the Stop and Go at this one tree, a scraggly something-or-other struggling against the concrete and gas fumes to survive where Mom had managed to hang a bird feeder.

I was about to get up and dress for school when a flash of brilliant white caught my attention. There, perched on the feeder, was a bird the size of a robin. It was shaped like a robin, but instead of the usual robin colors, the bird was all white with pink eyes. Mom was looking at the bird too. Her eyes were teary. "An angel," she whispered.

Mom believed the bird was her guardian angel. That it would watch over her and carry her soul to heaven someday when she went. She was into stuff like that. Signs. Angels. That's why she named me Faith, I guess.

I didn't believe it. To hell with Faith. I Googled the white-feather, pink-eye bird when I got to school. I found out the bird had an albino mutation and that's all. No sign. No angel. Just a rare mistake of genetics. Mom wouldn't listen. In her mind the bird was an angel and that's all there was to it.

I blink away tears. Screw her birds and her angels. Screw her for giving me hope, for getting off junk only to refuse to see a doctor when she got sick. Screw her for dying and leaving this mess about what happened to her. Couldn't she at least have given me that—a normal, straightforward death, so I could have closure and move on?

I won't cry.

For sixteen years my life has been a matter of basic biology—adapt or die. Only the fittest survive.

The smell of curry lures me from my despair. While Mom was lucky if she didn't burn microwave popcorn, Aunt T can whip up a double-layer chocolate fudge birthday cake with her eyes closed. The cupboards, countertops, and fridge in Aunt T's place are an around-the-world culinary exploration for anyone brave enough to actually try something called wattle seed or fennel pollen or jicama root. I let my nose lead me from my room, down the hall, and toward the kitchen where Aunt T is standing at the stove in her stocking feet, working a frying pan with one hand, holding a glass of red wine in the other. Her boyfriend, Sam, still in work boots and Carhartts, stands beside her.

I stop by the door and study the domestic scene the way an anthropologist might study a foreign culture. The way he slips his arms around her waist and kisses the back of her neck. The way she slides out of his embrace with a girlish laugh and flits to the pantry. Like an anthropologist, I'm an outsider. This is a private ritual. I don't belong with this tribe.

I'm about to retreat to the refuge of my room when I hear Aunt T say something that keeps me rooted to the spot. I step into the shadow of the antique armoire where we keep Mom's ashes and listen.

"I tried to talk to her about her mother again," she says in a voice that carries all the ten-million things wrong with getting stuck with the job of child-rearing when the closest thing to a kid she's ever had was a cat.

"And?"

"And nothing. It's obvious how much she's hurting, but she won't talk about her feelings. The only thing she'll say about her mother is that she didn't die of an overdose."

"Give her time," Sam says. Like his personality, his tone is gentle. Not exactly what you'd expect from a firefighter who looks like he could bench a small car.

"She'll be eighteen in no time. And then she can do what she wants. How much time do I have? I'm not her parent."

"Why can't you be? Make it legal."

Aunt T lowers her voice and says something I can't hear. What did Sam mean, "Make it legal?" Is he suggesting Aunt T should adopt me? For a split second I hallucinate over what it would mean for Aunt T to become my parent and to have a permanent place to call home. No more eviction notices. No more fleeing the landlord in the middle of the night, our few possessions stuffed into the trunk of some friend's car. No more cold nights and broken promises. I shake away the feeling almost as quickly as I allowed it in. Why would Aunt T burden herself with such a thing?

I press my lips together and jam my hands in my pockets. What difference does a stupid legal document make anyway?

Once I'm eighteen, there's nothing holding me down. No reason to stick around here.

I start across the carpet toward my room. I've hardly taken two steps when I trip over Felix, a portly tabby with double cataracts and limited hearing. Felix makes his irritation known with a loud and somewhat terrifying hiss. My cover is blown. Aunt T and Sam step into the hall, and Sam flips on the light.

"Hey, Rock Star!" he says, using the nickname he coined the first time we met when he said I looked like Patti Smith from back in the day. "What's up?"

"Hey," I mumble. "I was just—"

"Dinner's almost ready," he interrupts, preserving my pride. We all know I was eavesdropping.

"I made curry," Aunt T adds, a hopeful expression on her face. "Your favorite."

"Yeah, I know." My stomach rumbles with the rich smell of spices simmering on the stove, but I remind myself of my outsider status and ignore my hunger. "Thanks anyway, but I'm going out. I'm meeting someone." I sweep my hair out of my eyes and flash a smile I hope passes for genuine.

"Is someone picking you up?" Aunt T asks, exchanging glances with Sam.

"Nah, I'm walking."

Aunt T opens her mouth to speak. I wait for her to call my bluff and insist I stay. "It's awfully cold," she says instead. "Why don't you let me drop you off? Better yet, I'll go with you and you can drive. You need those practice hours if you're going to apply for your license."

"Come on, I'm a city girl. I'm just going a few blocks. I'm used to walking. All that driving makes you soft." I laugh, hoping to depolarize the tension with light-hearted wit, but if laughter were food, mine would be filled with artificial ingredients. Nobody shares the chuckle.

Aunt T sighs. "Okay, if you say so." She moves to hug me, but my body tenses and she drops her arms.

I busy my hands with the lighter and look at my feet, wanting more than anything to feel my aunt's arms around me, but the barren wasteland Mom's death left inside of me is a roadside warning: *Caution! Unmarked obstacle ahead! Proceed at your own risk!* So instead of the hug, I say a quick good-bye, grab my coat, and dash out the door before I can change my mind.

I race down the steps two at a time and cross a patch of dormant grass to the driveway. It's freezing out, so I go for the shortcut, weaving through the backyards of the big houses on Orchard Street to get to Darby. I burrow into my leather jacket and shiver as I walk, wishing Mom and Aunt T could've picked a nice warm place like Florida to live instead of the glacial northeast. I mean living in hell would be better than this. At least it's warm there.

Once on the main drag, I pass the fast-food taco chain, then the fast-food chicken chain, the fast-food burger chain, and the other fast-food burger chain—greasy, while-you-wait, and cheap—the kinds of places Mom and I ate most meals. A feeling of loneliness and anger weighs me down as I think how Mom and I will never again sit in her car, me scarfing down bean-and-cheese-filled tortillas or greasy chicken nuggets, her drinking black coffee and ranting against the system, or telling me about some exotic place she'd take me someday. I didn't care that deep down I knew those dreams would never come true, because in those moments she wasn't drunk. She wasn't high or with some guy she'd met at a bar. In those moments she was mine.

I scurry past all the fast-food places, unable to face the memories, and instead go into the Wawa mini-mart to search for something to eat that's in an actual food group. I settle on a hotdog cooked in a bun. I'm slathering on the ketchup, wondering if ketchup counts as a vegetable, when someone taps my shoulder.

I turn and there he is, New Boy. He's holding an energy drink in one hand, his skateboard in the other.

"What's up?" he asks, grinning.

I shrug. "Nothing."

"Got the munchies?" He points his drink at my hotdog. "Good choice. Did you know Reagan wanted to classify ketchup as a vegetable so schools could serve it to poor kids instead of real vegetables?"

"Reagan?" I snort. "You weren't even alive when he was president."

He drops his skateboard and tugs at his jeans, which have sagged below his bony hips, so I can't help but notice the narrow blue band of his boxers.

"Yeah, well how about this—did you know that ketchup comes from a Chinese word that means brine of pickled fish?"

I bite off a piece of hotdog. "What, are you some kind of ketchup expert?"

"Nah, I just like random facts. Did you know that the first known contraceptive was crocodile dung?"

"Gross. You're making that up."

"No way. It's true. Or how about this: Dueling is legal in Paraguay as long as both people are blood donors."

I fold my arms across my chest. "Wow, you're right. You are random."

"So, what's your name? You do have a name, right?" he asks, stepping onto the skateboard and rocking from wheel to wheel. "Because before when I asked, all I got was the finger and only some sick parent would name their kid F-you."

"Faith," I say, laughing. "Even *my* mom wasn't *that* sick."

"Wasn't? Like she's not around anymore, or she wasn't that sick when you were born?"

This kid is sharp. Doesn't miss a thing. It doesn't hurt that he's slamming down an energy drink, and he's probably all hopped up on sugar and caffeine.

"First one. As in not around anymore. As in dead."

For the first time since I met Jeffrey or Jim, or whatever he's called, he looks serious, genuinely serious. I guess kids with dead mothers can really have an effect on a person.

"I didn't know, sorry," he says.

"You don't have to be sorry, and I don't want to talk about it. What's your name, anyway? I was so busy hating you before, I blocked it out."

"Jesse," he says, reaching out for a handshake. The gesture is cool in an old-fashioned, formal sort of way, and I offer my hand. "Just like Jesse James, the badass outlaw," he explains, pumping my hand until I think it's going to fall off. "Only my last name's Schneider, and I'm not such a badass."

"So Jesse Schneider, the not-such-a-badass, I'm guessing you're not from around here."

"Nope. Grew up in Philly."

An argument breaks out at the checkout counter. I turn to see a girl who looks about thirteen trying to convince the pimply faced boy at the register to let her buy beer. She flashes some plastic card in his face, and he tells her his three-year-old niece could make a better fake ID and threatens to call the police.

I throw my last bite of hotdog into the trash and roll my eyes. "Underage drinking, our local entertainment—that and watching the grass grow."

He laughs.

"No, really. I'm serious. If you like historical and quaint, then live it up. Otherwise you have no idea how boring life out here in suburbia is. I mean we're just half an hour from Philly, but we might as well be on another planet."

"Well then you just have to make your own fun." Jesse kicks off and skates up the aisle, belting out the lyrics to "We Built This City" by Starship.

Although my fondness for eighties music isn't something I readily admit, I love this song. It was number three on the top-ten playlist Mom and I used to rock out to when she was feeling silly. Jesse screeches to a halt an inch from my nose, and I realize I've been singing along under my breath.

I cough into my fist and look down.

Jesse doesn't seem to notice my embarrassment. He hops off his skateboard and slides into the plastic booth by the coffee maker and stale donuts.

I slide into the booth across from him, beneath an obnoxiously bright strip of overhead light that showcases every blackhead and blemish a girl might be trying to hide, thank you very much.

"So how did you end up in Haverford?" I ask, trying to discreetly cover the zit on my left cheek.

"It was Doc's idea," he says, pulling out a bag of peanuts from his pocket and offering me a handful.

"Doc?"

"Yeah, my dad, Doc squared actually. MD, PhD. Knows everything there is to know, serious overachiever." Jesse starts drumming the table. His fingers are long and I notice his nails are trimmed to a manicured perfection—funny, given his torn jeans and hair that appears to have been styled with a butcher knife.

"Doc decided the city wasn't good for me," Jesse continues, bringing the finger tapping to an abrupt halt and leaning forward on his elbows. "I knew all the spots in Philly, man. That's the thing, the city—it's alive. People are making art, music, love—you name it, it's happening. So I stopped going to school. The real education's on the streets. You ever spend much time downtown?"

"No," I lie. I've spent lots of time in seedy downtown places with Mom. Places kids aren't allowed. Somehow she'd always know someone who'd watch me. Someone who'd cover for her. But I don't know Jesse enough to tell him this stuff. And besides, I'm guessing there's another downtown he's talking about. Places with signs above the doors and daylight coming in through windows.

"Well, I'll take you. Show you some places you won't forget." Jesse's face goes pink when he says this and he stuffs a handful of peanuts into his mouth.

"So, I'm guessing Doc…your dad…your parents…whoever, freaked when they found out about you ditching school," I say, changing the subject.

"Went mental. Moved us out here in about one second. Doc already has my sister Stacy locked up at Harvard. According to plan, I'm next." Jesse stretches his arms above his head and yawns. "So, I guess I'm rotting here for a year and a half until I graduate. That's my story. What's yours?"

"Mine?" I wrap my fingers around the lighter and think about Marlee Gomez, my best friend at West Philly High until one day she came over and there was Mom, passed out on the couch, needle on the floor, the tie-off still stretched around her arm. Marlee and I could never really go back to being friends after that. I was no longer myself. I became the girl with the junkie mom.

It would feel good to actually have a conversation about these things. To actually open my mouth and tell someone my story, like how sometimes I feel so lonely I think I might die. Instead, I look down and say, "No story." I expect Jesse to push, to insist I tell him something, like why I live with my aunt instead of my dad. He doesn't.

"That's cool," he says. "Some other time."

"Yeah, sure, some other time," I mumble. "I have to go, anyway. It's getting late."

"Totally, man." He's out of his seat and passing the motor oils and air fresheners before I've even said good-bye. He stops at the trashy magazines by the door and turns back to me. "You on foot, or did you drive?"

"Foot," I say, joining him. "I don't have my license yet. What about you?"

He holds up his skateboard. "Got a car, but I rode." There's something edgy in his voice I hadn't heard before. "I'm kinda under house arrest. My parents don't exactly know I went out. Didn't want to make a lot of noise escaping. Which direction you heading?"

"Toward Orchard."

"Cool. Me too. I'll walk with you."

He doesn't wait for my approval. He just pulls out his iPod, offers me an earbud, and pushes through the door.

"Punk rock," he says when we're in the parking lot. "That's where it's at. Some people say punk is dead. No way, man. My bud, Clyde, he's a magician on the guitar. He plays in this band, Flesh. It's raw stuff. Pure energy. Check it out."

He hits play, and we listen to fast guitar and aggressive drumbeat as we walk, but being connected to one iPod by a set of earbuds while trying to synchronize our steps is like trying to perform the three-legged relay from elementary school track-and-field day. After stumbling forward to a few bars of Flesh, we take out the earbuds and instead of listening to music, we talk about it, or rather Jesse talks about it, and I listen. He's in the middle of an elaborate explanation on the political and economic roots of England's punk scene when he stops in front of a two-story stone Colonial with an expansive front porch and detached garage and breaks from his dissertation.

"This is my pad," he says, "but I could walk you home. I'm not tired, and I don't have anything better to do."

Instantly the wall goes up. I reach for the lighter. Showing someone where you live is what friends do, good friends. I haven't even shown Anj where I live. Not to mention I've never once set foot in her place. Every time she's suggested we do the normal chilling-at-home thing, I've made an excuse. Never let her in too close.

"Nah, I'm good," I say, stepping off the sidewalk onto the empty street.

I slip into the darkness before New Boy can say another word.

Four

Friday morning at school when I get to my locker, Anj, fashion princess extraordinaire, is waiting for me, wearing a t-shirt featuring a cartoon carrot lifting a barbell beneath a logo that says *Veggie Power*.

"What's up with the shirt?" I say, lifting my eyebrows.

Instead of explaining why she's traded in vintage cashmere for a one-size-fits-all tee with a picture of a talking vegetable, she winks and says, "I heard about your hot date."

"What date?" I open my locker and take out my books for first period. English with Laz, short for Lazzio, as in Mr. Lazzio. I remember now I was supposed to finish *For Whom the Bell Tolls*, but last night when I got Melinda's note I forgot all about it, so I guess I'm busted.

"So?" Anj says with a coy smile. "Tell me about it."

"God, you're like a dog on a bone. Drop it. There's nothing to tell."

"Oh, I see, it's a secret."

"Anj, come on, get off it." I kick my locker closed. "I didn't have a date."

Anj cocks her head and her eyes widen. "Then why did Jennie Potter say she saw you nestled into a cozy little booth at the Wawa last night with Jesse what's his name?"

"Schneider, his last name's Schneider, and we weren't nestled."

"Aha! But you were there." She claps her hands and sounds absolutely delighted with herself. "You admit it! Jennie was right. She wasn't positive it was you."

I roll my eyes at Anj and remember the first Judo class during my two-week stay with Aunt T last summer. When Anj strolled into the studio, I took one look at her perky ringlets, pearl necklace, and peace-sign tie-dye and figured I'd kick this upper-class hippy-wannabe's ass.

Kung Fu chick took me down in about two seconds.

Anj didn't care about my five silver hoops, black nail polish, and grimace. Maybe she felt guilty about nearly breaking my back, but at the end of class, she said she needed new jeans and invited me to go shopping. I had nothing better to do, so I said yes, figuring I'd tag along as she checked out the racks of Macy's or J Crew at the Suburban Square Shopping Center. Maybe I'd even scrounge enough change from the bottom of my gym bag for a Frappuccino. Anj skipped the whole mall scene, though, and drove us straight to The Attic Thrift Shop in Broomall, then to Take Two in Ardmore where we discovered a joint love for gaudy costume jewelry (her pearls—overstock. com, $9.99), Wonder Woman memorabilia, anything purple, Ben and Jerry's New York Super Fudge Chunk, and *Gone with the Wind*.

By the end of the day Anj had became a proton to my electron. Her positive can-do attitude attracted my negative force, and soon we were orbiting each other's worlds, transmitting our relationship via Internet radio waves, and becoming friends without even realizing it was happening.

I stuff Hemingway into my bag and drape an arm around Anj's shoulder. "Look, Anj. You might be my one and only friend in this entire school, maybe in the entire world, but sometimes you're a real pain in the ass."

"I do my best." She pecks my cheek. "So?"

"So nothing. I went to the Wawa to grab something to eat and I bumped into Jesse. He was all hopped up on caffeine and I shared some peanuts with him. There. That's it. Satisfied?"

"Peanuts, how romantic. Sounds like a real Prince Charming."

We both laugh because at that moment Prince Charming himself comes barreling down the hall in his skinny jeans, black Converse high tops, and t-shirt silkscreened with the word *Flesh* in big letters across his chest.

"Hey, what's up?" Jesse grinds to a halt in front of us, taking out his earbuds and dropping them around his neck. The music's still playing, and I hear the unmistakable sneer of Johnny Rotten belting out "God Save the Queen."

"Did you get busted last night?" I ask over the thrashing drums and bass guitar.

Jesse turns off the Sex Pistols. "Nah, Doc was locked in his office, and Mom…" His voice trails off. "Let's just say nobody heard me come in."

"Well, I'll leave you two lovebirds alone," Anj says, slipping out from under my arm. "Three's a crowd."

Before I can punch her out cold, Anj skips off down the hall and joins up with Tara Henderson and her gang of socially conscious friends who are currently organizing a campaign called Happy Cows to raise awareness about factory farming. I'm sure Anj knows nothing about cows and hasn't once thought about where the plastic-wrapped grocery store meat comes from, but she's got the kind of personality that fits in anywhere. I'm betting within days she'll be lead vegan heading up the campaign for animal rights.

I shake my head as I watch her leave. "Sorry about that. Anj is really into setting me up. She thinks I need a boyfriend."

Jesse leans against my locker, arms folded across his chest like he's the king of cool and the question means nothing to him. "So, you don't have a boyfriend then?"

"No, and I'm not looking for one." I hoist my bag onto my shoulder and change the subject. "What English class are you taking?"

"Lazzio, first period." He grabs a well-worn paperback from his back pocket and flashes the title. *For Whom the Bell Tolls.* "Great book. I've read it three times. Hemingway's the man. You like his stuff?"

I shrug. "It's okay. I like Fitzgerald more."

Someone bumps into me. For the first time since meeting up with Jesse, I look around and realize it's morning rush hour. The halls are bloated with students completing last-minute locker checks and urgent social obligations before the bell rings.

"Well, see you later, then," I say, setting off toward homeroom.

Jesse doesn't give up so easily. "Ernest Hemingway," he says, trotting along beside me. "Born in Oak Park, Illinois. Won the Nobel Prize in 1954." He weaves around a herd of cheerleaders without breaking from his speech. "Seven novels, six collections of short stories, and two nonfiction books published before he died. And three novels, four collections of short stories, and three nonfiction books after he committed suicide in 1961."

I stop outside my homeroom and plant a hand on my hip. "And I suppose you know his middle name too?"

"Miller," he answers, grinning.

"What do you do, spend all your free time looking up this stuff so you can impress girls or something?"

"No, I'm just determined. Or compulsive. Once I start something, I can't stop until I know everything about it. Like did you know—?"

"No, I don't, and right now I don't want to. Tell me about *For Whom the Bell Tolls*. We have about three minutes before homeroom, and I didn't finish it."

Jesse tells me enough about how the book ends so I can answer today's essay question without getting an F. When it's time for English, I do my work and answer the question, but when Laz starts his lecture, my mind wanders.

I look at Jesse, or rather I look at the back of his head, because he's sitting in the front row debating Laz. I look at the other guys in class, too. Most of the guys at Haverford spend all their time trying to impress each other, bragging about how much they drank, how many points they scored at the game, how many girls they slept with, and who's easiest to get into bed. It's a total drag, like the date I went on at the end of the summer with Bruce Washington. Anj set it up. If I had to listen to Bruce talk about himself another second, I would've screamed. And then he tried to put his hand up my shirt. I kneed him in the balls, and the date was over.

It's not like I want a boyfriend anyway. Mom provided enough shitty examples to slow the whole hormone-sex-drive thing way the hell down. Mom was as addicted to losers as she was to heroin. Frank. Joe. Bob. Didn't matter. Different name, same guy.

Those guys were always hanging around our house, hiding in the shadows like spiders. When I needed to pee or get some water in the middle of the night, I'd wander out of my room in a t-shirt and boxers. More than once I'd found one of those boyfriends stoned on the couch with a cop show rerun playing on TV and a look in his eyes that made the mere act of being a girl feel dirty. So I learned when to stay in my room. When to lock the door. And to wear sweats to bed even in summer. Just in case.

I look at Jesse again, more like listen, since he's holding court now. "My dad's great uncle's friend had a sister who lived in Key West and knew Hemingway," he tells the class.

"Dude!" Jason Wallace, a bleary-eyed slacker who, according to Anj, was voted class clown two years running, shouts. "That, like, practically makes you Hemingway's best friend!"

Even Laz laughs.

Jesse starts to say something else, but the bell rings, cutting off the finale of his one-man show. Books slam shut. Chairs scrape the floor. Cell phones come out. Jesse follows me out the door and squeezes through the halls next to me.

"That was some act you put on in there," I say, barely avoiding a girl who's simultaneously talking to her friend, texting, and trying to dig something out of her pocket.

"Yeah, well, you have to liven things up, right? Otherwise it gets dull. 'Hemingway lived in Key West in the 1930s...'" he drones, holding his arms out in front of him zombie style. We reach the stairs and he stops. "I'm heading up for Pre-Calc. What about you?"

"History," I mutter, avoiding Jesse's eyes because having History next means my math is lowly Algebra instead of Pre-Calc.

Pre-Calc is the math I should be taking. I mean I could be taking it. I'm smart enough and always have been, especially at math, because whenever life got too chaotic I went for the books—the math books—where the problems had answers that I could solve. But because of Mom and the fact she could never hold a job for more than a few months at a time, we moved around a lot. New places meant new schools. Between four high schools, lost transcripts, starting and stopping mid-year, I've repeated Algebra like three times.

Jesse doesn't question my math status. He reaches out for a parting hug at exactly the second I lift my hand to wave. The end result is I poke him in the eye. I stammer to say something, but Jesse makes a joke of it. He pretends to poke my eye, and that's our good-bye: A see-you-later and an eye-poke.

I travel the rest of the hall solo, a voyeur, taking in all the sordid happenings of high school life outside the classroom: Chip Walker—*Mr. Duuuuude-I'm-So-Wasted*—gropes a girl who turns around and slaps him in the face. A knuckle-dragging Neanderthal in a football jersey sticks out his foot and trips a small Indian-looking kid, causing the kid to tumble to the ground and his books and papers to go flying.

"Did you see that?" Neanderthal laughs, punching his friend, Cro-Magnon, in the shoulder.

Cro-Magnon yuks it up with his buddy. "Check this out." He bends down and scoops up a bunch of the kid's papers from the floor.

"Thanks," the kid says, standing and reaching for the papers.

Cro-Magnon waves the papers above his head, so the kid has to stand on his tiptoes and twist and twirl like a trained circus dog to reach them. "Not so fast little guy," he says. "I have a joke for you first. If you know the answer, I'll give you back your stuff. What do you get when you cross an Indian with a—"

"Leave him alone," I blurt, stepping out of the crowd and squaring off with Cro-Magnon.

Cro-Magnon looks at me, his frog eyes bulging, and keeps the paper in the air. Neanderthal looks ready to turn my face to pulp. Even though I'm tall, I'm a dwarf compared to these two. These guys are big. Meat and potatoes big.

I should save my ass and shut up, but I've never been good at keeping my mouth shut. "I guess it must be hard to find someone your own size to pick on. Not many guys around here have taken as many steroids as you."

"Go fuck yourself," Neanderthal says, curling his hand into a fist and taking a step toward me.

"Try it and I'll—"

"You'll what?" He laughs. "Grab your broomstick and wand and turn me into a toad?"

I look around at the crowd that's gathered and feel my confidence wane. I won't back down, though. This I know from experience: *Look tough and act tough.* It's the name of the game. If you don't show your fear enough times, you actually start to believe you don't have any.

"No," I say, lifting one foot and showing him my Operation Desert Storm shit kickers. "I'll shove my boot up your butt and rip you a new asshole."

For a second nobody says anything, but then Cro-Magnon pulls his friend away from me and says, "Leave her alone. She's just some dyke. She's not worth it."

Cro-Magnon drops the papers, and he and Neanderthal laugh and bump fists and male bond over the brilliance of their final diss. That's it. The little show is over. I help the kid pick up his stuff, and I move on to history class where I find Anj hunched over her desk, working on our project, "Rediscovering Columbus," to show the negative impact of first contact on indigenous people, worth sixty percent of our grade for the term.

"We need to do more for this if we're going to get an A," she says without looking up when I reach her desk.

I stand towering above her. "More?"

"Maybe we could have a bake sale of First People's traditional foods. You know, show what it was like before Burger King?"

"But the project's due in less than two weeks. Isn't our PowerPoint presentation enough? I mean we've already edited, what, seventy-five slides?"

"Or we could put on a benefit concert for indigenous people's rights," she goes on, ignoring me completely. "Or make a digital movie reenacting Columbus' arrival. Wait! I've got it!" She perks up and beams at me. "We can each learn an Arawakan language! We'll decide when we meet next Tuesday. Don't forget. The library before school. The earlier the better."

"Anj," I say, slapping her desk, causing her to jump and her pencil to roll to the floor. "I think you're getting a little out of control on this thing. I mean it's a big deal, but not *that* big of a deal."

Anj shoots me a look and doesn't answer. I notice, though, that she exchanges glances with Duncan, her ginger-haired boyfriend, here on the foreign exchange program from Scotland.

"Whatever," I shrug, narrowing my eyes at Duncan. "It's your life. But I'm not learning to speak a new language in like ten days."

———

The rest of the day passes quickly and soon it's seventh period. On Fridays, I have seventh free, so I pack my books to head home. I'm just outside the front door when Jesse nearly runs me over with his skateboard. His hair is doing a good job of covering his eyes, and I'm wondering if there shouldn't be some kind of law against skateboarding blind.

"Finally. There you are," he says, sounding all annoyed like he's been waiting a really long time for some rendezvous we'd planned.

I burrow into my turtleneck and shiver. "Don't you have someplace to be? Like maybe a class?"

"Skipped," he says, as the front door opens and Mr. Torley, the drama teacher, comes out with lead thespian Max Browner, who's unabashedly practicing his Romeo for an upcoming school production: *But soft! What light through yonder window breaks?*

"On what, your like second day of school?" I say, resisting the urge to answer Romeo's declaration of love for Juliet— *Romeo, Romeo, Wherefore art thou Romeo?* "What will Doc say?"

"Doc won't know."

I pull an apple from my bag. "Aren't you worried about failing?"

"Nope. I'm not going to fail."

"How do you know?"

"I'll make up the work later. Always do." He tilts his head toward a mountain of books lying on the steps, which I assume is the work to be made up later and then some. "Hey, I have an idea." Jesse starts skateboarding again, rolling back and forth along the top step. "I'm going to the city tomorrow to hang. Want to come? I could show you some places."

I bite into my apple. "I thought you were under house arrest."

"Time off for good behavior. I get the day in Philly as long as I promise to get all my work done, be a good boy, and be back by ten."

"And do you promise?" I tease as he glides past me. It's hard to talk to a moving target.

"Depends."

"On what?"

He stops in front of me and raises his eyebrows. "On you. Are you going to be a good girl?"

I bat my eyelashes and clutch my hand to my chest, pretending to swoon. "Are you flirting with me?"

"Most definitely. So, is it a deal?"

I don't answer. I look toward a stand of tall poplar trees, their naked limbs crowded with a flock of noisy blackbirds. Tomorrow is Saturday. The day I'm going to see Melinda. I'm not about to take skater boy with me on that mission. He'll want the scoop on everything, like how I know Melinda. That means telling him about Mom, and that topic is off limits.

I take another bite of my apple, but it tastes mealy now. I toss the fruit to the frozen grass for the birds to peck, then close my eyes. Once you start getting personal, things change. Your heart opens and it hurts that much more when your friend disses you. Or you have to switch schools again. Or your mom can't make rent and you move to a place where you can't keep your new dog. Or someone gets sick. Walks out of your life. Dies.

Anj is the one person where my rule gets fuzzy. Last summer when Mom packed me off to Aunt T's, I cracked. Two weeks away from Mom usually spelled disaster when I got back. No big deal if you didn't mind coming home to the smell of puke, beer, and cigarettes, and the occasional furry, four-legged creature that you absolutely did not purchase at the pet store scurrying around in dark corners. I needed some-one to talk to. Someone my age. So when I met Anj, I gave her the cheater notes on my life, the chapter overview, but I left out the details, the parts where I actually told her how I felt.

I open my eyes and look back at Jesse, who's now sitting on his skateboard, a math book open on his lap, talking to himself as he tries to solve a problem. I have to admit, there's something about his in-your-face, take-it-or-leave-it attitude that I like, and his looks don't suck either.

It wouldn't kill me to spend a couple hours with him in the morning. I'm going anyway. Might as well try and have some fun, and like Anj said, take my mind off stuff. We'll have a good time, and then I'll bail early and see Melinda on my own.

"Fine," I say, "I'll go, but only for a while. I have something to do and I'm taking off early to do it, and don't even think about coming because you're not."

"Sounds mysterious." He jumps up and flashes a smile. "I like mysteries."

I don't return the smile. Instead I say, "You'd better get home, Harvard boy. It looks like you have some work to do."

"I'll pick you up at nine."

"Fine."

"Fine," he agrees, still smiling.

Now would be the time for a "later" or a "see ya" or whatever lingo kids like him use, but Jesse doesn't move. He stands there like Mr. Pizza Delivery Guy waiting for a tip

"Is there a problem?" I say a bit too defensively.

"Just a small one."

Great. I've known the kid one day and already there's a problem. Screw it. I don't need this. I don't need Jesse. I don't need anyone.

I'm about to leave when he says, "I don't know where you live."

"What?"

"Where you live. You know—your address? It usually starts with a number and ends with a street name."

"Oh," I say, feeling myself blush and hating myself for it, but before I can change my mind, I spew Aunt T's address. Then for the second time I turn to leave.

"Wait!" Jesse calls after me. "Aren't you going to poke me in the eye?"

I turn back around. "Nah. We have plenty of time for that tomorrow."

"Cool," he says, grinning. "It's always good to have something to look forward to."

Five

At nine Saturday morning, I've just slipped on my leather jacket when there's a knock on the front door, drumming to be more precise. I fling open the door and there's Jesse, hand extended, mid knock. "'Brown Sugar.' Rolling Stones, '71," he says.

"Huh?"

"The tune I was knocking. Recognize it? Classic stuff." He doesn't wait for my answer. "Nice pad. Ready?"

I try to slip out and spare the introductions, but Aunt T is hovering behind me. "Not so fast," she says, leading Jesse by the arm into the living room and giving him a serious once over, not even trying to hide the fact of her assessment.

I try to see Jesse through my aunt's eyes and imagine what she's thinking with his orange pom-pom ski hat, oversized flannel shirt, unlaced Converses, and torn jeans looking like he just robbed a Goodwill store. But there's something soft about Jesse, too, something honest in his indigo eyes that always seem to be looking behind what you're saying for something deeper. I'm sure Aunt T will see it.

Once she's completed her visual assessment, Aunt T begins the oral interrogation. Jesse answers each question with a polite yes or no ma'am. I guess he passes the test because Aunt T smiles at him, reminds me to keep my phone on in case she needs to talk to me, and we're off.

Jesse's car is a two-door hatchback in a nice shade of rust, and only the driver's side door opens.

"Nice car," I say as I wriggle over the gearshift to the passenger seat.

"Thanks, I bought it last month." He runs his hand over the steering wheel, completely missing my sarcasm. "Three hundred and sixty bucks. Best money I ever spent."

Something sharp pokes my thigh. I scoot onto one butt cheek and try to brush whatever it is off the seat, but I realize it *is* the seat. Two springs are sticking out, angling straight into my hamstring.

"Doc tried to buy me off," Jesse continues as I contort myself away from the rusty coils. "A new car if I made honor roll. Honor roll's easy, but I wasn't about to be bought off like a politician, so I got this baby instead." He turns the key. There's a click and then nothing.

"Cool," I say, trying to keep a straight face. "Good choice."

He shoots me a look and turns the key again. Still nothing.

"Maybe we'd better take the train," he says, when after the third try the engine shudders to life and the car hiccups down the road, barely clinging to life. "There's a ten o'clock that'll take us to Thirtieth. We can walk from there."

I agree, and he turns from the freeway and heads toward the train station.

The CD player's not working and there weren't even iPods in the seventies, or whenever this car was built, so Jesse scans the radio as he drives. He settles on something with a lot of clanging dissonance, and I'm not allowed to talk while he listens. Not that I could talk even if I wanted to since Jesse seems to think music has to be played at ear-splitting decibels to be enjoyed.

When the song ends, I turn down the volume and kick my feet on the dash. "You get accepted a year early to Harvard yet?"

Jesse doesn't take his eyes off the road, and he doesn't answer. For a second I think he didn't hear my question and I'm about to ask again when he says, "I was thinking of becoming a hippie and starting a commune instead." His voice is flat, and I'm not sure if he's kidding. I try to picture Jesse with long flowing hair, a bong, and a guitar, but then he laughs and says, "Let's not ruin the day and talk about college," and he turns the music back up.

I push Jesse's hand off the dial and take over the radio, scanning stations until I come to one playing classic Dylan. It's not the whole retro-1960s-protest-counterculture thing that makes me choose this station. It's that Bob Dylan reminds me of Mom. I learned to judge Mom's condition by the CDs she played. Velvet Underground if she was high, but not too high. The Jesus and Mary Chain when she was totally gone. Joni Mitchell for nostalgia. Bob Dylan for just about everything else. Neither Jesse nor I talk as we listen to Bob wail the lyrics to "Mr. Tambourine Man."

A lump forms in my throat as I lose myself in memory. *Dylan's on the radio. Mom's perched on the windowsill staring out at something only she can see. I stand at the edge of the room in Dora pajamas, even though I'm nine and too old for Dora. More than anything I want Mom to notice the hour and put me to bed. She doesn't notice. She's a million miles away. I back out of the room, my footsteps lost to the music, as if I hadn't been there at all.*

That was the beginning of life in the heroin era.

I lean my head against the window and watch the haze of picket-fenced homes blur past, then the new community center, a city park where a pack of toddlers chases after a balloon, mothers at their heels.

How did it happen? I wonder for the zillionth time. Was it at a party? Did Mom just say what the hell and stick a needle in her arm? And then some addiction gene kicked in and that was it, she was hooked?

Not that life before heroin was exactly a picnic. Mom drank too much, ran around with too many men, and she wasn't a stranger to pills—but she was alive. Spontaneous. Passionate. She'd wake me up in the middle of a summer night and drag me to the edge of the Schuylkill River to walk the trails in the rain. She loved to sit by the bronze lion in Rittenhouse Square and people watch, or go to the art museum and admire the Picassos. She'd talk to me about big things that were wrong with the world, things I was too young to understand, and when those things got to be too much, she'd retreat into her head and seal herself off in silence. Then the drinking would begin, the men, the pills.

Too sensitive for this world, that's what Aunt T once said. Bullshit. She could've done something with all that sensitivity. She could've worked to make the world better instead of throwing it all away.

A terrible emptiness settles into my chest, but I do what I always do when I feel this way—clamp off all emotion. Only when I'm sufficiently numb do I open my eyes.

Jesse, who's been lost to some music-induced trance, turns off the tunes.

"We're here. Ten minutes until our train." He starts to tell me something else, but a glance in my direction and he blinks back a look of surprise. "You okay?"

"Sure," I lie, digging up a smile. "Let's go."

———

The train ride is uneventful, and by the time we're downtown at the Thirtieth Street station, my feelings don't exist at all. We cross the platform and cruise through the central hall gleaming with a marble floor, high ceilings, and bronze statues. The place screams with the sound of trains and announcements. People scurry around like worker ants. We pass the food court, and soon we're out on the traffic-clogged congestion of Market Street. We head east under an overpass and dart along the busy roads, passing bars and hotels, metallic skyscrapers, and boutiquey shops with windows of politically correct, racially diverse, fashionably anorexic mannequins. A couple places look kind of hip and I wouldn't mind stopping, but Jesse's on a serious mission and window shopping isn't on his agenda.

"Okay, I could use a rest," I say after we've sprinted like a hundred blocks without stopping. "Is this the fun part, or is that coming later?"

"God, I'm such a lame ass," Jesse says, hitting his forehead. "I wasn't thinking. I get so focused on what I'm doing some-times—let's stop somewhere and get something to drink. Want to? This isn't where I hang, so I don't know what's around."

We find a coffee shop, an artsy kind of place where the amateur paintings on the walls are for sale and red velvet couches take the place of chairs. I've just managed to arrange myself on an overly cushioned loveseat without spilling any coffee when Jesse snaps a picture of me with his phone.

"Sorry," he says when I scowl. "I've been wanting to do that since I met you. You have a really interesting face."

"Interesting?" I ask, unsure if this is a compliment.

"Yeah, well." His cheeks go red, and he declares war on the napkin in his hand. "Pretty."

Jesse turns the screen to me. For a second I like what I see. It's a different me, someone softer, but almost instantly I recoil, feeling anxious and far too exposed, like I just arrived at school in my underwear.

"Wow. Phone photography as art. Who would've thought?" I say, making light of my discomfort. "Have you invaded anyone else's privacy with that thing?"

"If you mean have I taken other photos, the answer is yes." He leans in close to me and scrolls through what must be dozens of portraits.

"Hang on, who was that?" I ask when he passes a picture of a sexy blond girl with misty green eyes, her lips parted just so, as if blowing a kiss.

"Tia."

"Who's Tia?"

He glances at the picture and sighs. "That's a complicated question."

"Why? Is she an alien or something?"

"No," he says, pocketing the phone.

I wait for him to elaborate. "Okay, I see. You're going to make this hard," I say when he doesn't. "So, is she your girlfriend?"

He tears off a piece of pastry and stuffs it in his mouth. I listen to the French R&B song being pumped through the coffee shop speakers while he takes his time in deep, contemplative mastication.

"God, Jesse, you'd think I'd just asked you to explain quantum mechanics. Here's how it goes. You kiss. You go on dates. Maybe you have sex, I don't know. That makes her your girlfriend." I slump into the couch and kick my feet onto the coffee table with a loud thud. I have no reason to brood. This isn't a date. Jesse and I are just friends. Isn't that my mantra, the "just friends" rule? But it bugs me that suddenly New Boy's gone all distant and weird on me. "So, ring any bells? Is she your girlfriend?"

He washes down his pastry with a swig of coffee and finally gets around to answering. "No, Tia's not my girlfriend, but she's the girl everybody expects me to date." Then, just like that, he changes the subject. "What about you? You said you don't have a boyfriend. Why not?" He slips a hand onto my knee. "You're beautiful. Guys must ask you out all the time."

A torrent of warmth rushes from my belly to my thighs, but my brain runs interference, and I brush away his hand before I lose myself to the feeling. No way am I going to snuggle up and get close to Jesse—or anyone for that matter. Closeness is just pain waiting to happen. Love and hurt. Opposite sides of the same coin. Like every dude I watched walk into Mom's life and out again. Sometimes it took days, sometimes weeks, but in the end every one of those so-called loves took what they wanted and left. No thanks. I'm doing just fine on my own.

"Well?" he asks again. "Why don't you have a boyfriend?"

I shrug. "I just don't."

"Okay. Fine. How about this? Truth or dare. I go first." Before I can even agree to play, he fires off the first question. "What are you afraid of?"

"Alien invasion," I say, hoping to fill the achy void between desire and fear with a joke. "My turn. What do you want to do after you graduate?"

"Study photography." He pulls his phone back out of his pocket and snaps another picture of me. "But unfortunately, Doc puts picture-taking in the same category as quilting or doing bonsai. Things you do for fun. Not for real. My turn again. Are you a virgin?"

I punch him in the shoulder. "Pass."

"No way. Total violation of the rules. No passing."

"Too bad. Personal information. Not telling."

The stupidest night of my life plays its little movie in my head. *There's a boy I like. I think he likes me too. Mom's out, so I invite him over. After one night in the sack it turns out he likes Mary just as much as he likes me. And Jamie. And Chloe. And Elsbeth. And Marta.* I pull the plug to the projector. "What about you?"

He flashes a mischievous smile. "Depends how you define virgin." I don't have a chance to get him to elaborate before he's on to the next question. "What do you want to be when you're older?"

"A vampire. What's the most embarrassing thing that's ever happened to you?"

"I walked in on my parents having sex. What's a secret fantasy you have?"

"To be a weatherman on TV."

I hide each of my answers behind a wall of humor, and soon we've drained our coffees and exhausted the well of truth or dare. We leave the coffee shop and go back to our journey through the city. The energy buzzing between us pushes away the other worries I have about the day. I walk next to Jesse not thinking of Melinda or the note or Mom, but of his hand grazing my hip, the smell of coffee on his breath, the blueness of his eyes.

We travel half the city as far as I can tell when all of a sudden we stop. Just like that. I look around and wonder what we're waiting for because it doesn't seem like we're exactly anywhere. I raise my eyebrows at Jesse as in, Uh, dude, we sprinted half of Philly for *this?* But Jesse doesn't seem to notice. I guess this park, this little slice of nowhere, is somewhere to Jesse, so I look around and check it out.

The first thing I notice besides the trash and chain link is a big graffitied wall and the words *Blessed are the cracked for they let in the light.* I don't know what it means exactly, but I like it. The cracked. The whacked. The funky. The free. The nonconformists. The music makers. The artists. This is Jesse's world—gritty, but alive. A different urban scene than the one I'm used to.

Then I start really looking around. At first, it's like everything's all black and white, but the more I look, the more it comes into color. I start to see that it's not about the place. It's about the people. A woman with a purple Mohawk and three eyebrow piercings sells paintings. A guy sitting on a bench rips out the blues on a beat up guitar. A wall, that anywhere else might be just a wall, has been turned into art—a skyscraper mural stretching halfway to the sky. I start to see why Jesse brought me here.

"What do you think?" he asks. I can tell he's nervous. Like maybe I won't see the color, just the black and white.

"Awesome," I say. He looks relieved.

Jesse shows me around, giving me a gastric tour of his favorite Philly street foods. We spend most of the morning eating, apparently Jesse's favorite activity—not that you'd ever know given the fact the kid is like crossed with a string bean.

By afternoon we've turned our attention from food to friends and Jesse introduces me to some of the people he knows. I meet Clyde, the genius guitar player from the punk band Flesh that Jesse raves about. Then Cyndi, a tattoo artist and homeless rights activist. There's Max, a self-professed Robin Hood, stealing from the rich and giving to the poor.

"Lock pick extraordinaire," Jesse says.

"Big words for thief," I retort, and Jesse changes the subject.

I like it here. I like the people Jesse introduces me to, even Max, with his misguided idealism. The place is raw, the people are real, and I find myself thinking about my mother again. This could've been her scene if she'd wanted. If she hadn't gotten into drugs instead. Mom had the urban vibe, the funky artist thing going on. She studied art for a year at Temple before she dropped out. She even had some pictures in a gallery once. And there were her causes, too. She was always involved in some social issue. Putting an end to war, animal rights, AIDS, ending hunger, bad hairstyles. She probably started college just so she could be pissed off at the institution.

Sadness and confusion spread through my body like poison. I plop onto a bench and close my eyes. The ghosts of heroin users past claw at my soul—Joplin, Morrison, Holiday, Basquiat—all dead, overdosed on junk. My thoughts change as fast as a Hendrix guitar riff, and I think again about the guy who came to our apartment the day she died and the heroin in the bathroom. Maybe Aunt T is right after all. Maybe Mom *did* die a junkie. Maybe it *was* an overdose that killed her, and it was her own damned fault she died.

My shoulder muscles tense, sending a ripple of pain into my neck and the base of my skull. Heat and pressure bubble up from my gut, turning sadness to anger like graphite to diamond, the hardest substance known to mankind.

I look around for something to smash my fist into, some way of releasing the anger before I burst. As my right hand curls into a fist, I hear the voice of Marta, the school counselor I was forced to see during my brief stint at Germantown Friends after giving Sarah Raye a fat lip for spreading rumors about my mom. *Feelings come and go like clouds in a windy sky,* Marta would say, quoting some Buddhist master. *Let conscious breathing be your anchor.*

Anchor my ass.

But I was given five sessions and I wasn't allowed to leave Marta's office, so I tried, and as much as I hated to admit it at the time, the longer I sat there, the calmer I felt.

I release my fist and concentrate on those words now, letting my breath be my anchor.

"What are you thinking about?" I hear Jesse ask as I take my second breath.

I open my eyes to find him on the bench next to me. "Nothing."

"Technically that's impossible because if nothing existed then that nothing would be something and therefore nothing can't exist."

A small smile forces its way across my lips. "Thank you, your holiness, for enlightening me with your wisdom. Any other profound matters you'd like to share?"

"Actually, yes. The meaning of—"

"Kidding!" I say, elbowing him in the ribs.

He elbows me back, and soon I've buried Mom deep in my mind and we're roughhousing like puppies. I swear Jesse even growls. This form of physical contact is so sixth grade. Instead of actually grabbing Jesse and making out with him, like my body's begging me to do, I punch him, call him a dork, and turn away.

We sit there for a while, listening to some rapper dude with a crocheted Rasta hat perched high on top of a mountain of dreadlocks doing his thing. He's actually pretty good and before I know what's happening, Jesse's on his feet doing the human beat box next to the guy, trying to lay down a rhythm. I look around, totally embarrassed because Jesse's not that good. But Jesse's not at all embarrassed. He doesn't give a crap about who's watching. He pulls me to my feet. At first I struggle and try to sit back down, but then I stop resisting and somehow, even though I don't have a musical bone in my body, Jesse has me next to him, making a total fool out of myself, trying to lay down the beat.

I have a moment of total uninhibited truth as I let myself make strange noises in a park I've never been next to a total stranger and a boy I hardly know. The song ends. Rasta man applauds us. We applaud him, and we all laugh and hug in one big feel-good love fest. Then, by reflex, I slip my hand into my pocket to touch the lighter. Instead of the lighter, I find Melinda's note. My stomach tightens. I check my phone. It's four thirty. Game over. Time for business. I turn to tell Jesse I have to go, but he speaks first.

"You know what I like about you?"

"My fantastic looks, charismatic charm, and outstanding musical ability?"

"Besides that."

"Okay, no, but I have a feeling you're about to tell me."

"You're so guarded and mysterious. Like there's this whole other person inside you. But then, out of nowhere you're on fire and just go for it. Like in biology the other day, or just now, you're fearless. You just don't know it. Anyway," he says, checking his phone, "it's getting late."

"Yeah. I know." I look at my feet. I should get going. I should turn my back right this second and tell Jesse that it's been real and I'll see him in school on Monday. I don't move though, and I realize it's because I don't want the day to end. Jesse Schneider with his loud music, shaggy hair, and in-your-face honesty has wedged himself into a corner of my heart.

I look up and search his face. "Okay, dare."

He flashes a wicked smile. "Bring it on."

"I dare you to go with me to meet a junkie who used to be friends with my mom."

His smile disappears. "Fine. My turn. Truth. Why?"

"Why what?"

"Why are you going there?"

"Because she has something to tell me about my mom who was a heroin addict and supposedly died of an overdose, and I want to hear what she has to say." Saying these words about my mother out loud clears away the whole feel-good, chemical-attraction-induced fog, and I kick myself for telling him this stuff. How could Jesse ever understand my life when, from what he's told me, the hardest thing he's had to deal with is turning down a new car from his dad? I jut my hip to the side and fold my arms across my chest. "So, if you're going to be an asshole and ditch me over this or feel sorry for me or say my mother died of an overdose, let's just get that part over with now, so I know where we stand."

Jesse puts one hand on his heart, and holds the other up like he's being sworn into office. "I, Jesse Schneider, do solemnly swear that I will not ditch you or say your mother died of a heroin overdose."

I drop my arms. "Fine. Coming or not?"

"Bus fare's on me."

Six

The stench of piss and trash is the first thing I notice when we get off the bus. If hopelessness has a smell, this is it. Neither of us speak as we stand on the corner beside a sign that says Dead End, and that's just how the neighborhood looks: a dead end for people with nowhere else to go. I think of any number of postings that could be here, like *Beware–Plague*, given the trash blowing around and the probable presence of rats.

"Okay, then," I say, trying to fill the nervous silence. I point to the east. "Fifth is that way."

A burned-out factory is the first thing we pass. All that's left is the charred frame, a skeleton of some old place. The only landmark Melinda gave was a liquor store, which isn't much help given the fact we've passed about ten liquor stores, but all my time spent with Mom in neighborhoods like this has given me some kind of ghetto sixth sense. Soon there we are, midway down a street of dilapidated row houses, staring up at number 2750 just like the note said. The place is seriously falling apart. Two of the three first floor windows are boarded up. Fungus-green paint is peeling off in long strips, and there's a milk crate instead of a step leading to the front door.

I hesitate for a minute as I look for the doorbell, remembering the last time I saw Melinda.

She's passed out on our bathroom floor. I stand at the door, paralyzed. Mom rushes out of the bathroom, back in again with a needle and syringe. She fills the syringe. Jabs. Again. Until Melinda sits up, looks at us, and comes back from the dead. Narcon, the junkie miracle drug, Mom explains later. Saves you from respiratory arrest. Mom shows me how to fill the syringe, how much to give. Just in case I need to bring her back from the dead too.

A bus screeches through a pile of sooty slush, spraying my legs and sending a chill straight to my bones. I wrap my arms around my torso and step onto the milk crate. My heart's beating wildly. What if Melinda isn't here? What if the note's a ploy and all she wants is money? What if I have the wrong address and piss someone off by ringing the bell? But there's no bell, and if I don't make a move I'm going to turn around and hail the first cab out of here. That is, if we can find a cab. So, I knock.

No answer.

"Maybe she's out," Jesse says.

I knock again. Louder this time. I call her name. Still, no answer.

Someone starts shouting at me to chill out. I look up and see a man hanging half his body out a second story window. The guy is fat and bald, and he's wearing a wife-beater tank even though it's winter. The shirt doesn't cover his gut, so the view from below is like staring up at the underbelly of some bloated sea creature.

"What the hell do you kids want?" he shouts down at us.

I clear my throat and reach for the lighter. "My name's Faith Flores. I'm looking for Melinda Rivera. She invited me. She was a friend of my mom's."

The man grumbles and slams the window.

I stand there for a second, unsure what to do, but there's no way I'm leaving until I find out what Melinda has to say about my mom, so I try the door. The knob turns and the door creaks open.

"Come on," I say to Jesse. "Let's go."

"Uh. That dude didn't exactly exude friendliness. Do you think it's a good idea to just walk in?"

"No," I say, and go inside.

Jesse sighs, then follows.

Our footsteps echo into the cold gray space as we climb a set of rickety steps to the second floor. We walk down a narrow hall lit by a single bulb dangling from an exposed wire until we reach apartment 2E. I glance at Jesse and knock.

The fat guy from the window opens the door and stands in the entranceway, his pants struggling against his belly to stay up. He sticks his face up to mine. "You wanna see Melinda?"

I nod, expecting him to tell me to get lost.

"Follow me," he slurs instead. The stink of his breath is enough to make me sick. "Your boyfriend coming too?"

I'm about to tell him Jesse isn't my boyfriend, but there are more important things to worry about, so I just nod and follow him into a dark, musty room.

Melinda's hovering at the edge of the room in baggy gray sweats and a faded Phillies t-shirt. I recognize her hair—black by birth, blond by the bottle. I recognize her emaciated frame and black eyeliner smudged around her haunted brown eyes. We stand there, neither of us moving. I can hardly breathe. Melinda's skin is leathery and blistered, like someone who's been in the sun too long. And what's worse are the red dots like zits or chicken pox covering her face. But the marks aren't zits. They aren't chicken pocks. I know that. They're scabs.

Melinda has the same scabby, blistered skin my mom had before she died.

Melinda nods at the fat guy, who disappears down the hall, then she takes a tentative step toward me. "Hi, Faith."

It seems like there should be a different word than "Hi." You say "Hi" to your friends in the hall between classes, "Hi" to the postman or the salesclerk. Not "Hi" to the messed up heroin addict who overdosed on your bathroom floor, stole from you, and then disappeared. There is no other word, though, and I return the greeting.

Now comes the awkward silence. What is there to say? You still doing smack?

I stand in the doorway and peer into the tiny cluttered kitchen, at the crusty dishes piled in the sink, at the beer bottles littering the table, and the overflowing ashtrays. I breathe in the stink of cigarettes, marijuana, and a room that hasn't had fresh air in about a decade. My heart tightens. This scene is too familiar. I'm about to turn and leave when Melinda speaks.

"Come in," she wheezes. "I have to talk to you."

Jesse, Mr. Chivalry, tromps across the floor, hand extended. I take a deep breath and follow.

Melinda shakes Jesse's hand, then fidgets around in her pocket and pulls out a fresh cigarette and a lighter. She lights up with trembling fingers and squints at me. Bones poke at her flesh as if her skin is nothing more than a thin sheet holding her skeleton in place.

"I got your note," I say, finding my voice. "You said it was about my mom. So what is it?"

Melinda hacks and paces the perimeter of the room. Her eyes dart from door to window like she's expecting someone else to show up. "I'm sorry," she says, letting the cigarette dangle between her nicotine-stained fingers.

"For stealing from me or for almost dying on our bathroom floor or because my mom's dead?"

She stares at me with her gaunt face and hollow eyes. Television voices murmur from behind the closed door where Fat Guy disappeared. "All of it." She glances at the window again. "What happened? How'd she die?"

"She was sick," I mutter.

Melinda rakes her fingernails over her cheek, causing a welt by her right nostril to bleed. "I need money," she pleads as a trickle of blood dribbles past her lip onto her chin. "You're the only one I could go to, the only one who could understand. I'll pay you back. All of it."

I slap my hand down on the table, knocking over an empty wine bottle. "Understand? You've got to be kidding. You're really asking me for money?" I shake my head and turn toward the window where a trapped fly buzzes between the cracked glass and screen. "I can't believe you had the guts to come to my aunt's house, leave me some bullshit note about my mom, and ask for money after you stole from us." I spin back around to face her. "I'm such an idiot. I knew I shouldn't have come here."

"Wait!" she blurts. "Please. There's more."

She takes a drag off her cigarette and starts to cough. She coughs so hard I think she's going to crack a rib. For a second I almost feel sorry for her, but I shake off the feeling. I'm not getting suckered into that charity case routine.

"Forget it. We're out of here. Come on, Jesse. Let's go."

I grab his arm and start walking to the door, but Melinda gets there first. She stands in the doorway, arms out, blocking us from leaving. I could easily push her out of the way if I wanted to—a flick of my hand and those birdlike bones would snap.

"They're telling me not to go to the doctor, like they told your mother," she whispers.

"Like who told my mother?" I hear my voice rise, feel my face burn.

Melinda cracks the door, peers down the hallway, then closes it again. She's acting like a paranoid drug addict. Big surprise.

"I can't tell you," she says.

"Oh my god. This is crazy." I try to push past her, but she's not letting me go without a fight. She grabs my jacket with more force than I would've expected, given her size and state, and gives me a hard shove. I stumble backwards into Jesse. He rights my fall and holds my arm for a second, but I jerk away. I'm angry enough to return the shove, but Melinda's scurried past us and is cowering by the couch, holding out a piece of paper.

"Read this. It'll explain."

I snatch the paper and read the heading out loud, "You can lead a heroin-free life." Jesse peers over my shoulder and we read the rest together.

> "Neurons are cells that transmit chemical and electrical messages along pathways in the brain. In the center of the brain sits the reward pathway, which is responsible for driving our feelings of motivation, reward and behavior. Drugs, such as heroin, activate this reward pathway, leaving an addict with a high and craving more.
>
> At the Twenty-third Street Methadone Clinic, we are working with researchers from PluraGen, a leading biopharmaceutical company, to run a clinical trial to deliver an experimental new drug to block this pathway. This will stop the cravings/pleasure cycle associated with heroin use, so that

normal brain function can be restored and you can once again lead an addiction free life.

Are you interested in participating in this groundbreaking clinical trial? Applicants must be over the age of 18 and fill out our prescreening registration form to determine eligibility."

I glare at her when I'm done reading. "What the hell is this?"

"The clinical trial."

"*What* clinical trial?"

"The one I was in with your mother, for addicts." Melinda's whole body is one jittery motion—foot tapping, fingers drumming, hands quivering. Hardly the bleary-eyed, heroin vibe I've seen so many times. High on some other drug is my guess. She stubs out her cigarette in a beer can and looks at me. "I'm clean now."

"Clean?" I laugh. "So this clinical trial is a miracle?"

She ignores my sarcasm and breaks into another coughing fit. "I'm the one who told her about it," she says when she catches her breath. "I'm not supposed to talk about it...but I thought if you knew, maybe you'd help. I think it's side effects from the drug making me sick." She picks at a piece of skin hanging from her lip and her nervous eyes dart to the window again. "So I stopped going in for treatment. That's why I need money. To see a doctor."

I raise my eyebrows at Jesse, who gives a helpless shrug. "You're saying my mother was in some clinical trial for heroin addicts?"

"That's right. They say they're the only ones who can treat the symptoms, but I don't believe them."

"No way," I say, in a less than convincing tone. And then, my voice now trembling, I add, "Mom wasn't in a clinical trial. She would've told me. Mom didn't keep secrets like that."

Melinda suddenly lunges at me. She pinches my chin in her scabby fingers and raises my face to meet her eyes. "Look at me." Her voice is low and controlled and for a second all that twitchy, strung-out energy dissipates. "Your mother and I look the same, don't we? Our skin—the scabs, the blisters—side effects, all of it."

Staring into Melinda's decomposing flesh, I see my mother and remember that final morning.

She's all elbows and knees standing in front of the bathroom mirror in her underwear and t-shirt, rubbing cream onto her scabs.

"You should really go see a doctor, Ma," I say, peering at her from the doorway.

"I'm fine, hon," she tells me, frowning as she checks her reflection in the mirror. "Just a little under the weather. Too much sun at the shore last week. Maybe I have a little cold. Besides, I don't trust all those fancy doctors and hospitals. All they want is money." She looks at me, sees the worry on my face, and smiles. "I'll be fine, Faith, really. I'm clean now. Everything's going to be okay."

There was a lie behind that smile. Even then I knew it.

I wonder if the lie was about being clean or because she knew she was dying.

A familiar voice whispers in my head: *She betrayed you. She lied because she didn't love you. She didn't care.*

Angry tears burn my eyes. I blink hard and swallow. Maybe there is a reason Mom wouldn't go to a doctor. Maybe Melinda *is* telling the truth and Mom was in some clinical trial, trying to get better, and something went wrong.

The effect of this thought is relief, but then I look at Melinda again—the washed-out skin, the dark circles beneath her eyes, her tangled mat of hair and trembling fingers—and I remember what she really wants. Money. I twist out of her grip and back away.

"Go to the hospital if you're so sick. Why are you bothering me?"

She starts to say something, but someone pounds on the door. A man calls her name, and she doesn't finish her thought. She looks at me, and in a loud panicked whisper says, "Quick, go. He can't see you here." She snatches the flier from my hand and scribbles a number. "Call Al," she says, pushing Jesse and me down the hall into the back room and pointing at Fat Guy, who's perched on the edge of the bed, holding a joint and watching a lion tear apart a gazelle on TV. She stuffs the flier in my bag. "He'll know how to get in touch with me."

"Wait! What's going on? You're not making any sense. Why—"

Melinda dashes out of the room before I can finish my question.

Fat Guy doesn't move or acknowledge our presence. He just stares at the bloodshed on TV and takes a hit off his joint as if two strange teenagers getting shoved into his room is an everyday occurrence.

I have no idea what to do, so I go to the door and peak out to see a tall, stringy guy, wearing a black leather jacket, black jeans, and black sneakers. His back is to me, but from the way his hand is clamped around Melinda's wrist you don't need to be on the AP track to tell he didn't stop by for a cup of tea and some biscuits.

"What's happening out there?" Jesse whispers, squeezing up beside me.

Before I can answer, the guy glances in our direction. I'm not sure if he sees us, but my heart stops all the same. I grab Jesse to keep my legs from buckling.

I can't believe it. It can't be, but it is. I couldn't forget those heavy-lidded charcoal eyes, that long, narrow face and pointy chin, that stubby, wind-burned nose and small, twitchy mouth. It's that same guy who came to our apartment the day Mom died.

"You have a debt to pay," I hear him tell Melinda.

My stomach curdles at the words. A hard chill runs down my spine. I close the door and spin around to face Fat Guy.

"Who's that with Melinda?" I blurt.

Fat Guy scratches the hairy strip of belly his shirt doesn't cover. "No clue. She calls him the Rat Catcher."

"The Rat Catcher?" I say, not understanding and not sure I heard him right. "What does he want?"

Fat Guy snorts, turns away from the TV, and fixes me with his bloodshot eyes. "You want my advice?" He doesn't wait for my answer. "Mind your own business."

I stand with my back against the door, unsure whether to go out and help or take Fat Guy's advice. I close my eyes, and when I do, the grotesque image of Melinda's face haunts me, death tearing at her flesh. Those words echo in my ears: *You have a debt to pay.* Melinda's face morphs into Mom's. The Rat Catcher's at our apartment now. It's Mom's wrist he's holding, and when he looks up and sees me peeking out from my bedroom, the glint in his eyes is enough to keep me cowering.

If Melinda's really in trouble, I have to do something, but when I open my eyes and crack open the door, they're gone.

I take a deep breath to clear my head, but there isn't enough oxygen in this smoke-filled pit to fill my lungs. I grab Jesse's arm and take off through the apartment. I fly down the stairs and break into a run the second my feet hit pavement. If it weren't for the fact I failed PE at my last school, okay got kicked out (you *cannot* play field hockey in combat boots, Ms. Flores!) and my cardiovascular deal is on par with about that of a sloth, I'd keep running. But my lungs are going apeshit on me, as in stop now or die—literally. I have no choice but to obey. I slump against a kiosk and double over.

"What's going on, Faith?" I hear Jesse say. I straighten up and catch his eye, then quickly look away.

"I don't know," I say, stalling for time as I figure out what to tell him. Um, gee, sorry about what happened back there. Looks like there was some drug dealer or pest control guy having a seriously bad day in Melinda's place. I had a great time, though! (Big smile!) Movie next week?

It doesn't matter what I say or don't say, and I know it. Why would Jesse stick around after what just happened? I brace myself for the I-like-you-but-hanging-out-is-just-not-a-good-idea excuse. Well, that's what I got for asking him to come with me.

"How about a coffee?" he says instead.

"Huh?"

"Coffee—you know, hot beverage? Originated in Ethiopia around the ninth century? Filled with caffeine? Gets you through first period? I could really use one. And from the look on your face, so could you."

"Right…okay, good," I stammer. "Coffee sounds good."

On the other side of the street there's a place with metal bars across the window, a torn green awning, and a sign that says *Breakfast Served All Day*. Not exactly the cheeriest scene, but it'll do. We go inside where a girl with long, greasy hair stands behind a glass-fronted bakery case displaying food that looks to have expired sometime around the time of the dinosaurs.

While Jesse stops at the counter for coffee, I take a seat in the back corner by an ancient pinball machine and root around my pockets for a Tylenol, even though I know it's ridiculous to think a painkiller could kill the fear and anger in my heart. All I find is Mom's lighter, some lint, and an unwrapped piece of gum.

I stick the gum in my mouth, and when I close my eyes, the questions start to flow. Is the Rat Catcher Melinda's dealer? Was he Mom's dealer, too? Did she owe him money? Did he have something to do with her death? And why's he called the Rat Catcher?

I run my hands over the grime of the sticky table and open my eyes. Then there's the clinical trial. How does *that* fit in? What if Melinda was telling me the truth? What if she was right and it was the side effects from some drug that killed Mom? That would mean she didn't OD.

I stare out the window into the last light of day, thinking about the word *truth*. Is there even such a thing? Mom was always about to get off drugs and get better. That was *her* truth. In the end it was all a lie. Even if it was true that she'd gotten off drugs, she didn't get better. She died.

I'm lost in these thoughts when Jesse comes back with the coffees. I ignore the mug he sets in front of me. "What if Melinda's being straight and my mother was in some clinical trial? Why didn't she tell me? Why keep that a secret?"

The question is rhetorical, but Jesse answers. "Maybe she didn't want to get your hopes up, you know, in case it didn't work."

"Yeah, like maybe she'd die," I say. "Anyway, it's bullshit. It has to be. Melinda owed the Rat Catcher money. That's why she looked so scared when he showed up. He's probably her dealer. That's the debt he was talking about—drug money."

Jesse doesn't say anything. He dumps three containers of cream into his mug, takes a sip, then dumps in another container along with about ten packets of sugar and sips again. Once his coffee expectations are satisfied, he picks up the flier I set on the table and reads it over. Then he reads it again. I'm wondering if he intends to memorize the thing and am about to snatch it out of his hands when he says, "Melinda doesn't seem capable of making this up."

"What are you talking about?"

"This," he says, waving the flier in my face.

"So?"

"So, I'm just saying, she did have this flier for the clinical trial. It has to be legit."

I roll my eyes. "She could've found it in the trash."

Jesse shrugs and sips his coffee. "She seemed pretty scared, though. Totally messed up, but scared. It seems possible she's telling the truth."

I lean forward, knocking over the sugar with my elbow. "So you think my mother was being used as a lab animal in some clinical trial that she never told me about?" My voice is loud, too loud, but I can't help it.

The girl behind the counter throws me a dirty look, like I might be some kind of teenage psychopath sporting a gun under my jacket.

"You're getting too emotional," Jesse says.

"Too emotional?" I burst, and then lower my voice, forcing myself to keep control. "It's my mother we're talking about. Not some lab animal."

"Yeah, well I'm just trying to help."

"Yeah, well I'm not a charity case."

"Yeah, well I'm not your punching bag."

I'm about to start another "Yeah, well..." but I look down at my hands folded in my lap and feel lame for my outburst. I want to say I'm sorry, but I don't have much practice in the field of apologizing. Mom and I solved most problems by pretending they didn't exist. In fact, she was an addict and her whole *life* was a problem. That meant our entire relationship was one big avoidance.

"Okay, fine. You're right. It could be true," I concede after several minutes pass, hoping this counts as an apology.

I pick up my coffee mug, but put it back down without drinking. I stare at the kid with the big eighties hair and duck tail who's passionately working the pinball machine. I watch the flashing lights, listen to the ping as the ball drops into the gutter. My thoughts bounce back to that last day. I try again to understand what happened.

Mom's in the kitchen attempting to scrape together something to eat. Dylan's "Tangled Up In Blue" crackles on the radio. I'm in my room, digging around the dirty laundry pile for a pair of jeans.

"Did you finish the peanut butter?" Mom shouts to me from the kitchen. "I'm trying to make PB and J, Faith! If you finish something, you gotta tell me."

I'm about to shout back and tell her there hasn't been any peanut butter for three days, that I threw out rest of the Wonder Bread, which looked like a science experiment, when there's a knock on the apartment door.

I hear Mom's footsteps as she stomps across the kitchen, then the squeak of door hinges. I'm still in my underwear, so I stay in my room, but when I hear a man's voice, I peek out.

"Come on," he says. "You're coming with me."

Mom's shoulders are hunched. Her head is down. At ninety pounds, she looks like a kid getting scolded by a teacher.

"I don't want to go," she tells him.

"You have a debt to pay," he says in a voice that leaves no room for argument.

"One minute...I...need my purse."

She's stalling, but why? Does she think she can get away from him? That she can call for help?

"Faith," she whispers as she passes my room. "I'm..."

But that's all she gets to say. He yanks her to the door, and then they're gone.

Was she trying to tell me something? Where did the Rat Catcher take her? What debt did she have to pay? I never got to ask. That night she was dead on the bathroom floor.

The front door opens with a loud clang. The Arctic blast slaps the memory-induced haze right out of me. I shift my gaze from the pinball player and look at the flier again: Twenty-third and Jefferson. I might not know who the Rat Catcher is or what debt she owed him, but there's one way to find out if Melinda was telling the truth about my mother.

"I'm going to the clinic," I tell Jesse.

Jesse looks at me with a blank expression.

"The clinic," I repeat, pointing at the flier. "I'll go Monday. Whoever's in charge should be able to tell me if my mother was in the clinical trial. And if she was, maybe they can tell me if the symptoms were side effects from the drug. At least then I'll know if Melinda was telling the truth, and maybe I'll find out what happened to my mom."

———

When I get home an hour and a half later, Aunt T and Sam are hanging out on the couch watching some show about mummies on the History Channel. Aunt T pats the couch and moves over, making room for me. I know how much she wants me to stay and tell her about my day, how much she wants to include me in things and make my life normal. But how can my life be normal? My mom was possibly used as a guinea pig in a clinical trial she never told me about. I just saw her strung-out former junkie friend who got led away by a possible drug dealer who might've once been Mom's dealer. How can I tell Aunt T what I think might've happened in the past when more than anything she wants me to let go and move forward? I smile and thank her for the offer, but tell her I'm tired and withdraw to my room.

Once in my room I pick up my iPod. I jam the earbuds into my ears and crank up the sound of waterfalls and singing birds, hoping the peaceful sounds of nature will still the restless demons pacing inside me.

The singing birds remind me of the white bird. I flop on my bed and stare at the ceiling.

Maybe that bird was Mom's guardian angel. Maybe it did watch over her and then carry her away to the stars, to the heavens, to someplace she believed existed. Mom always taught me there are some things you know, like the laws of nature; for other things, like souls and heaven, you have to have faith. Maybe she gave me my name as a reminder of this, so that whatever happened, my faith would carry me through.

But what kind of faith am I supposed to have? If an albino bird was Mom's guardian angel, then she never had a shot at survival. Albinos stand out in the wild. Forget being cared for and watched over. Her guardian angel would be attacked by predators and ripped to pieces.

Seven

I spend most of Sunday in my room, listening to music and obsessing about all that happened at Melinda's. First thing Monday morning, after a night of tossing and turning, I call the methadone clinic to see if I can get an appointment with whoever's in charge of the clinical trial. I figure it'll be days before someone can see me, that is *if* someone will see me. What if they won't talk to a minor? What if I need some kind of parental consent?

I'm working out a plan, which basically comes down to begging, when a woman answers the phone. I tell her that I'd like to make an appointment to discuss the clinical trial and wait for her to a) laugh, b) hang up, or c) ask to talk to my mother.

"Dr. Wydner's in charge of that," she says instead. "Hold please." She pushes whatever button turns on the really bad music, and after a round of put-you-to-sleep piano, she's back. "He can see you at one today."

"He can? Today? One o'clock?" I don't even both considering the consequences of missing school or the logistics of getting downtown. "I'll be there," I say and hang up.

A few hours later, I'm crossing the school parking lot, ditching the rest of my classes so I can catch a train and make my appointment when I hear someone calling my name. I turn and there's Anj bounding toward me. In her pink fluffy sweater and matching pink hat, she looks like she's been wrapped in cotton candy.

"What're you doing? It's freezing out here. Don't you have class?" she asks when she reaches my side.

"Skipping. What about you?"

"PE, but that's not a class. I told Mr. G it was that time of the month and I had cramps and he excused me. Works every time." Anj smiles. It's the smile more than anything that lets her pull this kind of crap. Big, bright, radiant, and oh so earnest. "So what's your plan?"

"I'm going to the city," I say, tapping my foot. I have an eleven o'clock train, and I'm late as it is. Laz cornered me after third period and wanted to know when I was planning on handing in my Hemingway term paper, due sometime last week. I promised I'd get it to him tomorrow and took off before he could protest.

"The city?" Anj bubbles. "Sounds fun. There's something I have to tell you. Mind if I tag along?"

"Well, actually—"

"Great, because Mondays are a total drag. I have three electives in a row. Spanish, German, *and* French."

I lean against the hood of a red car with a license plate that says GRLTOY and stare at Anj. "Since when are you taking German?"

Her cheeks turn the same color as her sweater, and she looks at me with a sheepish grin. "I started two weeks ago. What can I say? Romance languages look good on applications."

"But German isn't a romance language," I say as a boy driving a truck with purple racing stripes peels out of the parking lot. "And anyway, who takes three languages? That's crazy. You're going to get your *bonjour* mixed up with your *buenas dias* and your *buenas dias* mixed up with your *guten tag*. I can just hear it, *Guten jour*...or is it *buenas tag*?" I say, laughing at my joke.

Anj brushes a curl off her face and works me with the angelic smile. "Yeah, well, I'll worry about that if I ever actually speak any of the languages for real. So where are we going?"

"We're not—"

"Never mind." She grabs my hand. "You'll tell me later. Come on, let's go. I'll drive."

I check my phone. Ten forty-five. Good chance I'll miss the train even if I leave right now. The next one's not until two. "Fine," I tell her. "Let's go."

We head to the back of the parking lot and load into Anj's car, this enormous twenty-year-old Chevy with like 200,000 miles. She calls the car Hazel in honor of her grandma who left it to her when she died. Anj starts the engine and Hazel makes every bad car noise imaginable, sputtering and spewing enough smoke and fumes to increase the planet's temperature a full degree. But the car starts and a few minutes later we're on the West Chester Pike heading into the city.

At some point I'll have to give Anj directions and tell her where we're going, but I have some time before we get to that part because it's at least a twenty-five-minute drive, and Anj immediately starts updating me on her relationship with Duncan.

"He's not the type I usually go for," she reminds me. "It's the accent. I don't care what he's actually saying. I just like listening to him say it. What about you and Jesse?"

"What about us?"

Anj swerves into the next lane without looking and nearly causes a collision. "He's pretty cute in that grungy I-haven't-taken-a-shower-in-a-week kind of way," she says, smiling an apology into the rearview mirror at the woman behind us who's wailing on her horn. "Do you have the hots for him? Are you guys hooking up?"

"Anj, give me a break. The kid's been here all of four days. I don't work that fast."

I turn and look out the window, making it clear that the conversation about my love life, or lack thereof, is officially over.

Anj tries a few more questions, but when I refuse to say more, she drops the subject and starts telling me about the Happy Cow campaign, which I was right about and she is spearheading. She tells me all the campaign gossip, how they're trying to get the school cafeteria to go vegan, and how, of all things, the head of food services didn't even know what vegan meant! Then she starts telling me about something called mechanically separated chicken and pink slime, which makes my stomach turn. With hardly a pause for air, she changes the subject—classes, boys, teachers—whatever pops into her brain.

Twenty minutes later, the old-money, Main Line estates have been replaced by boxy rows of storage units, fields of crisscrossing train tracks, and abandoned warehouses—an urban, industrial gloom untouched by the historical tourist-Mecca of Franklin Square and Independence Hall.

Anj breaks from her monologue to offer a suggestion for our outing. "How about Society Hill? There's this awesome new vintage boutique Tara told me about."

How can I tell Anj we're not going shopping for retro out-fits and having our nails done? We're going to a methadone clinic to talk to someone about my mother. Anj has a dad who works at a marketing firm, a mom who sells real estate, and a little sister who plays on a basketball team. Anj lives in the same house she was born in. Once a year she goes on Club Med vacations with her family to places like Jamaica or Costa Rica. How could I expect her to understand?

"Turn left on Chestnut," I say instead. "And head to Twenty-third."

The bronze spire of William Penn gazes down at us from his heavenly position on top of City Hall as Anj drives past the treelined streets of Center City. "I totally suck at parallel parking," she moans when we reach Twenty-third and the only empty spots are in line with other cars against the curb. After a long and fruitless mission of searching for an easier solution, she gives in to the inevitable, bumping both the car in front of us and the one behind before finally managing to maneuver Hazel into a spot.

"Where to?" she asks, cheerfully cutting the engine.

I look at my hands knotted in my lap. The moment of truth is upon us and I search for a lie. "You can just drop me off and I'll meet you in a few hours," I say, unable to come up with a fib and instead going for vague.

Anj rolls her eyes toward the roof of the car. "You dragged me out here so I could hang out by myself?"

"I didn't drag you," I remind her. "You wanted to come."

Anj ignores this detail and pierces me with a stare. I swear the CIA could use her for counterinsurgency intelligence operations. She could get a terrorist to rat out his own mother with a single look.

"Okay, fine," I say, buckling to her silent method of inter-rogation before she pulls out the water board. "I'm going to a methadone clinic, but you don't have to come. You can go shopping or whatever and pick me up later, or I can take the train back."

Even as I say this, I realize how much I want Anj to come. Not so I can get all sentimental and teary eyed about my mother, but because Anj drags me out of the nightmares that play in my head when I'm alone and keeps me in the world of the living.

"A methadone clinic?" she asks without taking her eyes from my face. "What are you going there for?"

"Some unfinished business about my mom," I respond, offering just the right amount of information to keep the chemistry of our friendship in balance. Too many details and the relationship erupts in flame, not enough, it fizzles and dies.

For a minute I think Anj is going to break the formula and unbalance the equation with a question. Instead she switches her well-glossed lips to the side and reaches into her purse. "Okay," she says, handing me a brush. "But you have to comb your hair. You look terrible."

I do my hair as directed, and Anj announces that before she can go anywhere, she needs something to eat. We find a deli on Twenty-second where she apologizes before ordering a cheese steak sandwich and makes me swear I won't tell Tara.

"Okey dokey," she says when she's devoured the last bite. "Let's go meet some heroin addicts."

―――

The first thing I notice when we walk into the clinic is the nasal assault of chemical disinfectant, B.O., and cigarettes. The second thing I notice is the uniformed security guard. His presence is ominous and I guess that's the point, to make sure no badly behaved junkies lose their cool and start wielding a knife at anyone.

Anj takes a seat on a folding metal chair, plucks a magazine from the floor, and starts to read, as if sitting in the lobby of a methadone clinic is the most natural thing in the world. I, on the other hand, can't relax. It's been years since I went to a place like this with Mom. The memories are there though, burned into my mind, tattooed into my flesh. Every cell of my body holds a piece of her story. Some things you can't forget.

I drop into the chair next to Anj and watch a scrawny guy with a greasy ponytail and leather vest pace the floor. This is where I come from, I think, noticing his skinny, track-marked arms.

I stare at the wall, seeing nothing, and remember.

I'm ten years old, just home from school, the thrift-store Cinderella backpack I scribbled all over with black sharpie slung over my right shoulder. Mom's in a tank top and shorts, standing at the sink, washing dishes. I notice the row of red bruises following the blue veins on her arms.

"What are those marks on your arm, Ma?" I ask, rolling up my sleeves to inspect my own arms. "Will I get them, too when I'm older?"

Mom whirls around from the sink and grabs my shoulders. "No! You'll never have them. Okay, Faith? Promise. You'll never be like me."

"Do you have a light?" I hear someone say.

I blink and look up to see a hollow-eyed girl with a gaunt, angular face standing at my side. I realize she's talking to me.

"No," I murmur, fingering the empty Zippo in my pocket.

She turns and goes to a corner. I watch the dead look in her eyes as she sits on the floor, muttering to herself, and I think maybe the real issue isn't where I come from, but where I'm going. Is it enough to try really hard to be different, to try and do better, or in the end is it just a story of genes, and no matter how hard I try, I was screwed before I was even born?

I tear my mind from these thoughts and glance at Anj, the little piece of normal holding me up like a life raft. I didn't come here to wallow in self-pity. I have a purpose. I get up, cross the peeling linoleum floor, and go to the back of the room where a small corner is sectioned off with glass blocks. I assume this glass cubicle is the check-in. *Hello and welcome! Come lead a happy heroin-free life!*

I stand next to a poster of a sunset dangling from a single tack and tap on the window. A young black woman with her hair in cornrows and a name tag that says Veronica pinned to her blue smock raises her eyes from her computer without lifting her head and slides open the window.

I tell Veronica my name and appointment time. Her long, pink fingernails click the keyboard as she types my information.

"Doctor Wydner'll be with you soon," she says in an accent that makes me think of white sand beaches and clear blue ocean water. "Have a seat."

I slump into a chair next to Anj and burrow into my hoodie. The guy with the leather vest sidles toward me, aiming to strike up a conversation. I pick up an informational pamphlet from a dusty table and busy myself reading. I'm in no mood for chitchat.

> "The Twenty-third Street Methadone Clinic is a public health clinic offering low cost treatment choices to help stop substance abuse. We offer both counseling services and detox programs. We have two medical treatment options: Methadone and RNA 120."

I skip the part about methadone and read on to RNA 120.

> "For patients interested in a new, experimental approach to substance abuse, the Twenty-third Street Methadone Clinic is working with researchers

at PluraGen, a leading biopharmaceutical company, to offer a clinical trial to those who meet our eligibility requirements."

I've just finished reading when Veronica calls my name. She leads me out of the waiting area and down a long, mildew-stained corridor, past a cluttered desk guarded by two tall filing cabinets. A stocky, unsmiling nurse waits by the copying machine. A few others flock around the coffee maker. I trail after Veronica to the far end of the hall where she stops and knocks on a door beside a plaque that says: *Dr. Joseph Wydner, MD, RNA 120 Clinical Trial Administrator.*

The first thing I notice about the guy who opens the door is his hair, a do that reminds me of a big fuss in the news a few years back about a political candidate who spent like five hundred dollars on a haircut. This guy's hair is styled and combed meticulously into place and then gelled so carefully that even if a windstorm tore apart the city, I doubt a single one of his hairs would move. Maybe the hair is an attempt to draw attention away from the rest of his face, which is tired and weathered, skin sagging around his cheeks and neck as if he's about to molt.

"I'm Dr. Wydner," Hairdo says, offering a hand. "Please, come in."

He leads me to a folding chair opposite a large desk. I take a seat and look around. Besides a few framed photos of a girl about my age, there's nothing personal in the office. No diplomas or art or posters. Just a computer, some papers on his desk, and the obvious need for a vacuum and dust rag.

"So," he says, peering at me with tired eyes before sliding a form across the desk. "You're here about the clinical trial. Are you eighteen?"

"No," I say, unsure what my age has to do with anything.

"You have to be eighteen," he tells me, taking in my hoodie and faux leather skirt, my black eyeliner and the curtain of my bangs.

Suddenly it dawns on me—my clothes, my hair, the way I look. He thinks *I* want to be in the clinical trial. "You got it all wrong," I say. "I'm not here for myself. I'm here about someone else."

Dr. Wydner raises his eyebrows and steeples his fingers beneath his chin. I can tell he doesn't believe me. It's like going to Planned Parenthood for condoms and saying they're "for a friend."

"No, really. I'm not…I don't…" I stop and inhale, fold my hands in my lap, and start again. "I want to find out if someone by the name of Augustina Flores was in this clinical trial." I cringe hearing myself call Mom Augustina. She hated that name. She used to say it was too Catholic for a New Age Pagan like her. Everyone called her Auggie.

Dr. Wydner scrutinizes me like I'm a lab mouse and he's waiting to see which way I'll go in the maze. "I'm sorry," he says, without taking his eyes off my face. "That information is confidential."

"But, I'm her daughter," I protest, digging through the clutter in my bag for some kind of ID. I find my birth certificate crumbled at the bottom along with several other papers from school registration I never bothered cleaning out. "You can give the information to family, can't you?"

"Her daughter?" A look of surprise crosses his face.

I pull out the crinkled document, push it across the desk as proof of my existence, and sit patiently as I wait for the doctor to study my birth certificate and confirm I am who I claim to be.

When he's examined my documentation and lo and behold, I'm Faith Flores, he hands back the paper and clears his throat. "Yes, well I see. We can certainly release information to family members, but I don't have the information at my fingertips. I only have a number for each patient, not a name. I don't see the applications or work directly with the patients. The nurses do that. They register the patients and administer the treatment. I'm here to monitor the progress and analyze the data."

"Well, couldn't you find out about my mom? Ask a nurse or something? You are running the thing, aren't you?" I don't even try to hide my irritation. He's just like every adult who blows me off whenever I bring up my mom, who acts like the word teenager is a synonym for delinquent.

Dr. Wydner sighs, leans forward, and rests his fatigue on his elbow. "Why not ask your mother if she's in the study?"

I meet his eye without flinching. "Because she's dead."

He passes a hand over his jowls. For a minute he doesn't speak. There's something faraway about his silence. Like he's forgotten I'm here.

"I'm sorry," he finally says. I'm not sure what he's apologizing for—his silence? My mother? That he can't help me? "I know how hard losing someone is." He glances at the framed photos on his desk. "I have a daughter."

I look at the pictures of the smiling girl with brown curls and soft brown eyes. In one of the photos she's dressed for a soccer game, in another for a prom. She seems like someone who might be head of student council or editor of the yearbook, someone who's pretty enough to be a bitch, but whose warm smile tells me she isn't.

He clears his throat. "She's very sick....We might lose her."

For some reason, hearing this ignites my anger. What does he mean, "lose her?" Is he going to misplace her in some drawer? And why is he telling *me* this?

I peer at the doctor again and immediately feel bad. He's obviously hurting and, judging from his appearance, not doing too well. I mumble something sympathetic about his daughter and get up to leave, thinking our meeting's over.

"Augustina Flores, you said?"

I stop in my tracks, two steps from my chair. "That's right."

He lowers his eyes and starts typing. I stand there, wondering if I'm supposed to stay, or if he's moved onto something else and class is over and I'm dismissed. I'm guessing the second. I'm about to split when he pushes his chair away from his desk and looks up from the screen.

"I'm sorry. I didn't find anyone by that name."

Okay, well at least I have my answer. Melinda lied. Mom wasn't in the clinical trial. I'm not sure if the lie is a total relief or a total let down, but I'm not about to stand around all day dwelling on it. I thank Dr. Wydner for his time and turn to leave for real this time. I make it all the way to the door when something between a eureka moment and a hunch stops me. If Mom really was in this clinical trial and really didn't want me to know about it, wouldn't she cover all her bases to hide it from me?

"Archer," I say, wheeling back around to face Dr. Wydner. "Augustina Archer. Can you check that name?"

Dr. Wydner scratches his head (not a single hair moving) and gives me a look like you give the guy outside the Wawa who reeks of booze and just needs a few bucks for his pregnant girlfriend because his car broke down and he's stranded and his girl's gonna drop any second.

"I know what you're thinking," I say, running emergency ops. "Archer is a different last name from mine, and you can only release the information to family, so how do you know we're family? How do you know I'm not lying?"

"Something like that," he admits.

"Yeah, I understand, but Archer was her maiden name. Please," I add, when he doesn't respond. "This is really important."

Dr. Wydner picks up a pen and taps it on the desk. I wait. *Tap. Tap.* I stare out the window at an insurance agency building with a falling down sign that might've once said, "We have you covered" but now says, "We 'ave you 'overed." *Tap. Tap.* Finally Dr. Wydner puts down the pen and turns back to his computer.

"I found her name," he tells me after a minute. "Augustina Archer. Your mother was in the clinical trial. I see she died about six weeks ago. The report we received from the medical examiner said it was a heroin overdose. I'm sorry. It's always a disappointment when the treatment doesn't work." He looks at his daughter's picture again, and I wonder if it's his own disappointment he's talking about or mine.

"We normally don't take people with dependents," he goes on. "Any new medicine has potential complications and risks. This is an experimental treatment. For people with dependents, methadone is a safer alternative."

He leans back in his chair and rambles on, but I stop listening. My nervous system is jammed. Too many synapses are firing at the same time.

I close my eyes, and when I do, I see Melinda. I hear her voice. *Your mom and I look the same. Side effects, all of it.*

"Do patients ever have any side effects from the treatment?" I ask, opening my eyes.

Dr. Wydner stops mid-sentence and gazes at me. He pushes back from his desk and walks heavily to the window, like his whole body is a sigh. "I'm guessing you're looking for an alternate explanation of how she died," he says more to the window than to me. "That's not uncommon. But I'm sorry. I can't help you. I can only tell you that she was in the trial, and the documented cause of her death. I can't discuss the specifics of the treatment or the clinical trial. These things are confidential."

There isn't anything more to say. I know Mom was in the clinical trial, but without information on her symptoms and a connection to the treatment, I haven't gotten any closer to learning what was wrong with her. I thank him again for his time and gather my bag.

"How old are you?" he asks as I start to leave for the third time.

"Sixteen."

He comes around to the front of the desk and perches on the edge. "This must be very hard for you."

I don't know if this requires an answer, but I'm not about to get into it with a stranger, so I nod again.

He doesn't press the topic. He asks a few more general questions about my life, and for a few minutes we have a connection of sorts. I fill the daughter void, and he fills the caring-father void. It's playacting, but it works. We each get to fill a little of that emptiness, if only for a moment or two.

He's just asked a question about Aunt T when the door opens and Veronica sticks her head into the office. "Your next appointment is here to see you."

In about a second's time all that warm, fatherly stuff disappears, and Dr. Wydner morphs into something totally different. He's on his feet, handing me his business card and walking me to the door. "If there's anything else I can do for you, please call." He shakes my hand and ushers me into the hall as the next guy enters.

The rapid departure from the office has me disoriented, but not so much that I don't get a good look at the guy coming in. He's the love child of Wall Street and American Idol, polished down to his three-piece suit and shiny shoes, just the right amount of gray woven though his black hair. He smiles and says hello as we pass, but the smile doesn't reach his eyes. It's all teeth and no heart.

"Dr. Glass, it's good to see you," I hear Dr. Wydner say as I start down the hall. "I have the data you were asking about."

―――――

When I return to the waiting area, Anj, diplomat and peace-maker extraordinaire, is having a friendly conversation with a guy with a naked woman tattooed onto his shaved head. Anj's smile is a shining star in this dreary place, and she seems the happiest person in the world, sitting on the floor, chatting up some half-baked junkie.

"Come on," I say, tugging her to her feet. "Let's go."

"Back to school?" Anj asks as we leave the clinic.

I don't answer right away as I let an idea percolate. The thought has been a seed in my mind since her death, but it wasn't until I went to Melinda's and saw the Rat Catcher that it really took root: what if the heroin and the debt had something to do with Mom's death? I followed up on the clinical trial. Now it's time to follow up on the dope.

I look at Anj with her rosy cheeks and sparkly blue eyes and hesitate. I don't want to bring her there, to that place, but it's now or never. "Can we take a detour on our way back to school?"

Anj agrees and twenty minutes later we're at a place I never thought I'd see again. Nothing much has changed. The street scarred by potholes. Mad Dog in his Eagles jersey, selling hotdogs from his corner cart. The trash collecting around curbs and piling up in the gutter. The falling down Welcome sign above a boarded up store. The Pawn Shop. The torn Bud Light billboard. Welcome to paradise.

"Uh," Anj says as I direct her to an empty lot across the street from the last place Mom and I lived. "What are we doing here?"

"Stay in the car," I say instead of answering. "And lock the door. I won't be long."

Before she can protest, I dash across the street. I bite down hard and steel myself against the desire to bolt as I open the front door of my old building and trudge up the stairs, pretending the life I once led here life belonged to someone else.

I reach the apartment at the end of the second floor belonging to Wanda, the one person in this building Mom called friend. I hear music. Old R&B. Something sultry and sexy. Marvin Gaye I think. I raise my hand and knock.

"Who is it?" a muffled voice calls.

"Faith Flores. Auggie's daughter," I say to the closed door.

A second later Wanda opens the door just wide enough for me to notice that she's wearing something short and lacey with far too much exposed flesh for a Monday afternoon.

"Girl," she says, tossing her head and flipping her long black hair behind her shoulders. "I didn't think I'd see you again. What are you doing here?"

"I'm sorry to bother you. It's just…I have a question."

"Babe!" I hear a man call from inside the apartment. "Bed's getting cold."

Wanda glances over her shoulder. "Now's kind of a bad time."

"I'm sorry. I'll be quick." I bite my lip. "It's just that you and Mom were friends, so I thought maybe you'd know." I stop. Not sure I can ask. What if the answer is yes?

"Know what?"

I look into Wanda's eyes—black like obsidian, like something dark and shiny and beautiful—and find the courage. "If she was using heroin before she died."

"You came all the way here to ask me that? Aw, Faith, I'm sorry, but I can't help you. I hardly saw your mom at the end. She was acting so funny."

"What do you mean?"

"Wanda!" the man calls again. "I'm serious. Tell whoever it is to come back!"

"Look, hon. I've gotta go. I'm sorry."

"Wait! One more thing. Did you ever hear of someone called the Rat Catcher?"

The man comes to the door. Tall. Black. Gorgeous. And none too happy to see me standing here. "Wanda doesn't know anyone with that name," he answers for her. "Now we're busy. Come back when she's free."

He closes the door before Wanda can say good-bye.

I sigh and go back outside to the car. The wind's picked up since the morning. My hair whips my face. Pieces of trash swirl like snowflakes. A beer can rolls down the sidewalk and hits a wall with a metallic clank. Car brakes squeal, followed by a long honk. There's a siren somewhere. The whole city feels like an emergency, and I have a sudden need to get out of here, to quiet the thunder in my brain and try to fit together the pieces of this story. Melinda. Mom. Dr. Wydner.

Three different versions, and only one truth.

Eight

School's out for the day by the time we get back. Groups of students amble around getting ready to attend whatever afternoon clique they're part of—yearbook, football, cheerleading, art club. I say good-bye to Anj and wander toward a small grove of trees on the east side of campus at the corner of Leedam and Mill.

I sit under this granddaddy hickory, listening to a woodpecker working a tree somewhere, watching the clouds shape-shift as they float across the sky. A chickadee flutters onto a branch, investigates my presence with a cock of its head, then flits off to forage somewhere else. A red-tailed hawk circles and vanishes into the gray. Mom taught me the names of birds. She knew the names of flowers and insects, too. I asked her once why all those names and labels mattered. Knowing what things are called gives order to the world, she told me; makes the whole damned ride less lonely. I didn't understand back then. Maybe now I do.

"What happened to you, Mom?" I say to the sky. "You're dead, but I still have so many questions."

The only answer is the chatter of a squirrel.

I rest my head against the tree and think about Melinda. She didn't lie about Mom being in the clinical trial, but what about the side effects? Blaming her symptoms on a clinical trial I knew nothing about and saying she needed to see a doctor would've been a pretty clever way to pull my heartstrings and get me to give her money.

Then again her symptoms were the same as my mother's. That hardly seems like a coincidence. Suddenly I have a dozen question for Melinda, a dozen things that don't make sense. I find the flier in my bag where she wrote Al's number, get my phone, and dial. The phone rings and rings. Just as I'm about to hang up, he answers.

"Uh, hi…this is Faith Flores. I met you the other day. Melinda gave me this number and said I could get in touch with her."

"Well, you can't."

I pick up a pebble and rattle it in my fist. "Um. Okay, well then, is there another number where I could reach her?"

Al makes a disgusted grunting sound. "Not unless you know how to communicate with the dead."

The pebble slips through my fingers and drops to the ground. I press the phone to my ear and lower my voice. "What happened?"

"Shit, kid, how should I know? That woman was so messed up. Said she was clean, but cops say there was heroin. Who the hell knows? I wasn't there when she kicked it."

"Wait! What about the side effects from the clinical trial?"

"Was she feeding you that shit?" he sneers. "That woman was always going on about one thing or another. Paranoid about everything. All that junk'll do it to you. Thought everyone was out to get her. One time she thought I was putting poison in her water and she didn't drink nothing till she got so sick I had to drop her at the hospital. Side effects, my ass. She swore she wasn't using, but why else would that creep show up?"

"You mean the Rat Catcher?"

"Yeah. That's him. Lowlife scum."

"But what if Melinda really was clean?" I say, thinking about my mom. "Maybe the Rat Catcher had been her dealer in the past, and maybe she was going to rat him out to the police. Maybe he came to stop her."

"Just forget about all that," Al says. "A kid like you don't need to go messing around in this stuff. It's dangerous. Forget you was ever at Melinda's place." I hear something on the other end that could be a sigh or a sob, or maybe just a nose blow. Whatever the bodily function of Al's sound, when he speaks again, he's lost the angry edge. "Forget you ever saw anything. I'm sorry I couldn't help."

Silence, and the line goes dead.

I sit there, staring at the phone, my heart hammering until I realize I'm shivering. I grab a beanie from my bag, but it doesn't take away the chill. If only the weather was my problem. The problem is Melinda's dead. Mom's dead. The Rat Catcher was at both their places, and it's all a little too much to be a coincidence.

What was Mom doing? What kind of dangerous thing was she messed up in? What didn't she tell me?

I've struggled on my own with the questions for almost two months. I can't listen to the solo conversation in my head anymore without going crazy. ("What do you think Faith?" "I don't know what do *you* think, Faith?") I have to talk to someone. I can't talk to Aunt T about the past, and bringing Anj to my old place was bad enough. I'm not telling her about some drug dealer called the Rat Catcher. That leaves Jesse.

I gather my knees to my chest and taste the cold winter air on my lips as I consider the possibility of bringing Jesse closer into my life. He already knows my mom was an addict. He knows about Melinda and the Rat Catcher. He's smart. Energetic. Not shallow. Pretty cute (okay, nothing to do with it.) All in all, New Boy seems like the real deal—non-asshole material that might be worth trusting.

I decide to go look for him and see what he thinks.

———

I find him in the library, sitting in front of a computer, studying a picture of a DNA molecule. His face is reflected in the screen, so it looks like the double helix is printed on his forehead.

"It's a miracle something so small could hold the entire instructions for growing an organism," he says without looking up.

"A miracle?"

"Yeah, but not in the Jesus-walking-on-water kind of way, more like the holy-shit-how-did-that-happen kind of way."

Sunlight filters in through cracks in the blinds as I slide into the seat next to him. "Okay, sure, but if you don't mind me asking, why are you sitting here contemplating the miracle of life at 4:30 in the afternoon?"

"Extra credit for bio. I got a B on my last science paper at my former school." He looks at me with a grimace. Before I can ask what's so terrible about a B, he says, "We don't *do* B's in my family. I'm making up for the crime."

I watch as he rifles through a notebook and clear my throat. Then I clear it again.

"You need something to drink?" he asks, tossing me a plastic water bottle without looking up when I clear a third time.

"No, I'm good. Just a tickle."

I'm getting ready to begin my story, to tell Jesse about Melinda and the conversation with Al, about the appointment with Dr. Wydner and what I found out, when someone at the table behind us squeals. I glance over my shoulder just in time to see a senior girl I recognize from the halls throw her arms around a girl I've never seen and shriek about her acceptance to U Mass. They giggle and hug until the librarian, Mrs. Carter, wags a finger at them, and they lower their voices to whispers.

The details of my day slip away as this reminder of a different anxiety rushes in—college. I mean a year and a half and then high school is over and then what? I'm not about to parasitize Aunt T and linger around her place forever, mooching handouts. Sure, I'd love to go to some killer college like everyone else around here, but it's not like Mom left a pot of gold hidden somewhere for me to inherit. I have what? Two hundred dollars? From what I've heard, college costs a bit more than that these days. I scroll through my mental list of life-after-high-school possibilities: community college, applying for financial aid, a job, riding off into the sunset and nobody ever hearing from me again.

Jesse pokes me in the arm with his pencil. "I think you were about to say something. Either that or you were going to clear your throat again."

"What? Oh, right." I will away the post-high-school turmoil and turn my attention back to more immediate concerns, but before I can utter a syllable, another squeal erupts from the college crew as the girl delivers her news to a boy who's just joined them. This time Mrs. Carter lays down the law. She tells them if they can't keep their enthusiasm to an appropriate level, she will personally escort them to the gymnasium where Coach Johnson will be glad to run them until they're too tired to talk.

Once Mrs. Carter has delivered her dissertation on library etiquette and the glee club goes quiet, I lean in closer to Jesse. "Melinda's dead," I begin. I give Jesse a detailed description of what happened today, including what Al told me about Melinda and the Rat Catcher. I omit the part about visiting my old place and my fear that Mom might've still been a junkie and skip to Dr. Wydner and what I learned at the clinic.

"I asked Dr. Wydner if there were side effects from the treatment, but he said he couldn't comment." No sooner have the words left my lips than something occurs to me. I sit up and reach for the keyboard. When in doubt, Google. "Just because Dr. Wydner said he couldn't discuss side effects doesn't mean there aren't any."

"RNA 120?" Jesse asks, standing up behind me and reading over my shoulder as I type. "What's that?"

"The name of the treatment in the clinical trial," I say, staring at the screen.

The search brings up a few technical research papers with words like antisense RNA and protein encoding and adenovirus. Might as well be Chinese. There's one thing that might be of use: a name. I click on it.

> Dr. Monroe, assistant professor in the Department of Human Genetics at Philadelphia University, has recently patented a new antisense RNA drug therapy called RNA 120 to help break the cycle of heroin addiction.

I look up Dr. Monroe's name and find out that the professor's still at the university, then I slide my hands off the keyboard and turn to Jesse. "It looks like I'm going to the city tomorrow. You in?"

Jesse rocks back on his chair, kicks his feet on the table, and sighs. "Sorry. Tomorrow's out. I have an alumni interview on Friday. Some Harvard lawyer whose kid goes here. Doc wants me to get an early start on the whole brown-nosing thing. Most people wait until senior year to rub shoulders with the elite. Not me. Doc set up a meeting for me with the college guidance counselor tomorrow morning, so she can coach me on what to say. He wants to make sure I don't screw up and actually sound like a real person."

I hear the eye rolling in Jesse's voice. Try as I might to imagine him in a shirt and tie, spewing bullshit about how excited and qualified he is for the Ivy League, I can't. He seems so willing to bow to Doc. Jesse might be all Rage Against the Machine on the outside, but I wonder how much rebel he really is on the inside?

I turn off the computer and shake my head. "Shit, Jesse, do you even want to go to Harvard?"

"Not really," he says, scribbling on his jeans with a pen. "Maybe someday. I have other things to do first."

"Like what?"

He doodles down the length of his thigh and traces circles around the tear on the knee. "Live. Travel. See shit."

"Well then, maybe you should try telling that to Doc."

Jesse gives a bitter laugh. "You don't tell Doc things. He tells you."

"Fine, but—"

"There are no buts." His chair clanks to the floor. "That's the law of the Schneider universe. Doc makes rules. Everyone else follows."

Mrs. Carter calls out, breaking her vow of library silence, and tells us it's time to get going. She's closing the library, and if anyone would like to check out materials they should please do so now. Jesse throws his things into his backpack and checks out a book about the discovery of the double helix. I gather my stuff, and we leave.

"I'd give you a ride," Jesse says, stopping when we reach the front door, "but I'm meeting Seth, from bio. He's doing the extra credit, too."

Before I can decide if I'm ready for a good-bye hug, or if I'm still in the eye poke phase, Jesse wraps his arms around me. At first the embrace is your ordinary give-your-pal-a-hug variety, but quickly it becomes more than that. He pulls me so close I can feel the beat of his heart, smell the spice of his shampoo.

"Good luck, tomorrow," he whispers into my ear. "Text and tell me what you find out."

He drops his arms and trots off down the hall to find Seth, leaving me standing there, still wobbly from the hug, thinking it's not luck I need. It's answers.

Nine

My phone rings the next morning before it's light out. I fumble around for where the ringing's coming from and finally find the phone on the bedside table under *The Sun Also Rises*, compliments of Jesse.

"Surprise! It's me," comes Jesse's voice before I'm even alert enough to say hello. "Wake-up call. I have an idea."

"Don't you ever sleep?" I mumble, rubbing my eyes.

"Sleep, what's that? Read about it once." He sounds far too chipper for whatever ungodly hour it might be. "Okay, here's the deal. I'm coming to get you and we're going out to breakfast. You dressed?"

I bolt upright and check the clock, then groan. "You really are crazy. It's five o'clock, and it's dark out, and if wearing flannel pajamas counts as being dressed, then yes, I'm dressed. And no, I am not going out to breakfast, and besides, what's open this early?"

"Denny's—come on. I'm outside."

"What?" I leap out of bed, awake now, and run to the window. I can just make out the rusty hatchback parked outside the house. Jesse flashes the one working headlight, illuminating the fact that not only is it pitch black out, but it's snowing.

"You coming or what?"

"Coming." I sigh and laugh. Somehow Jesse has a way of making anything sound like a good idea.

I throw on the same clothes from yesterday, grab my bag, and tiptoe into Aunt T's room to leave a note about where I've gone.

In the subtle glow from the hall light, I can just make out the sweep of Aunt T's blond hair, the slight upturn of her nose, the way she sleeps with her hand draped across her forehead. I stand there for a second, disoriented—it's like seeing Mom, only older. I look away and wonder how two sisters, same gene pool, raised in the same house by the same people, could have such different outcomes?

If I were to write the story of Mom and Aunt T, I'd call it *A Tale of Two Sisters* and the synopsis would go like this: Once upon a time there were two girls who lived in a small house by the Hudson River. The older sister was level headed and calm, born of a soft September breeze, while the younger sister was wild and angry, born of ocean waves and thunder. The older sister listened to female singer songwriters and R&B. The younger sister listened to death metal and rap. The older sister liked to stay in and read. The younger sister liked to stay out and party. The older sister turned eighteen and got into college. The younger sister turned eighteen and got into drugs. The end.

Just as sadness and anger stick their nasty little fingers into my chest and get hold of my heart, the phone vibrates in my pocket. I grab it and check the screen. *U coming or not?* I reach into my bag, thankful for the distraction, and find a piece of paper. I use the light from the phone to scribble a few lines to Aunt T about getting to school early to do some work, then drop the note on her dresser and leave.

I hear Modest Mouse blaring from Jesse's car the second I open the front door. I'm surprised someone hasn't called the cops for noise violation. I'm surprised the dude has any hearing left.

"You're insane," I say, climbing into the car and turning off the stereo. Like me, Jesse's wearing the same clothes as last night. The difference is, his appear slept in. His hair has seen better days, too. The back is sticking straight out and the top straight up. His eyes are red, but he's smiling.

"You got that right. Hungry?"

"Starving."

"Then Denny's it is." He twists his head to the left and backs out of the driveway. "Home of the twenty-four-hour Grand Slam."

The snow is falling harder now. The roads glint slick and silver. Besides a few semis, we're the only ones out. I watch a ribbon of orange break through the black sky. Maybe it's because I'm still half asleep, or maybe it has to do with sitting next to Jesse, but for the first time in forever, I feel still inside, like a prayer.

A few minutes later, Jesse pulls into the Denny's parking lot and the spell is broken. I open the door to the outside world and follow him into the restaurant.

The second we're seated he slides a green spiral notebook across the table. "Read this."

I glance at him and open the notebook. The first page is filled with notes under the heading *Gene Therapy*, so is the second page and the third. The notebook is at least a quarter filled with scribbled notes. "What *is* this?"

"Research."

"On what?" I ask, though from the title it's obvious.

"Gene therapy," he says from behind a menu. "Vectors."

"Whose is it?"

He peeks up over the menu. "Mine. I looked it up last night."

"Wow, you weren't kidding about the OCD thing. What did you do, stay up half the night?"

He drops the menu to the table, stretches his arms over his head, and yawns. "All night. Insomnia rules."

A tired-looking girl with spiked blue hair arrives to take our orders. I order two blueberry pancakes, Jesse orders the Grand Slam breakfast special, and the girl plods off to the kitchen to place our orders.

"Okay, here's the thing," he says the second she's gone. "After you looked up that RNA 120 stuff, I started wondering what it was. I did some research, and I found out it's kind of like a gene therapy. Check this out." He grabs back the notebook, flips through a bunch of pages, and somehow in all the scribble manages to find the one he's looking for. "'The first step to gene therapy is designing a delivery system to introduce a new gene or turn off the old one. The delivery system for gene therapy is called a vector. Viruses are the favored vector.'"

"Viruses?"

"Like flu, mumps, HIV. That sort of thing."

"HIV, as in AIDS?" I massage my temples. "Are you saying they were injecting my mother with the HIV virus, so they could get a new gene into her body to make her heroin cravings go away?"

"Not HIV. But yeah, something like that." Jesse closes the notebook and chugs his entire glass of water without stopping for a breath. He wipes his mouth with the back of his hand and keeps going. "They take out the bad genes from the virus, put in some new ones, and let the virus do its thing."

"Which is?"

"To get the new gene to the cell, so it can make more copies of itself." He holds my eye for a second with his. "Sometimes the body can react to the vector."

I reach into my pocket and draw my finger over Mom's initials engraved into the lighter, the groove of the A, the blunt lines of the F. "React like how?"

"Like die. I read an article about this eighteen-year-old kid who volunteered to be in a gene therapy trial to treat this rare liver problem he had."

"And?"

"Four days after the vector was injected he died."

"That's really depressing," I mumble as the waitress arrives with our food and we stop talking.

"Anything else?" the girl asks, already looking to the next table where a group of five promises a bigger tip.

"Nothing else," Jesse says and digs into his eggs.

I pick at my food and look out the window, thinking about the boy and wondering if what happened to him is what happened to my mother, if her death was—as Jesse calls it—a "reaction." But if that's the case, why did her death certificate say heroin overdose?

I stare out the window, lost in these thoughts, and watch the falling snow. It's coming down hard now. Big, fluffy flakes temporarily cover everything ugly beneath a glistening white surface.

"And what about other side effects?" I ask, clinking the ice in my glass. "Did you find anything like my mom had?"

"Not exactly." He grabs the knife and smears a glob of butter big enough to have its own zip code across his toast. "But it's possible. I just ran out of time. Give me another few hours and who knows what I'd come up with." He rips open a packet of strawberry jam, slathers it on top of the butter, and licks the knife. "But I did find out something else." Jesse slides the notebook back across the table, the page open to a newspaper article from the Trenton Times printed off the Internet. "Check it out."

> May 4, 2013, Trenton, NJ; Mary Wydner, the sixteen-year-old daughter of a local doctor, Dr. Joseph Wydner, was found unconscious last night after a party at a hotel in Lawrenceville. Trenton Police Detective Keith Hadley said investigators determined the girl's blood showed overdose levels of opiates. According to friends, the girl had spent two months last year in rehabilitation for heroin, but had a relapse and recently started using again. She is in Trenton hospital in a coma, and is currently unresponsive

I've barely processed this latest information when Jesse points to the notebook. "Turn the page."

I do as instructed and find a different article from the same newspaper.

> July 3, 2013, Trenton, NJ; Dr. Joseph Wydner was charged with injecting bodybuilders with illegal steroids. The New Jersey State Board of Medical Examiners suspended the medical license of Doctor Wydner pending further investigation.

I fill in the blanks as I read, what the article leaves out. Dr. Wydner's heroin-addicted daughter ODs and goes into a coma. He falls apart, loses his job, starts selling steroids and gets busted, so he takes a job running a clinical trial for a biopharmaceutical company at a run-down methadone clinic. The end. No wonder his office was so empty.

A deep sadness shudders through me. The world at this moment seems nothing more than sorrow and death. I pour about a gallon of maple syrup over my pancakes and watch the excess liquid pool around the edges of my plate.

"I have a theory," Jesse says, stabbing a potato with his fork.

"A theory?" I ask, but my heart isn't in it.

"Dr. Wydner's hoping his kid's going to wake up, right?"

I shrug. "I guess."

"Come on, man, think about it." He sounds miffed about my lack of enthusiasm. "It's his kid. He'll do anything to save her. Why not hide the fact that some people might have side effects, so he can help get the drug on the market? If she wakes up, he can get her off heroin and they'll live happily ever after."

He stuffs the potato in his mouth, and that's the end of the discussion—at least for the time being. He's all about his food now, thank God, because even though his theory about Dr. Wydner covering up the side effects makes sense, there are still the unanswered questions about the heroin and Mom's death certificate and my mind has officially declared itself in overdrive. I need some time to reboot and clear my head before I meet Dr. Monroe and find out what the professor has to say.

Something nags at me, some unsettled business. For a minute I'm not sure what that something is, but then I remember the other day, when after meeting Melinda, Jesse offered his help. Instead of thanking him for his ideas and concern, and for being the first person to take me seriously about my mother, I had an outburst of assholeitis and told him I wasn't a charity case.

I clear my throat and fidget my hands in my lap. "Thanks for doing all this research. I mean I know you have a ton of homework. You didn't have to—"

"I know I didn't *have* to," he cuts in. He drops his fork onto his plate with a loud clang that makes me raise my eyes. "But I wanted to. I like you."

"You stayed up all night blowing off your homework because you like me?"

"What's wrong with that?" he asks, meeting my eyes. Looking into those maddeningly blue blues my brain goes murky, but it's not just his eyes that disarm me—it's the idea that Jesse might really see me for who I am.

I know he wants me to say more, like how I feel about him. I want to tell him I think he's cool and fun to hang around and smart, but I can't. It would mean I want something from him, or worse, that he could have something from me. Instead, I mutter, "Nothing's wrong with it," and shove a forkful of pancake into my mouth.

We go quiet again. It's hard to shoot the shit after someone's just confessed they like you and your response was to stuff your face with food.

"What was your mother like?" Jesse asks just as I'm about to say something about the weather to try and fill the awkward silence.

I groan. Any conversation but that. It's one thing to talk about how Mom died and what happened to her, another to talk about her as a real person, as in who she was, and what it was like to be her kid. Then again, this is my chance to say something real about how I feel. Like I miss her. Like half the time *I* was the mother, and I hate her for that. Like no matter how bad it got, she always made sure I had clothes. Food. A place to live. Like she always said she loved me and, despite it all, I loved her, too.

I pick at my black nail polish, thinking of the mile long list of things I could tell Jesse. She was impulsive, funny, hardheaded, selfish, a dreamer. None of that seems the right answer, though.

"Everyone called her a junkie," I finally say, "but it's not the right word."

"What's the right word, then?"

"I don't know." I look down at my half-eaten food. "Screwed-up addict. Functional fuck-up." I give a hollow laugh. "She did everything she could to hide her addiction from the outside world because if someone found out the truth, they could take me away from her. So hiding her addiction was a way of loving me. Some logic, huh?" I feel the familiar aching void like hunger only no amount of food will make it go away. I reach for the lighter. "She hated herself for it. I know that. I hated her, too. But I also loved her. I don't get that part. How can you love someone who you hate so much?"

I stop talking. I've said too much already. "What about you?"

"What about me?"

"I don't know. Anything. What were you like as a baby?"

"Bald without teeth."

"Come on, Jesse, I'm serious. You get to ask me all these questions about my life. What about your mother? You never talk about her."

"Fine. About six months ago she wouldn't get out of bed. The end."

"The end? That's your story? She wouldn't get out of bed? Was she sick?"

Jesse looks out the window. In the long pause that follows, I realize how much easier it is for him to do the asking than the telling. It's harder when you're the one baring your soul.

"Sick, yeah, but not physically," he finally says. "Depressed."

"Depressed?"

"Look, this isn't something I want to talk about, so how about we—"

"Don't talk about things that are hard? Yeah, I haven't done any of *that* today." I say it as a joke, but Jesse doesn't laugh. "Look, I'm not going to get all Dr. Phil on your ass. I'm all for repression and denial, but fair's fair. I told you something. Actually, I told you a lot of somethings. It's your turn."

It's like sticking a tack into a balloon. Jesse goes flat. His shoulders slump. Even his face seems slack.

"My mom always tried to be the perfect wife and mother," he begins slowly, as if the words have to fight their way to the surface. "She had to keep up appearances and all that crap. She had to do it for Doc." He drops his eyes and settles his gaze on his lap. "I guess she couldn't take the pressure anymore. Let's just say our family's in free fall right now, and without Mom there isn't any parachute to slow us down. Doc's dealing with the whole thing by channeling Stalin. 'Didn't do your homework? To the Gulag!'"

"How's she doing now?" I ask, wishing I knew how to bridge the canyon between my hurt and his. "Is she getting better?"

"Depends what you mean by better. Better than she was when we were in the city, yeah. Like she was before? No way." He balls his hands into fists and presses them to his eyes. "Doc blames me for how she is. He never says it, but it's what he's thinking."

"How on earth could it be your fault?" I feel like a hypocrite for asking. How many times have I blamed myself for what happened to *my* mother, told myself I could've done something to help—made her see a doctor, given her vitamins, herbs, crystals, prayed, hired an exorcist?

"According to Doc, I'm the original fuck-up. He says I make her life hell—skipping school, not giving a shit. Maybe he's right. But every time I try to be his college-bound-Ivy-League-wet-dream, I feel like I'm going to kill someone." He pushes his plate away and it skids across the table. "Mom's the real reason we moved out here. It wasn't for me. I'm just the excuse, so Doc doesn't have to admit to anyone that his wife's plunged off the deep end. Gotta keep up appearances, you know?"

He stops talking. I search for something to say. I could tell him not to worry—that it'll all be okay and none of this is his fault. Isn't that what people do when you fess up to your problems? Try to make you feel better? It's bullshit though. Trite platitudes just make you retreat deeper and feel less understood.

"I'm sorry," I murmur, offering up the only words I can think of.

Jesse looks at me for the first time since he started talking about his mom. In the look that passes between us, something inside me shifts. His world isn't so different from mine after all.

He reaches out and touches my hand. I let his fingers join with mine. The touch is our bridge. For the first time I feel my way across the divide.

Ten

A half hour later Jesse drops me at the train station so I can go meet Dr. Monroe, and we say good-bye with a hug. This time the hug isn't so much a current in my belly as a connection in my heart. I hold back on a kiss, though. I'm not ready for that. The bridge might be there, but there's still a speed limit.

I sit on a bench with a few student commuters once Jesse's gone and imagine what it would be like to be a college student, to study biology or some other science, physics maybe. Not that I'd ever fit in with the AP physics clique and their quarks and N-dimensional space and inside jokes. *Two atoms were walking across a street when one said, "I think I lost an electron." "Really?" the other replied, "Are you sure?" "Yes, I'm absolutely positive."* Give me life science any day. If you can see it, you know it's real. Maybe I'd study genetics, and like Mrs. Lopez said, be in the forefront of scientific discovery. The problem is when I follow the thought and go through the list of steps needed to actually becoming a scientist— steps which begin with college, which begins with applying, which begins with dealing with financial aid—my internal hard drive crashes and rebooting just gives me a headache. So I push it all away.

I take out my iPod, close my eyes, and tune out to Bob Marley until the train arrives. I listen to "One Love" all the way to Sixty-ninth, where I get the Market Line to Thirty-ninth. From there, I turn off the tunes and walk, letting the sounds of the city be my music.

Last year the school guidance counselor at West Philly High took every sophomore on a campus tour of Philly U, and I remember seeing the human genetics department, a complex of impressive-looking buildings with lots of glass and steel and elevated walkways, so I know where I'm going—at least generally speaking.

I pass a vegetarian taco place, an all night pizza parlor, and a vinyl shop with posters of The Grateful Dead, Miles Davis, and Eric Clapton decorating the front window. Just as I pass Sydney's Second Hand Clothes, someone creeps up behind me and grabs my elbow. Judging from the strength of the grip and the size of the hand, I'm thinking some testosterone-fueled bastard is about to mug me. The IMPACT personal safety You Tube video with the man in the padded suit and the woman attacking him and screaming, "GROIN! EYES! ELBOW!" flashes through my mind.

I whip around to take a swing at the guy's nuts. He seizes my free arm before I can make contact, but not before I get a look at his face and discover it's not some mugger after the three quarters, lint, and lighter in my pocket. It's him. The Rat Catcher.

"Shouldn't you be in school?" he hisses into my ear as his grip on my elbow tightens, and he forces me down the side-walk around a girl with a messenger bag slung over her chest.

I wriggle my arm and try to struggle free, but his hold is too tight. "What do you want from me?" I say in a taut voice I hardly recognize as my own.

Instead of an answer, he pulls me off the sidewalk into an alley and now I'm thinking, great, he's going to kill me, and the real panic sets in. My heart hammers furiously as I check out the scene for an escape. Dead end to my left, and Mr. Drug-Dealing-Thug is blocking access to the right. I wait to see what happens, which, unless you count the Rat Catcher lighting a cigarette and blowing smoke in my face as something happening, is nothing.

With the Rat Catcher this close, I notice he's younger than I first thought. I realize the erosion of his face isn't so much a byproduct of time as a byproduct of a life hard lived. The acne scars on his right cheek. The yellow teeth and empty space where an upper left canine should be. His unwashed hair, the ashtray of his breath. I almost feel sorry for him. He seems more like a street bum than a drug dealer.

But then our eyes meet, and my nanosecond of pity hemorrhages and suffers instant death. The look he gives me is nothing to feel sorry for. The look in his eyes is a mix of madness, determination, and something else I don't even have the word for, but makes me shrink back against the wall and look again for an escape.

"I heard through the grapevine that you've been poking your nose around in your mother's death," he says in a low voice that reminds me of the kind of snarl a dog gives when warning an intruder off his territory. I start to respond, but he holds up a finger and continues. "Listen to me and listen carefully. Your mother was a drug addict. It's bad business, and if you keep asking questions, you're going to end up meeting some people who, I can assure you, you don't want to know." He drops his cigarette, stubs it out with the toe of his boot, then smiles showing off those big, unbrushed yellows. "This is where

I come in. I'm here to give you a little friendly advice, Sweetie. You don't want to get involved in this. Do you understand?"

"No. I don't understand," I snap, conjuring up defiant, tough-girl Faith. It's all smoke and mirrors, though. The real me, the one behind the assertive voice and FU attitude, is terrified. "Who are you? Her dealer?"

The Rat Catcher studies me with dark, unblinking eyes. "Let's just say I work for some powerful people who do not favor a kid poking into their business. As long as you stop asking questions, you'll be fine. Remember, I know where you live and how to find you."

Before I can say anything else, he steps out of the alley and into the street.

"Wait!" I chase after him, but I've taken just two steps when the light changes, and I'm nearly flattened by a taxi.

I jump back onto the sidewalk, and he disappears into the crowd.

Fear and adrenaline blast my legs into action. I take off running toward the university. I don't care how stupid I look sprinting down Spruce Street in combat boots and a leather coat. I don't stop running until I'm on a campus quad surrounded by turreted brick buildings like medieval castles. I lean against a wall to catch my breath. What people was the Rat Catcher talking about? Who doesn't want me poking around? Who was Mom messed up with? A drug mob?

Something pegs me in the chest. I scream, certain I've been shot, and then flush from head to toe when I realize the "bullet" was a Frisbee and it must belong to the smiling blond guy trotting toward me like a golden retriever.

"Sorry," the bearded blond says when he's a few feet away. "Didn't mean to scare you." He opens his hands and I'm thinking what, you want money? And then I realize he wants me to throw his toy to him.

I pick up the Frisbee and fling it lamely in his direction. He calls thanks over his shoulder and goes back to the grass to join the other Frisbee-playing college coeds.

As I watch the Frisbee game, my breathing slows, my heart beat returns to a nonlethal rate, and I consider my options: Stay safe, abort the mission, and forget asking questions, or take the risk, continue to Dr. Monroe's office, and find out what I can about the clinical trial.

The choice is obvious.

I pick up my pace to meet the professor.

A few streets later I'm in front of the genetics department. I follow a hedge-lined path past a stone statue of some serious-looking bald guy whose head is covered with pigeon shit. A bunch of the offending birds roost on his shoulders and arms. *Immortalized in pigeon shit—every scientist's dream.* Finally, I reach what appears to be the main building. I enter a vast circular lobby with three sets of elevators and overhead walkways jutting out in all directions like tentacles.

I'm standing there, literally scratching my head, when a short, curly-haired guy wheeling a metal cart packed with microscopes passes. I stop him, half expecting him to ask me for ID or something to prove I belong here. He doesn't, and I tell him who I'm looking for.

"Next building to the right. Third floor. Room 310."

What's left of my adrenaline propels me up the stairs two at a time to the second floor. I take the elevator up another level to the third floor and start down the main hall, reading room numbers and course titles as I go: *Molecular Basis of*

Human Genetic Diseases. Genomic Technology. Developmental Biology and Genetics. Statistical Analysis of Biological Data. Model Organisms and Epigenetics. I recognize individual words, but string them together and I've landed on another planet.

The hall ends in a T. I turn right and follow the numbers until halfway down this new hall I find room 310. The door is closed and covered with cartoons of talking bugs, mad scientists, and cows that stand on two feet. Next to the door is a plaque that says *Dr. Monroe: Molecular Genetics of Drug Addiction. Office Hours: Tuesday and Wednesday 10:00–11:00 and by appointment.* I check my phone. 9:30. I plop to the floor and trace circles in the dust with the toe of my boot, checking the time approximately every five seconds as I wait for the professor to arrive.

At ten, a small, ponytailed woman wearing jeans and sneakers walks down the hall and unlocks the door. She turns when she sees me sitting there and asks if I need any help.

"I'm here to see Dr. Monroe," I say, jumping to my feet.

"You're in luck. That's me. What can I do for you?"

I white-knuckle the lighter in my pocket and take a breath. "I'm here about my mother. She was in the clinical trial for RNA 120 at the Twenty-third Street Methadone Clinic."

Dr. Monroe's eyebrows rise above her pale green eyes. She's pretty, I notice, but not the kind of pretty that's self-conscious or put on. She has an earthy confidence about her. "I see," she says. "Come inside and we can talk."

I follow Dr. Monroe through her lab. The walls are plastered with diplomas and white boards scribbled with equations and notes. Every inch of counter, table, and desk space is occupied with notebooks, papers, books, and weird looking machinery. The weirdest piece of machinery though, is this large appliance-like white box attached to a computer. The thing takes up half a counter. I stare at the blinking lights and listen to its hum.

Dr. Monroe follows my gaze. "Pretty cool, huh?"

"I guess. What is it?"

"A DNA sequencer. I can pop in a sample of DNA and a day later the sequence for whatever gene I'm looking at is emailed to me."

"Emailed?" I blurt. "So, like if you have a mutation or something it comes to your inbox along with discount offers to Target and Facebook messages from your friends?"

Dr. Monroe smiles. "It's a little more complicated than that, but basically, yes." She goes into the office connected to the lab. I follow and wait as she riffles through about a zillion pages scattered on her desk. She plucks the one she's looking for from the mess and hands me a paper filled with what must be thousands of A, T, C, and G's, the letters of the genetic code. "AGS3," she says, as if this might mean something to me. "It's a gene that plays an important role in opiate craving."

I stare at the rows of tiny letters until my eyes go blurry. "So just like that you could put some of my blood into that machine and sequence my DNA, and I'd find out if I had that gene?" I say, handing back the paper.

Dr. Monroe laughs. "It's not quite that easy, but yes. I could sequence one or all of your genes, depending on how much time and money you had."

I can hardly speak. Standing here, staring at the real deal, a machine that can actually sequence my genetic code, I think about Mrs. Lopez's question again. Would I want to know? *Do* I want to know? I thought the answer was yes, but now I'm not so sure I want my A, T, C, and G's appearing in somebody's inbox.

"Now, how can I help you?" she asks, attempting to bring order to the anarchy of her desk. "You said it was about your mother."

An image flashes through my mind—a blustery March day and Mom's taken me to the Morris Arboretum, blocks from here, to admire the blooms of the witch hazel, their ruby red flowers a promise of spring. No sooner does the image appear than it mutates. The red flowers turn to blood, her sleek hair to tangles. She's scabby and emaciated, hunched over the kitchen table wheezing for breath. I blink and look at Dr. Monroe.

"Right before my mom died she got really sick. Everyone tells me she had side effects from the heroin, but I was wondering if maybe there could've been side effects from the clinical trial." I pick nervously at a piece of lint on my sweater and look at the floor. "I mean from, you know, your drug. RNA 120?"

Dr. Monroe stops moving. Even though I'm studying the pattern of grain in the wood floor, I can feel her eyes on me. "What kind of side effects?"

"Like her skin," I say, glancing up. "It was all blistered and scabby. And she started getting short of breath, wheezing all the time."

Dr. Monroe adjusts the fold of her turtleneck and doesn't answer right away. "I suppose it's possible she had an immune reaction to the vector," she finally says, but before she can elaborate, there's a knock on the door. "If you'll excuse me." She crosses the office and opens the door to a trim, gray-haired guy in a striped shirt and khakis.

"I'm sorry to interrupt," the man says, looking past Dr. Monroe and smiling an apology at me, "but I've been reviewing your dossier and I have some questions about the NIH grant." He hands her a thick document in a brown file folder. "You'll want to review that before the tenure meeting."

She takes the document and flips through a few pages, nodding as she goes.

"Also, I have a question about some data in the AGS3 paper. I heard Bickwell's lab is submitting a similar manuscript to *Nature*. I don't want you to get scooped on this. How soon can we meet?"

"I have office hours and class until three," she says, tucking the folder under an arm.

"Fine, let's say four o'clock in my office. I think that's about it, at least for now. You all set for the conference next week?"

"Once I get through this," she says, holding out the folder. "And the tenure meeting. And that." She points to a table in the corner of her office where a pile of papers is stacked underneath what must be a week's worth of empty Chinese food take out boxes. "Not to mention two sections of intro genetics, office hours, and senior seminar." It's the to-do list of a small empire, but if the workload is a stress to her, she doesn't show it. "Then, I'll think about the conference. I'm just glad Glass is presenting RNA 120 and not me."

I look around the room as she talks, but this time it's not the machinery and books I think about. It's Dr. Monroe. She's a real scientist, a professor, someone who does research and teaches classes and has office hours. What would it be like to be the one sitting here, the one inventing new cures and analyzing DNA? For the briefest moment I see my life stretch in front of me, and in that flash it *is* me sitting here. It *is* me with the big degree. I'm no longer Faith Flores, junkie's daughter. I'm Faith Flores, PhD.

"Well, I'll leave you to it," the man says, snapping me out of my fantasy. "I'll see you this afternoon."

Dr. Monroe comes back into her office once he's gone and drops the folder on the table, knocking over one of the Chinese food boxes. "You know you're up for tenure when the delivery kid at Beijing knows your office address by heart," she says, tossing the box at the trash and missing. "Okay, where were we? Immune reactions I believe." She sits in the only seat not being used as storage and clears textbooks from the other chair for me. "An immune reaction happens sometimes when the body rejects the virus carrying the DNA strand. It might see the vector as foreign material and attack it with antibodies. That can, of course, cause all sorts of problems."

"Vector?" I ask, remembering Jesse's discourse this morning. "Is the drug some kind of gene therapy?"

"It sounds like you've done your homework." She picks up a pen and taps it on the table. "The drug is like a gene therapy, but a little different. What I use in this treatment is something called antisense RNA."

"What's the difference?"

"The difference is that in gene therapy, you replace a defective gene. What my drug does is work to shut a gene down." She looks at me to see if I'm following. "In addicts, we want to shut the gene down that causes the craving. But both things use a modified human virus, a vector, to get the DNA into the body. Does that make sense?"

"I guess," I say.

"None of that really matters, though, does it? It's a bunch of scientist talk. The important thing is your mother. How's she doing now?"

I'm sure she's hoping for some kind of success story. My mother quit smack, got a job, and we lived happily ever after. I feel ashamed now, coming here to trouble some professor about my mother's death. I look at a poster about the human genome on the wall above her head when I answer, so I don't have to meet her eyes.

"She's dead."

"Dead?" Dr. Monroe runs a hand through her hair, pulling loose her ponytail. I notice lines around her eyes I hadn't seen before when she was smiling. "I'm so sorry. What happened?"

"The medical examiner's report said it was a heroin overdose, but she was clean. I know she was." I try to sound scientific, or at least factual, as I explain what I believe about the end of my mother's life, but the truth is, no matter how I spin the story I don't have any facts to back it up.

"She could've stopped going in for the treatment and relapsed," she says when I've finished my tale. "You have to inject the drug weekly for several sessions for it to work. But even if she did relapse and had morphine in her blood, with the symptoms you described, I think you're right to be skeptical. There was probably an underlying problem."

I don't say anything. We sit in wordless silence, listening to the whir of the sequencing machine as it works to decode some person's inner mystery, to reveal the secrets of their health, sickness, longevity, whatever it is scientists understand from reading the order of those four letters.

"Well, I'm sorry I couldn't be more of a help, and I'm terribly sorry for your loss," Dr. Monroe says at last. She pushes the chair back from the table with an abruptness that makes me jump.

"Wait! Please. There's one more thing. I wouldn't have come down here and bothered you about my mother if it didn't seem strange."

"If what didn't seem strange?"

"My mom had a friend who was in the clinical trial with her. I saw her a few days ago. She said she was clean, but she had the same symptoms as my mom, and then she died too."

Something cold flashes in Dr. Monroe's eyes, but before she can respond there's another knock. She walks briskly across the room and opens the door.

"Carla," she says to the skinny, dark-haired girl waiting in the hall, "I'll be right with you." She closes the door and turns back to me, but leaves her hand on the knob. "Look, I don't know what you're hoping to find out, but I can tell you there is nothing wrong with RNA 120. I spent the past six years developing this treatment. Do you know how many post-docs have worked on this? How many lab techs and research assistants? NIH money. Grants. There's no evidence in all my years of preclinical studies to support any symptoms like you're describing." She draws a sharp breath and glances at the folder on the table. "The symptoms your mother and her friend shared were a coincidence. Addicts are susceptible to all sorts of problems: liver disease, respiratory issues, viruses, collapsed veins, abscesses, pneumonia...." I think she's done talking, but then, in a softer voice, she says, "I don't know you, but it seems to me maybe it's best if you accept that your mother died of an overdose and move on. I'm sorry." She opens the door to a pack of students gathered outside her office. "Is there anything else?"

"Nothing else," I say, standing.

"Then if you'll excuse me. It's office hours."

I walk past the students without making eye contact and beeline for the bathroom where I lock myself in a stall. I sit on the toilet, head in my hands, and think about how silly it is to be disappointed that the symptoms my mother had weren't connected to the treatment in the clinical trial, but I can't help feeling let down. At least the clinical trial gave me a direction to pursue, a possibility of finding an answer, even if it was an answer I didn't like.

I'm still sitting in the stall, working my brain cells for how all the pieces fit together, when I feel my phone vibrate against my thigh. I yank it from my front pocket and see a text from Anj: *Are you totally ignoring me or what?*

I'm confused until I notice the two other messages—one text, one voice. I check the text first: *WHERE ARE YOU?????* *WE WERE SUPPOSED TO MEET THIS MORNING!!!!*

I cover my face with my hand and groan. I'm so busted. The social studies project. Today's Tuesday. I promised to meet Anj in the library before school to work on it.

I have to hold the phone about a foot from my ear so I don't go deaf when I listen to the voice message. *IT'S EIGHT O' CLOCK AND THE BELL'S RINGING* AND *YOU WERE SUPPOSED TO MEET ME IN THE LIBRARY AT SEVEN THIRTY!*

My head fills with this new crisis. Anj might be all sugar and sweetness on the outside, but stand her up, or burn her in some other way, and all her volatile chemicals release. She caramelizes into something hard and brittle. I have to get back to school and talk to her. Maybe she'll forgive me if I promise to go home and learn Arawak.

———

An hour and a half later I'm in the cafeteria, expecting to find Anj at the center table with Tara and crew, eating organic vegan sandwiches and plotting the overthrow of all things unjust. Instead, I find her nestled at a corner table with Duncan, her Scottish lover boy. I loiter in the corner of the cafeteria between the table shared by the Goths and emos and the milk cart station and watch. Duncan, with his coppery hair sweeping across his blue-gray eyes, laughs at something Anj says, showing off his perfect chin dimple. Anj, in her flirty off-the-shoulder tee and mock diamond choker, basks in his attention.

I'm thinking of leaving the lovebirds alone and blowing off the whole apology thing until later when Anj looks up and catches my eye. I give a little smile and wave, but she doesn't return the greeting. Even from across the cafeteria I can tell she's still pissed. I take a deep breath and go over to make amends.

"Where were you this morning?" she demands the second I get to the table.

"I'm—"

"You're what? Sorry?" she interrupts, shoving her lunch aside. Her chocolate pudding splats to the floor, but she ignores the mess. "Because for your information I need an A on this project from Mr. Robertson, and it happens to be due next week, and I can't do it without you. So, what's your story?"

"I was—"

"And don't even tell me you had something more important to do."

"Anj, will you let the lass talk?" Duncan says. The lilt of his words gives the sentence a musical quality that for a second makes me blank and forget why I'm here.

"Fine." She folds her arms across her chest and gives me the death stare. "I'm waiting."

I stand on the sticky floor, next to the smear of chocolate pudding slime, brain dead about what to say. I could follow the path of least resistance and make up something (Great sale at Wanamaker's! Couldn't miss it!), so I can avoid the whole mother thing, but Anj has a BS barometer that can detect even the tiniest rise in bullshit. If I want a friend five minutes from now, I have to tell her what's going on.

"Well?"

A denim-clad dude from the ghetto crowd looks up from his table and checks me out as if assessing my suitability for recruitment into their cult of suburban gangster wannabes. I ignore him, take a deep breath, and give Anj, and by proximity, Duncan, the scoop on the last few days: Melinda, the RNA 120 clinical trial, my visit to the university. I don't want to send Anj into a panicked tizzy though, so I spare them the part about the Rat Catcher and his threats.

Anj clasps my hand in both of hers when I'm done talking. "Ohmigod, Sweetpea," she moans. "I can't believe all that! Why didn't you tell me what was going on yesterday when we went to the clinic?"

I start to answer, but she cuts me off.

"Never mind. It doesn't matter. I know now." She pauses and lowers her eyes. "I'm *so* sorry I freaked out on you. I guess I'm just really stressed about this project. It means a lot to me."

"But why's it such a big deal?" I ask, snagging a jalapeño-flavored potato chip from her lunch and sitting down, relieved to move on to a topic that doesn't have to do with me.

Anj glances at Duncan, who gives a barely perceptible shake of his head. "No reason," she says, twisting the pink plastic gemstone on her right index finger.

"I'd want to know what happened if it was my mum," Duncan says, changing the subject. "I remember when my cousin Andrew died in Wales and my aunt needed the coroner to give her every detail of what happened to him before she could—"

"Wait. What did you say?"

Duncan lifts an eyebrow. "I said when my cousin Andrew died, my aunt needed the coroner to go over every detail of his autopsy report before she could accept his death."

"That's it!"

"*What's* it?" Anj asks, pulling out a compact from her purse and checking her teeth.

"Why didn't I think of it before? Duncan, you're brilliant!" Anj snaps the compact shut and looks at me. "Hel-lo. Earth to Faith. What are you talking about?"

"Don't you see?" I lick the artificial orange coloring from my fingers. "The coroner, well we call them medical examiners here, but whatever. The medical examiner's the perfect person to talk to. All I saw was the death certificate after Mom died. If you're doing research, always go to the primary source."

I think of Dr. Monroe's words: W*ith the symptoms you described, I think you're right to be skeptical. There was probably an underlying problem.* Then I think of what the Rat Catcher said: *You don't want to get involved in this. I work for some powerful people who do not favor a kid poking into their business.* How could talking to the medical examiner count as poking my head into their business? It's not like the medical examiner killed my mom.

I snag another potato chip and grab a carrot stick as a healthy chaser. "Maybe there's some subtler condition the medical examiner ignored or missed because the police report said they found heroin and Mom looked like a junkie and calling it morphine was so obvious. Maybe he could read through the autopsy report with me. See if anything was overlooked."

"Uh, I don't mean to sound unsupportive," Anj says, a lead-in to why she's about to be unsupportive. "I know how much this means to you, but you can't just walk in and talk to the medical examiner. You were living in Philly when she died."

"So."

"Think about it. *West Philly*. I'm sure the guy has like a million deaths and murders a day to deal with." She shivers and scoots closer to Duncan. "I just think maybe you're taking this too far."

"Taking what too far?" Jesse asks, arriving from god knows where and nearly taking off my fingers with a textbook he drops onto the table.

"What happened to her mother," Anj says. "Faith wants to go talk to the medical examiner."

I do my best to ignore the sizzle of warmth shooting through my stomach as Jesse squeezes onto the bench next to me, and I update him on what happened at Dr. Monroe's office. I still leave out the part about being followed by the Rat Catcher and the whole you'd-better-stop-asking-questions thing. More like stuff it down and pretend it never happened. Two of my favorite survival strategies: avoidance and denial.

"Cool," he says when I'm done. He reaches into his backpack and digs out a peanut butter and jelly sandwich from somewhere on the bottom. "Total CSI. Can I come?"

I twist in my seat and put my hands on my hips. "What about your appointment with your speech coach?"

"Done deal. We met this morning. As long as I follow the college automaton script and don't say anything original, I'll ace the interview, so I'm free until Friday. We can go tomorrow."

"Yeah, mate, there's just one problem," Duncan says.

"What's that?" Jesse and I ask at the same time.

"It's like Anj said. I doubt you can just walk in on the medical examiner without an appointment."

The lunch period must be almost over because the custodian's started to mop at the far end of the cafeteria. The group from the in-crowd table gets up and leaves as a single unit. Somewhere in that herd is a conductor whose winning smile and stellar personality coordinates the exodus, so not a single blond hair is out of sync or left behind.

"Well, I don't see how I'm going to get an appointment," I say, slumping over the table and trying not to actually breathe the smell of Pine-Sol, garbage, and whatever food product was served today. "I can just imagine the call." I clear my throat and talk into my fingers like a phone. "Yes, hello, I'm a sixteen-year-old whose mother supposedly died of a heroin overdose, and I don't believe it. I'd like to make an appointment to go over her autopsy report with the medical examiner."

Duncan rocks his hand side-to-side in a not-too-bad-could-be-better kind of gesture. Then he breaks into his dimpled smile. "What about this? Good day. This is Dr. Bell from University of Glasgow." He pours on the accent thick and lowers his voice. "I'm on sabbatical and I have an urgent medical matter I'd like to discuss with you concerning the toxicology report of a recently deceased woman who died while participating in a clinical trial."

I nearly fall off my chair laughing. The voice and the content are so good that if I weren't looking right at Duncan, I'd believe the voice really did come from a doctor.

"Sounds good, there's just one problem," I say, wiping a tear from my eye.

"What?" Duncan ducks as a cupcake sails over his head. The frosting glues the cupcake to the wall for a second before it slides to the floor like a slug leaving a trail of vanilla goo. Someone on the end of the cafeteria opposite the custodian yells "Food fight!"

"Say you do get me the appointment. What happens when I show up without Dr. Bell?"

"It's easier to ask for forgiveness than ask for permission," Jesse says, tossing the rest of his sandwich into his backpack and kicking an orange that's landed at his feet back in the direction it came.

Anj rolls her eyes. "Which, you realize, is just a fancy way of saying this is a ridiculous idea and it'll never work."

Jesse shrugs. "Never know unless you try." A clump of spaghetti hits the wall to our right. "Now let's get out of here before this turns ugly."

We slip out the back door just as a wall of teachers close in on the place.

A minute later the four of us are outside on the front steps where nobody will overhear the phone call. It's stopped snowing and turned into the kind of brilliant afternoon that looks warm and sunny when you're sitting in class dreaming of freedom, but the second you're outside you realize the sun's tricked you. It's the wind calling the shots.

"It's cold enough to freeze the balls off a brass monkey," Duncan says, shivering in his t-shirt and jeans.

"C'mon, Dunc," Anj moans, burrowing under his freckled arm. "You promised you'd help me make the Happy Cows flier." She turns to me, her teeth chattering. "No offense, Faith. But Dunc really shouldn't be helping you. Impersonating a doctor is probably illegal. He could get deported or something. I mean it's not like I don't want to help, but—"

"Haud your wheesht, you!" Duncan interrupts. If he's speaking English, I have no idea what he's just said. I don't ask what he means though, and neither does Anj, but the vibe is enough to shut her up.

Jesse offers me his favorite orange pom-pom hat, which I gladly accept, pulling it low over my ears, while he whips out his phone and Googles the number.

"Here you go, Dr. Bell," he says, handing the phone to Duncan. "The office of the Philly medical examiner."

Duncan turns his back to the wind. We all freeze our butts off while we wait to see if Dr. Bell can land us an appointment.

A few minutes later he turns to us, goose bumps prickling his flesh, but smiling. "Pure deid brilliant! You have an appointment with Dr. Carlisle tomorrow morning at ten thirty."

Anj drags Duncan back into school to work on her flier before I can say thanks. I'm about to follow and get to my locker before bio when a black Mercedes pulls up to the curb. A man with a buzz cut, wearing a navy jacket, tan pants, and shades gets out and starts walking toward us.

"Check out the FBI agent. You think we're under terrorist attack?" I say, pointing my chin toward the guy, expecting Jesse to laugh.

He doesn't laugh. He doesn't even crack a smile. He just stares at the guy and shrinks about two inches as he approaches. "Dad, what are you doing here?" he asks when the counterterrorist agent reaches us.

Doc? I feel my jaw unhinge and straighten my skirt, as if straightening my skirt will cover the fact I'm wearing a five-dollar fake leather mini, orange pom-pom ski hat, and combat boots.

Doc gives a tight-lipped imitation of a smile and puts his hand on Jesse's shoulder. "What are *you* doing out here, son?" he demands, casting a disapproving look in my direction. "Don't you have class?"

"Yes...I mean, no," Jesse stammers, wiggling out from Doc's grip.

"Yes or no? I assume you know if you have a class or not? It's not a difficult question."

"It's lunch, Dad."

At that moment the blond from the photo on Jesse's phone tumbles out of the car. She runs to Jesse and throws her arms around him. With her pouty red lips, tousled blond hair, and tight black turtleneck clinging to her curves, she's even sexier in person than in the photograph. I've gone rigid. A step away from rigor mortis. I can't do anything but stand there and stare like an idiot. Everything about me suddenly feels wrong—my height, my clothes, my dark hair, skin, and eyes.

"Hey, Tia," Jesse says, returning the girl's hug.

"Hey, Tia, nothing." She smiles and plants a kiss on his cheek, leaving a big red lipstick stain. "I was supposed to wait in the car and surprise you, but I couldn't stand waiting another second!" She nods in my direction. "Who's that?" she says, as if I'm mute and can't answer for myself.

"My friend, Faith," Jesse mumbles, his arms still around Tia's stupidly small waist.

"Oh," she says, ignoring me. "I have so much to tell you!"

"Tia got into Stanford," Doc says, somehow managing to make this sound like a criticism of Jesse.

"That's great, Tia," Jesse says, beaming into her pretty face. "I'm psyched for you."

"I couldn't wait to tell you. Premed. I've already decided. I know I wasn't supposed to arrive until tomorrow, but when I found out I was so excited, I had to come a day early. Let's go." She takes his arm and leads him toward the car. "Your dad's signing you out early. We're going to celebrate. He's taking us to the city, and tonight we're having dinner at Rittenhouse Square."

Jesse peels himself away from Tia and comes back to the top step where I'm still standing. "I'm sorry, Faith."

I soften. Sorry works. It's a start anyway.

"But I have to go."

I feel like someone's knocked the wind out of me, but I play it cool. "Yeah, whatever," I say, reaching for the lighter. "See you later."

I start down the steps, my shoulders straight, trying to project a confidence I don't feel. Jesse calls after me, but I don't stop. I keep walking until Jesse, Barbie, and Doc are out of site.

Only then do I sit on the edge of someone's lawn and cover my face with my hands, my feelings tumbling from jealousy to hurt to anger. I have no right to be jealous. New Boy and I aren't a thing. I've known him for less than a week. The disappointed ache in my gut tells me this is a lie, though. How long you've known someone doesn't matter when you have a real connection—or thought you did.

But it's not just plain old petty jealousy getting to me. It's that New Boy's not who I thought he was. Why's he acting like such a shallow charmer and a flirt, not to mention a chameleon? He doesn't want to go to the Ivy League, but he'll do the interview. He doesn't want Harvard, but he won't tell Doc.

And then there's this business about Tia not being his girlfriend. What a cowardly load of crap. Uh, hello? You don't go around hugging someone who isn't your girlfriend like that unless you want to get arrested.

I thought I understood New Boy. Worse, I thought I could trust him.

Now I'm not so sure.

Eleven

I wave hello to Mrs. Dunnings as I walk down Aunt T's street. She throws me her usual sour look, and Rosy, the rodent mutt, growls. Great. Now even dogs are shunning me. The second I get home, however, I'm flooded with dog love as Goldie, Sam's Irish wolfhound-golden retriever mix, bounds across the yard to greet me.

"What are you doing here, girl?" I say, staggering backward as she flings her paws onto my shoulders and slobbers my nose.

Goldie barks and runs off to get her ball. It's then I notice both Aunt T's car and Sam's pickup parked in the driveway. Sam must be in between one of his overnight shifts at the fire station, but what's Aunt T doing home this early?

I throw the slobbery tennis ball Goldie's dropped at my feet and watch with serious dog envy as she chases it across the grass. Imagine being that happy just from chasing a ball. While Goldie settles on her stomach to chew her prey, I trudge up the porch steps, hoping Aunt T and Sam are busy in the bedroom or taking a walk, so I can avoid conversation.

No such luck.

The door to the kitchen is open. I see them at the table, Sam on the far side in jeans and a blue flannel button down.

Aunt T, still wearing her name tag pinned to her blazer, sits across from him.

"Faith," Aunt T calls as I tiptoe past the room. "Come in. I need to talk to you."

I plaster on my happy face and head onto the stage for some playacting. "You're home early," I say when I get into the kitchen. The false cheer in my voice makes me sick. I might as well add *golly gee, Auntie T, good to see ya!*

I wait for Aunt T to explain why she's home early, but she just exchanges glances with Sam who gets up as if he'd been about to leave, which, judging from the barely eaten plate of food in front of him, I'm guessing he wasn't.

"Where are you going?" I ask.

He scratches the gold-gray bristles on his chin and looks at Aunt T again. "I'm taking Goldie for a walk."

"But you didn't finish your food."

"You can save it for me, Rock Star," he says, tousling my hair. "I'll eat it later."

I shrug. "If you say so." I slip into his seat and reach for the basket of muffins that look far too healthy to taste good.

The second the front door closes, Aunt T turns to me. "I got a call from a company called PluraGen today," she says. "Ring a bell?"

My hand freezes in midair. "I don't think so."

"Well then let me refresh your memory. They're in charge of a clinical trial for a heroin addiction treatment called RNA 120, and you were at the clinic that's been hired to administer the treatment yesterday."

"Oh, that PluraGen!"

I turn and focus my attention on a bird that's landed in the maple tree outside the window…too small to be a robin…

wrong season for warblers…not the right behavior for a nut-hatch…. My aunt's voice breaks into my avoidance strategy.

"Okay, Faith. No more looking out the window and evading the topic. You skip school. You go to a methadone clinic, and I only learn about it when I get a call from a biopharmaceutical company. *What* is going on?"

She sits down and strokes Felix, who's jumped into her lap, and waits for me to speak. Other than the lines of strain on her forehead, her expression is unreadable. Forget lying. She already knows I was there. The crystal prism hanging in the window casts rainbows of light on the walls and ceiling as I tell the story about going to Melinda's place, then to the clinic and meeting with Dr. Wydner.

"I never knew about the clinical trial until I talked to Melinda," I say quietly. "It was some secret Mom was keeping from me."

I squeeze the lighter and wait for Aunt T to have a shit fit about me digging around in the past and looking for an explanation for something she believes has already been answered.

"I knew," she says instead.

I break off a piece of muffin and bring it to my mouth. "You knew what?"

"About the clinical trial."

"What do you mean you *knew*?" I sputter, gagging on a walnut piece.

Felix jumps off her lap, and Aunt T gets up to pour herself a cup of coffee without answering. I look down, my face burning with shame. How could I lie to my aunt, the one person I have in the world? No sooner do I have this thought than anger swoops in to take its place. She knew about the clinical trial and she didn't tell me! How could she keep that a secret?

"Last summer your mother told me about a new drug treatment for heroin addiction," she says, bringing her coffee back to the table. "She said it was in phase one of a clinical trial study and she was going to sign up, but insisted she didn't want you to know about it. She didn't want to give you false expectations. She made me promise not to tell you."

"So you listened to her and kept it a secret, even after she died?" My feelings go supernova as all the anger, disappointment, and hurt from the past two months fuse. The combined energy is more than I can contain. I push back from the table and jump to my feet, sending the chair clattering to the ground and terrifying Felix, whose claws scrape the floor before he gets enough purchase to flee.

Aunt T's grip on her mug tightens, but her voice stays calm. "I told her you should know, but she wouldn't be persuaded. Once she died, I didn't see the point in telling you."

"It's always a lie isn't it? First her and now you."

"It's not a lie," Aunt T murmurs.

"Oh yeah, and how do you figure that? Mom was farming herself out to some drug company to test a drug that's never been used on people before and nobody thought to tell me?"

"I tried to reason with her, Faith. You don't have to believe me, but I'm telling you the truth. You know how she was in the end, completely irrational. She wouldn't go to the doctor. She even stopped participating in the clinical study. Stopped getting her treatment. She said the drug was making her sick. It was another excuse, just like every time she tried to get clean and couldn't do it."

For a second I think I see tears beading in Aunt T's eyes, but she turns away and when she looks at me again, her eyes are dry.

"Anyway, that's behind us." She reaches to the floor for her work bag and brings out a folder. "I got a call from a woman in the legal department at PluraGen this afternoon. Apparently you made quite an impression on the doctor administering the trial."

"What do you mean?"

"He put in a call to the company on your behalf. Look. They faxed me this." She puts on glasses, opens the folder, and hands me a sheet of paper with the name PluraGen printed in the upper left hand corner.

The antique clock by the stove chimes the hour. I pick up my chair, drop back into the seat, and read.

Compensation Structure for Human Research Subjects in Clinical Studies

PluraGen will arrange for medical care for any injury or illness that occurs while participating in one of our clinical studies. Dependents of study participants who incur disability or death may be eligible for compensation.

"Apparently your mother checked the box on her application that said no dependents, so until you showed up at the clinic, you didn't exist," she says when I look up. "I was listed as her emergency contact, so they called me to see if I knew anything about you."

I crumble the edge of the paper in my fist. "She said I didn't exist?"

"Honey, it's not like it sounds. She told me they were screening applicants and preferred those with dependents stick to more traditional treatment methods. She was desperate. You know just as well as I do that she'd already been through methadone twice and both times relapsed." She lets the word "relapse" hang in the air like a bad smell, then says, "The amount isn't set yet. There's a process, a review board, but my understanding is that this could be enough money to start a college fund. All you have to do is sign a waiver saying you won't hold the company accountable for what happened and that no further compensation will be sought and the money is yours."

The energy from my outburst has dissipated, leaving me inert and contracted. "So I have to agree not to ask questions and not to sue if I want the money?" I ask, sinking down into the chair.

"I guess you could interpret it that way, but why would you have to ask more questions or think you'd have to sue someone?"

Instead of answering, I glance at the paper again, at the paragraphs of disclaimers and clauses that you need a law degree to understand, and slip even lower into my seat. "It sounds like they're trying to buy me off."

Aunt T laughs. "What would a company be trying to buy you off for? That doesn't make any sense. You have to stop being so paranoid." She regards me for a moment, still smiling, but when she realizes I'm serious, the smile disappears. "It's a good policy, Faith. This could be good money."

"Yeah, well a lot of things could be good money—selling dope to kids for example, and I think we both agree that's a bad idea."

"Okay, let's forget the money for the second. Let's talk about college." She reaches across the table, but I retract my hand before she can touch me. "You're a bright girl. You should go to university. I want to help you with tuition, but you know I hardly have any savings as it is."

I run my fingers over the lighter and sigh. The black hole of my brain sucks me in further. Maybe Aunt T *is* right. Maybe

I am being paranoid. God knows I could use the money for college. Isn't that what Mom would want me to do? Take the money and move on with my life? But then again, why do I care what she wants? Why would I listen to her when she said I didn't exist?

"I'll think about it," I say and excuse myself to my room just as Sam returns with Goldie.

———

It's not until dark that I'm ready to talk to someone. Jesse's out with Tia, but even if he wasn't, after what happened today I don't really want to talk to him. I don't actually even want to think about him.

I pop my knuckles trying to decide if I should call Anj. She already knows what's going on. The relationship would've combusted by now if it were going to. I pop a final knuckle and dial her number.

"Turn down the music!" she shouts into the phone when she answers.

"Uh, what?" I say, looking at the level-two volume of nature sounds playing on my boom box.

"Not you…. Ugh…Chrissy! Will you turn down your music! Sorry about that. My sister has a new CD of some boy band, and she's been torturing me all night by blasting their pimply voices at my door. My parents are out and I'm babysitting, so if I don't show up at school tomorrow it's 'cause I killed my sister." The boy band blares in the background, so loudly I can make out the words—*baby, baby, oh yeah, baby*—followed by a shouting match and a door slamming. "Oh-kay, that should take care of it," Anj says happily as the background noise ceases. I imagine her sister tied up and gagged in a closet.

I'm about to ask if everything's all right on her end, but she speaks first. "So what's going on?"

I stretch out on my bed and stare at the yellow water stain on the ceiling. "Well, remember the methadone clinic we went to the other day and the clinical trial I told you about?"

"Uh, yeah. It's not like I'd forget that."

"Well, it turns out that Dr. Wydner, the doctor I met at the clinic, is running the trial for some big company called PluraGen that manufactures the drug." I quickly explain about the contract, the waiver, and the money before Chrissy can free herself from her hypothetical bondage and the music can start again.

"Sweetpea, that's great!" she says when I finish talking.

"You don't think it sounds a little…" I pause and search for the right word. "Suspicious?"

"Suspicious? Girly, you watch too many movies. Maybe this is just something good, and you don't have to ruin it by turning it into something bad like the world's some big, sinister plot against you. Maybe it's time to look ahead and stop looking at all the bad things that are behind you."

A wave crashes on the CD player. The ocean stirs my agitation. I get up and start to pace. I stop in front of the window and gaze at the star-filled sky, at that silvery light from millions of years ago that's traveled through the vacuum of space to reach us, a cosmic reminder that no matter what, we're always looking back.

"Maybe," I say, "but I still want to talk to someone at PluraGen before I sign. I was thinking of going over tomorrow morning before my appointment with the medical examiner. I Googled the company. They're not that far, just in King of Prussia. You think you could give me a ride?"

"I hate to go to King of Prussia and not visit the mall, but I can't miss first period." She sighs dramatically as if the no-shopping-versus-driving-me conundrum is whether or not to nuke an enemy nation. "But I suppose I could take you and do retail therapy another time." Before I can thank her, she says, "But there's one condition."

"Let me guess? I learn the Arawak language on the way?"

"Gosh no. Not the whole language," she says, sounding shocked. "Just five or ten words. I'll bring a vocab sheet in the car."

For the first time all evening I smile. "Fine. A few words and you've got a deal." I give her Aunt T's address and we hang up.

Twelve

At seven thirty Wednesday morning when I climb into Hazel, a pair of hands, smaller than Anj's but adorned with as many fake jewels, covers my eyes.

"Surprise!" Chrissy squeals, releasing her hands and popping up over the seat. She grins at me with her red-tinted braces and matching red rubber bands.

Anj glares at her sister as she backs out of the driveway. "Will you sit down please and put on your seatbelt and pretend you aren't here?"

"Anj is skipping scho-ool!" Chrissy sings.

Anj stops Hazel in the middle of the street. "I am *not* skipping. I'm taking Faith to an appointment, then I'm dropping you off, and then I'll go to school, but if you don't stop acting like a five-year-old, I'll let you out here, and you can walk." Anj turns to me and rolls her eyes. "Sorry. I forgot I had to take Chrissy to school today. It's too early to drop her off, so she's coming with us. I already forged the tardy note."

"Yeah, and Mom will kill you if she finds out!" Chrissy pops up again and smiles, as if this is the best news in the world, then slips on a pair of heart-shaped sunglasses and slides back down into her seat.

Anj starts driving again and grimaces. "She swore she wouldn't tell if I promised to take her to Justice this afternoon and buy her one of those neon satin shirts with the puffy sleeves the fifth-grade girls call fashion."

Chrissy springs back up. "And take me to the Sweet Factory!"

"Right. Now sit back down, be a good girl, and make yourself invisible."

Chrissy obeys and sings along with her iPod the rest of the way to King of Prussia.

"Sorry I can't wait around to take you back to school," Anj says, when we pull into the PluraGen parking lot fifteen minutes later.

"No prob." I hop out of the car, relieved to get away from the off-key-sing-along concert tour of teenybopper pop taking place in the backseat. "I'll catch the bus. I already checked the schedule."

"Okay, then." She blows me a kiss. "Good luck. Oh, and before I go, take this." She hands me a sheet with two columns of Arawak words. "Don't forget to learn these. You promised."

I put the sheet in my backpack, close the door, and wave good-bye.

I glance nervously over my shoulder for the Rat Catcher as I cross the parking lot. If he knew how to find me yesterday, why not today? I push away this fear and head toward the PluraGen building, a gleaming pillar of tinted glass and metal columns, a high-tech monument to money worlds away from the Ben Franklin-era brick shops and homes of Society Hill and the poverty-stricken neighborhoods of North Philly.

I head into a slick, two-story lobby where all the doors and elevators have security panels, and all the people entering the building carry identification cards. I'm wondering if you have to take off your shoes and empty your pockets to get into work when a receptionist, who looks like she's just been plucked from the front window of Macy's, asks if I need any help.

My boots squeak on the slippery tiles as I cross the lobby. "I'd like to speak to someone in the legal department," I say when I reach the woman's desk.

"The legal department?" She raises one perfectly shaped eyebrow. "Anyone in particular?"

I take the folder from my bag and plunk it onto her desk, realizing that Aunt T never mentioned an actual name or contact person when she told me about the deal. I'm about to explain my situation, but I lose my train of thought when a man in a gray suit and paisley tie passes the desk and smiles. There's something familiar about the smug way his lips part to reveal a set of chemically white teeth.

"Good morning, Carla," he says to the receptionist as he scans his ID card and opens the door leading into the bowels of the company.

"Good morning, Dr. Glass," she replies.

Dr. Glass. The guy from outside Dr. Wydner's office. My brain goes high speed, streaming snippets of conversation from the past few days. *These things are confidential.…I have the data you were asking for.…I'm just glad Dr. Glass is presenting RNA 120 and not me.…*

I snatch my folder off the desk, race across the lobby, and grab the handle of the door marked personnel that's about to swing shut behind Glass.

"You can't go in there!" Carla calls after me.

I ignore her and go in anyway.

"Dr. Glass!" I shout into the quiet corridor as I rush to catch up with him.

I've just reached his side when I hear the scuffling of feet behind me. I look over my shoulder and see a security guard with a face like a baked ham heading my direction. "Everything okay, sir?" he asks, settling his meaty frame protectively in front of Glass.

"Wait, please!" I beg before Glass can give the order to have me hauled off. "I need to talk to you about the clinical trial for RNA 120."

Glass steps out from behind the security guard and we lock eyes. He holds my gaze for so long I start to feel uncomfortable, but I don't look down.

"Thank you, Bernie," Glass finally says, shifting his focus from me to the security guard who waits obediently at his side like a trained dog. "Everything's fine."

Bernie lingers for a second, his tiny chocolate-chip eyes darting from Glass to me, as if assessing my risk factor and whether I've come to blow up the place. I guess I pass clearance, but only just. He plants himself next to a window a few feet away where he can still come to Glass' rescue, should I cause a fuss.

"Are you in charge of the clinical trial for RNA 120 being run at the Twenty-third Street Methadone Clinic?" I ask, trying not to let on to how nervous I am.

Glass' dark eyebrows creep up his forehead as he examines me. I tug self-consciously at my black t-shirt, wishing I'd worn something without a skull on it.

"I'm in charge," he finally says. "What can I do for you?"

I slide my hand into my pocket, unsure how to proceed. I hadn't thought this through when I chased after Glass. Standing here now, smack center of the PluraGen mother ship with Rent-A-Cop a few feet away, it's hard to imagine confronting Glass with my theory on side effects of the drug his company is paying Dr. Wydner to test.

"My mother was in the clinical trial, and she died," I say at last.

"I'm sorry to hear that," Glass replies. He glances at his watch. "And I'm terribly sorry, but I'm late for a meeting. If you're here about our compensation fund, you'll have to speak to someone in legal. If you'd like to discuss the clinical aspects of the treatment, you're welcome to make an appointment." He reaches into his pocket and pulls out his wallet. "Here's my business card. If you'd like to set up something, my receptionist would be glad to help you. Now if you'll excuse me."

He turns his back and starts off down the hall. I escort myself out before Bernie can do it for me. The receptionist is on the phone when I get back to the lobby. I figure she might not be so keen on helping me after I ignored her directive and ran after Glass, so I hop on the elevator and ascend into the clouds until I reach the floor marked legal.

Legal is a cubicle nightmare. Like which cubicle worker to talk to? The one sitting in front of a computer, or one of the other zillion sitting in front of a computer? I stop a young woman with a smart haircut and a smart suit and a smart water bottle and ask for her help. She gives me a blank look, so I cut my losses and figure I'll try legal another day. I leave PluraGen, Glass, and this sleek world of legal drugs and their profit behind for the improbable task of convincing the medical examiner that I'm connected to a nonexistent Dr. Bell.

———

I check my phone as the bus whisks me from King of Prussia back to Philly. Between yesterday afternoon and this morning Jesse has sent three texts and left four voice messages, all begging me to call him back. For a second I consider calling, but then no way. It's not hurt silencing the cell-phone waves. It's not jealousy. It's something far more basic. I'm pissed.

If I hadn't ditched first yesterday, what would Jesse have done? Let me stand on the front steps alone as he and Doc and Tia drove away? Waved good-bye from the Mercedes? The whole thing was embarrassing and stupid, but really, if I think about, it's myself I should be pissed at. I should've known better than to start liking New Boy and to think I could trust him. I'm a fool. A total fool.

———

At ten fifteen, I'm sitting in the waiting area of the medical examiner's building, the same building where Mom was sliced open, her rib cage sawn apart, her tissues cut and examined before she was turned to ash. Sadness, with an atomic mass heavier than plutonium, settles in my chest. I pick up a *People* magazine, hoping that pictures of pregnant movie stars and stories of the rich and famous and their troubles will chase away the heaviness and fill me with a lighter element. The lives of the glamorous are no match for the raw wound of my loss though, so I flip on my iPod.

"Both Sides Now," a Joni Mitchell tune my mother used to play and sing over and over when she was nostalgic or sad, comes on. The melody is sweet, but the words lonely, a song about illusions and love. That always seemed ironic, how something so sweet could hold so much pain. Those sad Joni Mitchell words are singing in my head when someone taps my shoulder.

I nearly fly out of my skin as I lurch around, thinking for sure it's the Rat Catcher, but when I open my eyes, it's not him.

I yank out my earbuds and drop them around my neck.

"What are *you* doing here?"

Jesse looks taken aback as if it's not totally obvious that I wouldn't want him here after what happened yesterday.

"What do you mean what am I doing here? We had a plan, remember?"

"Yeah, well that was before you took off with Doc and your girlfriend to play polo or dine at Chez Five Star or whatever," I say, shoving my earbuds back in. I'm being a sarcastic bitch, and I know it, but anger drives my mouth.

Jesse says something, but I missed the class on lip reading. I jerk out the earbuds again and glare at him.

"You think we could go outside and talk?" he says.

"No." I'm about to put my earbuds back in yet again, but Jesse grabs my arm and pulls me to my feet before I have the chance. "Come on, Jesse, my appointment's in ten minutes."

"This'll take five."

I wriggle my arm, but he's not letting go. I want to hear what he has to say, though, in the infinitesimally small chance I got it wrong yesterday and Tia is like, what? His cousin? Not that it matters. Still. I let him pull me through the lobby and lead me through the front door.

Only once we're outside and he plants himself firmly on the sidewalk does he let go. He kicks a soda can into the street and watches as it gets flattened under the wheels of a passing car.

"So?" I say, shivering. "Is there something you actually wanted to talk about, or are we just going to stand around and watch traffic because in case there's something wrong with your short-term memory and you forgot I have an appointment in a few minutes."

Jesse leans against the post of a street light and fidgets with the string of his sweatshirt. Then, in a voice hardly louder than the breeze, he says, "I just wanted to say sorry I didn't tell you the truth about Tia and I."

"I'm listening."

"That's it. I'm sorry."

"That's it? You're sorry?" I look at a plastic bag tangled around a tree limb like some kind of fungal growth and then look back at Jesse. "You know what I think about sorry? I think sorry is an excuse to do whatever you want and then think you can make up for your behavior with this one tiny word that frankly, without a little more to go on, means nothing."

In a split second, Jesse goes from cozy herbal tea to high-octane espresso. He springs away from the metal post and starts to pace, short jerky steps—three in one direction, turn, three in the other.

"Okay. Fine. You want more to go on, here it is. Tia's parents and my parents are best friends. I've known her since I was five. Last spring we started going out, then her family moved to New York. She's a senior and she's going to college next year. With the distance and the college thing I didn't think I had to cut it off. I just figured it would end on its own, you know?"

"No."

Jesse stops in front of me. He throws his hands in the air and looks skyward as if pleading with some deity to make me understand his self-inflicted quandary. "Tia's a great girl. She's pretty and we have fun together, but I'm not in love with her. Going out with her is like going out with my sister—not in some sicko way—but it's like she's family." His hands flop to his sides, and under his breath he mutters, "She's Doc's dream girl."

I wait while Jesse studies his feet. When finally he looks up at me, I offer up my biggest smile and say, "Okay, then I have a great idea."

"What?" he says, a hopeful note in his voice like I might actually solve his problems for him.

"Your dad can go out with her. That should make everyone happy. And then you don't have to live the world's biggest cliché."

"Funny."

"I wasn't trying to be. God Jesse. It's your life. Try living it."

He digs into me with his eyes. "You don't get it," he says, kicking the curb. "Doc wants me to be someone else. Tia. Harvard. It's all part of his plan. It's impossible to stand up to him."

"You don't think I understand having to stand up so I can be myself and not someone else's version of who they think I am or want me to be? My whole life is about standing up for myself, Jesse. Most people assume I'm some kind of druggie kid just like my mom, so spare me the 'I don't get it' crap."

I'm ready for a good knock-down-drag-out fight, and I arm myself with another verbal punch, but suddenly I realize I'm exhausted. It's his life. Why should I care what he does? I have bigger problems to deal with. Instead of saying anything else or waiting while Jesse comes up with his next line, I turn and start walking back to the medical examiner's building.

Jesse trots along next to me.

I stop in front of a kiosk loaded with promos for some benefit concert at the Art Institute. "What are you doing?"

"Coming with you."

"No you're not."

"Am."

"Not."

"Am." He walks back to the building, opens the door, and calls over his shoulder, "And if you keep arguing you're going to miss your appointment."

———

Just as we enter the lobby, a heavyset woman with molded gray hair and glasses dangling down the front of her unibosom from a beaded chain calls Dr. Bell's name. I race across the room and tell the woman that I'm with Dr. Bell, but that he's running late and I'd like to start the appointment without him. She buzzes me through the door and leads me to the elevator without asking questions. Jesse follows.

"Where are we going?" he asks as the elevator door dings open.

"Administrative. Second floor." She must glean something more from Jesse's question because she adds, "Autopsies and forensics are on ground level."

"Bummer," Jesse says under his breath.

The elevator door slides open. Even though she's just told us that this floor is for administrative purposes only, the place smells like biology lab on dissection day. My legs go weak. More than once I think of turning back, but I force myself to follow the woman down the corridor, past a row of offices, to family services, a somber room with dark wood paneling, a large bookcase, and heavy blinds. She tells us Dr. Carlisle will be right in and leaves.

"Cheery place," Jesse says once she's gone.

I don't answer. Not because I don't want to or because I'm still thinking about Tia and Doc, but because I'm afraid if I open my mouth the only sound to come out will be a sob. I drop onto the leather couch and dig my nails into my palms, concentrating on the physical pain as a distraction from my emotional pain. I'm examining the half-moon impressions etched into my skin when a balding man with wire-rimmed glasses and pockmarked skin the color of boiled potatoes enters through a door opposite the couch.

The man crosses the floor in two big steps and extends a hand like a bear's paw. "I'm Dr. Carlisle, medical examiner." He looks around the room, then looks back at us and frowns. "I'm sorry, but I was expecting someone else. I'm supposed to be meeting with a Dr. Bell from Glasgow."

I'm instantly on my feet explaining. "You are. I mean *we* are. I mean we're all having a meeting. Only Dr. Bell's not here. The woman we're here to talk about was my mother and Dr. Bell was a friend of hers, but he got called away on some other business and sent us on our own. I brought the death certificate with me. You can look at it yourself." I glance nervously at Jesse, who smiles encouragingly, but leaves the fibbing to me.

Dr. Carlisle tugs at his chin. "I see. Well, this is most unusual."

Before he can decide that "most unusual" means "most unacceptable," I launch into the story. I tell him my mother's name and when she died, then explain her symptoms and the circumstances of her death, what the death certificate says, and my belief that she didn't OD.

"So, I thought maybe there was something else wrong with her," I say, finally stopping to catch my breath. "Something that got overlooked when they found the morphine. I was hoping you could review the full autopsy report with me."

Dr. Carlisle peers at me through the thick lenses of his glasses. "The results of a full autopsy report can take a few months to complete, and legally you have to be an adult to get the report. Are you eighteen?"

My chest tightens around the question. "No," I mutter.

He opens and closes his mouth like a goldfish. No words come out and his hand flies to his chin again where he pulls at the bony nub as if searching for a beard to tug. Finding no beard, he transfers his agitation into his feet, scuffing the floor with a brown loafer.

"Well, I'll see what I can do." He hurries across the room and disappears through the door connecting to what appears to be his office.

"I wonder where they store the bodies?" Jesse asks the minute the door clicks shut. "Do you think they put them in a walk-in freezer? Or maybe they keep them in drawers. Or maybe—" He looks at me and stops. "Aw, man, shit, sorry." He hits himself on the forehead. "Major insensitive. How're you doing?"

"Okay," I say, trying to constrict thoughts of my mother, so her image is no more than a pinhole of light at the back of my brain; trying not to think of her naked flesh frozen in some freezer, a bar code and case number Sharpied onto her arm.

Jesse picks up a pamphlet from the coffee table and reads. "'How to deal with the death of a loved one. Step one: Seek the support of family and friends.' You want one of these?"

"Nah, I'm good."

"No really, you should take one. Check it out. In just five short steps you'll start to feel better. Imagine that. 'Step two: Keep busy.' Man, whoever wrote this is some kind of friggin' genius. He should write a book or have his own TV show. Maybe he could start a church."

He rambles on with a critique of the generic self-help literature, and I don't think he notices that I've turned on my iPod and have stopped listening. I watch his lips move and his hands gesture as I advance through my songs until I find an upbeat Jimmy Cliff tune that I hope will drive away the gruesome image of my mother's body on the autopsy table and replace it with a positive reggae vibe. I'm listening to "I Can See Clearly Now" when Dr. Carlisle returns. I turn off my music and put my iPod in my bag at my feet.

"I'm sorry, but the complete report isn't available yet," the medical examiner tells me. "As soon as it's available, you can bring an adult, and I'll be glad to meet with you and go over all the details. Now is there anything else I can do for you?"

Jesse turns to me. His eyes are a question. I shake my head. "Nothing else," I say.

Dr. Carlisle nods, then turns and vanishes into his office with hardly a good-bye.

I follow Jesse out of the dark room into the harsh florescence of the overhead lights, a penetrating white that turns skin so pale it's easy to imagine ghosts wandering these halls. We follow the corridor back to the elevator. We've just gotten to the first floor when I reach for my bag and realize it's not with me.

"I left my stuff in the room," I say. "I'll be right back."

I retrace my steps, but when I get back to family services, my bag isn't on the couch. It's a few seconds before I find it on the floor beneath the coffee table. I drape the strap over my shoulder, and I'm about to leave when Dr. Carlisle's voice startles me. The door leading from family services into his office is cracked open. I can just make out his back, a phone pressed to his ear.

"It's about Augustina Archer," he hisses.

I freeze at the sound of my mother's name, the way it spits off his tongue like the name Augustina Archer is some kind of curse. I think of yelling out, telling the dude to respect the dead, but there's something anxious in his tone that warns me to keep quiet, not to move, and to listen.

"You didn't tell me she had a kid. If you want me to lie to some teenager, you're going to have to pay more."

The stress beat of my heart pounds against my chest and temples. A sickening tremble ripples through my body. What lie?

"Yes, I did an autopsy report....Yes, a real one, and I have the proof right here. If you don't give me more money, I'll show the girl."

He slams down the phone after that and slaps something onto his desk, then puts his hand to his chest like he's having a heart attack. He's studying whatever it is making him so upset when I hear a knock on what must be another door at the far end of his office, and a woman tells Dr. Carlisle that he's needed right away in the pathology lab. He shuffles some papers around his desk, then follows the woman out.

I don't have time to think or to plan my next move. I dart across the floor, slip into his office, and head straight to his desk where I immediately start sifting through papers and folders slopped across the surface. I'm peeling through some medical file when I hear Dr. Carlisle's voice at the door leading to the hall.

"I must've left it in my office. I'll be right back."

I glance around for somewhere to hide. There isn't a closet or even a bookshelf. My only hope is to make it back to family services before he opens the door. I've hardly taken the first step when Dr. Carlisle speaks again.

"Wait a minute. Here it is. Let's go."

My heart jackhammers and my hands shake, but once I'm sure he's gone, I continue to search, desperate to find whatever he was talking about and get out of here. His proof could be anywhere, anything. I'm about to give up when a red folder peeking out from beneath the keyboard catches my eye. I snatch the folder off the desk and turn it over. Augustina Archer is written in black marker.

I tuck the folder under my arm and force my nonathletic and now trembling legs on an aerobic sprint for the first floor.

Thirteen

My stomach's taken a parachute dive, and my heart's still racing when I get back to the lobby and find Jesse waiting for me.

"Let's get out of here," I say, pushing through the front door.

I set a brisk pace down the sidewalk the second we're out of the building.

"What's going on?" Jesse pants, dodging a woman pushing a baby stroller. "What's that folder under your arm?"

I glance over my shoulder. It would be just perfect if the Rat Catcher chose this moment to show up. "Keep going. I'll tell you later."

We take a few turns, carving a circuitous path through city streets, putting distance between the medical examiner's office and us. Seven, maybe ten, blocks later I stop on a busy street filled with suit-and-tie-wearing clones who jabber into cell phones without making eye contact with any of the other clones.

"Over there," I say, pointing to a department store, the last place I figure the Rat Catcher would track us.

Jesse follows me into the store, past cosmetics, through a maze of consumer's paradise until I find a dressing room in the women's department. I motion for him to follow me into the changing area, and we slip past a saleslady sporting what must be half the gold in the jewelry department and half the makeup in cosmetics as well, giving her an Avon-lady-meets-streetwalker kind of look.

The fitting room is one of those extra big deals with a couch and mirrors on three sides for people who take their shopping seriously. Jesse looks so ridiculous sitting here in über-feminine pastel land that I should laugh, at least crack a joke about a guy in the women's dressing room, but there's nothing funny about the situation.

"Dude, we're like Marathon Man." Jesse gives me the thumbs up and makes himself at home on the couch. "Dustin Hoffman, Laurence Olivier, 1976."

I know Jesse well enough to understand this non sequitur is a lead-in to why we just ran out of the medical examiner's office and then high speeded it down all those blocks, so I squeeze onto the couch next to him and explain what happened. It's only then, the fight-or-flight pump of adrenaline no longer flowing through my veins, I realize the implications of stealing a file from a medical examiner's desk: police investigations, jail.

"Here. I can't look," I say, handing Jesse the folder, a queasy feeling about whatever's inside.

Jesse opens the folder and pulls out a thick envelope with my mother's name printed in big black letters. He glances at me, then opens it. Inside is a smaller envelope.

"What is this, Russian dolls?" I snap.

Jesse doesn't answer. He takes out the smaller envelope, tears it open, and removes something that looks like a shiny white matchbox. He slides open the drawer of the box and peers inside.

"What the hell is that thing?"

Jesse studies the contents for a few seconds, then closes the drawer and looks at me. "A microscope slide. Could be some kind of tissue sample from your mother's autopsy." He catches the look of surprise on my face. "What? I saw something like it on a crime show once. Who said TV was a waste of time?"

He slips the glass slide back into the smaller envelope and reaches into the bigger envelope again. This time he brings out a thin stack of photographs rubber banded together and finally a bunch of papers. He puts the photos on the couch, grabs the top paper, and reads the heading out loud. "Toxicologist's report."

I tap the floor with the steel toe of my boot. Crack my knuckles. This report is no big deal I tell myself. I already know what it's going to say: cause of death heroin overdose. But still my breath is shallow; my heartbeat too fast: *I have proof right here. If you don't give me more money, I'll show the girl.*

A shopping soap opera takes place in the dressing room next to us. Woman A complains about how a pair of jeans makes her butt look fat. Woman B tries to convince her she looks gorgeous. Woman A debates if the jeans are really worth two hundred dollars. Woman B delivers a sermon on the value of the newest, must-have designer.

Parallel universe theory. That's what I'm thinking. How can two groups of people so close in time and space occupy such different realities? I drift away on a head trip about the nature of reality, of sitting in a woman's changing room in an upscale department store, looking at my mother's flesh reduced to a microscope specimen and reading her autopsy report, while listening to someone in the next room mull over jeans worth more than my mom earned sometimes in two weeks. I hardly hear Jesse when he asks if he can check out the photographs.

For a minute I have no idea what he's talking about. I stare at him with a blank expression.

"The photographs?" he says, eyebrows arched. "Is it okay if I look at them?"

"Oh, those, right," I say, with a tight smile, pretending I'm not teetering on the edge of an internal Mount Everest. "Sure."

Jesse picks up the photos from the couch and holds them close to his chest, so all I can see is the scrawl of my mother's name on the white backside of the photo paper. He looks at the first image, then the second. Watching Jesse study the images, the way he exhales small puffs of air, each one a sigh lifting the hair from his forehead, I have a bad feeling that the Richter scale of my soul is about to record a level nine seismic event.

Next door the jeans dilemma is solved. Woman A decides to make the purchase. I grab the toxicologist's report and start to read. I'm picking off what remains of my black nail polish when I come to a page that makes me gasp.

Jesse puts down the photos and turns to me. "What is it?"

"According to this, my mother's blood test was negative." I hand him the report with shaking hands. "There was no morphine in her blood. That means my mom didn't overdose."

I feel instantly lighter, as if someone pumped helium through my veins and sent me floating off into the cumulus-filled blue. Mom didn't die a junkie. She didn't take her life and leave me.

I start creating a mental list of all the people I get to say, "I told you so" to, but then an inky black feeling crawls over me, and I crash back down to earth.

If Mom didn't have morphine in her blood, why did the death certificate say she did? The medical examiner said he had the real autopsy. Does that mean the death certificate Aunt T and I saw was fake?

"Let me see the pictures," I say, wheeling around to face Jesse.

Jesse mutters something before spreading the photographs face up on his lap. The first image is of my mother's face in profile. An up-close shot capturing her reptilian-like skin. The blisters. The flaking scabs. The dry scaly puckering.

The next three pictures are of some organ that looks like a lump of uncooked meat. A rush of nausea overtakes me. I feel color draining from my face, but I force myself not to turn away. The organ is badly scarred and disfigured, blackened, as if by tar. Even if I had paid attention during ninth-grade anatomy, it would be hard to say what organ this was.

"Cancer?" I ask. The word feels messy, my tongue thick in my mouth.

"I don't think so," Jesse says. He's been scanning the report, and now he holds out a single piece of paper for me to see. "According to this your mother had something called IPF, idiopathic pulmonary fibrosis."

"Idiopathic pulmonary fibrosis? What the hell is that?" I hear hysteria in my voice. Come on, Faith. Now's not the time to lose it.

"No idea. Never heard of it."

"Well, how could that be? How could they have overlooked something like that?"

Jesse doesn't reply, but the truth hovers in the silent space between us: they didn't overlook it. Dr. Carlisle lied about my mother's death.

I want to say a dozen things at once, but words skitter away like cockroaches. I close my eyes and inhale the heady scent of perfumes and colognes, sprayed and dabbed, trying to hide the natural odor of human flesh. Behind my eyelids is a picture of Mom. Spread on the bathroom floor. Dead. All the time her insides diseased.

I have to get out of here. Out of the easy-listening Muzak, soft lighting, and must-have materialistic bullshit. I throw open the door and step out of the dressing room. Jesse files out behind me. Together we pass the startled saleslady who calls after us, asking if we need any help with sizes.

I race through this fantasy of happiness, winding my way through hangars of push-up bras, flab-squeezing camisoles, and other undergarment devices of torture and deception, then through shoes and jewelry, juniors and cosmetics until I'm outside, standing on the sidewalk next to a tree. A white bird perches on a limb. My breath catches. Mom's bird. A blink of the eye, and the bird is gone.

Happiness, joy, love. They're all just illusions. A trick of brain chemistry. I look down, trembling, and focus on a rivulet of oily snowmelt trickling into the gutter. The sun hits the water and reflects a shimmery rainbow that swirls into patterns of red, green, yellow, and blue. I remember, as a kid, thinking the patterns cast of oil and water were magical, like tooth fairies and Santa Claus. Now they're just ugly, a sign of pollution and nothing more.

I feel a hand curl around my shoulder. I turn to see Jesse looking at me. His thumb presses against my scapula. His fingers graze my collarbone. His hand on my body is an anchor, and at this moment I don't care about Tia or Doc. I just need a friend.

I let his hand stay there—something solid and organic to hold me down and keep me from drifting away. A quote by some dead philosopher that Marta had on a poster in her office pops into my head: *For a tree to become tall it must grow tough roots among rocks.*

That was the only quote among all her self-help posters that meant anything to me. I always saw myself as that tree:

lanky in body, resilient in spirit. Or ornery, depending on who you talk to. That's what I need now, resilience. If I'm going to figure out who Dr. Carlisle was talking to and who paid him to lie about my mother, and more important, *why*, I need tough roots in all these rocks.

The problem is I have no idea what to do next. I've been an expert at making up stories, at skipping school and running around and asking questions. It's been a game of distraction until now. It's not a game anymore.

"Do you think it could be Dr. Wydner who got the medical examiner to lie?" Jesse asks, ESPing in on my thoughts. "He's giving the treatment. How hard would it be to fake the data? I mean, he's got the whole gotta-save-his-daughter motive going, right?"

"Maybe," I say, peeling back a strand of hair from my face and looking up at the dark and troubled sky. The peaks of buildings disappear into a haze of low hanging clouds and smog like an urban mountain range.

Jesse stops at the corner where an old black guy in a down jacket and earmuffs is selling soft pretzels from a glass-enclosed cart. "You like these things?"

"I only used to live on them."

Jesse buys us each a steaming hot pretzel. I slather mine with mustard, then bite into the chewy dough. For one blissful moment, my taste buds rule the world. But as I finish eating, my thoughts curdle and my food-related ecstasy turns to gloom.

"None of this explains why there was heroin in our apartment the night my mom died," I mumble.

Jesse dabs my nose with his napkin then shows me the yellow mustard splotch. "Not following," he says, tossing the napkin into the trash.

I sit on the curb with my back against the garbage can. Jesse sits next to me and listens as I tell him the rest of the story, the parts I haven't been able to say out loud: how mom swore she was clean. How the Rat Catcher came to our apartment and told her she had a debt to pay. How there was heroin in the apartment the night of her death.

"I'm sorry to say this," Jesse says when I'm done talking, "but don't you think you're being a little thick?"

I swallow back the urge to tell Jesse to f-off, but I was the idiot who brought up the topic, so I guess I'm the idiot who gets to listen.

"Kind of sounds like your mom was still using," he goes on, giving me a sideways glance, "like she bought the heroin and owed the Rat Catcher money for it."

Leave it to Jesse to snub tact and skip right to the painful heart of the matter. I chew my pinky fingernail and concentrate on a withered leaf blowing across the road. "Or maybe the Rat Catcher planted the heroin after she died," I say, too stubborn to let truly accept the possibility that Mom died an addict. "He could've come back to our place that night. When I left."

"Why would he do that?"

I stand up and start to walk. Jesse follows. "I don't know. The guy's a dealer. Those dudes are whack jobs. Maybe he's trying to hide something. I just have no idea what."

"Well then maybe you should go to the police."

I stop walking and spin around to face Jesse. "Why would I want to do that?"

"Why? Hmm." Jesse scratches his head in an exaggerated motion. "Let's think about it. We have no idea what happened, but we do know that someone's bribing the medical examiner to lie about your mother's death. Last time I checked it's the police who deal with illegal things, so you might reason that you should tell them about what's going on."

"No way." Anger like magma pours through my blood, hardening my face to stone. "The cops didn't give a shit when my mom died. They looked at us like we were scum. They didn't lift a finger to investigate. I wouldn't be surprised if they're getting paid off, too." Jesse tries to say something, but I cut him off. "Besides, even if they did care, what am I going to say? Um, gee, sorry, but I stole this file from the medical examiner's desk. Please don't arrest me."

"Fine. The police are out. Do you have a better idea?"

The truth is, I don't have a better idea. I don't have any idea. But if I'm going to refuse to see the cops and deny the Mom-on-drugs scenario, I have to come up with something.

"Okay. I've got it," I say, flip-flopping back to the clinical trial. "We're going to learn more about RNA 120."

Fourteen

"Remind me again why we're here," Jesse says thirty minutes later when we're walking down the hall to Dr. Monroe's office.

I stop in front of the computer lab where a lone student, armed with a supersized caffeinated beverage, hunches over a keyboard. "Because when I talked to her the other day, she said there was probably an underlying illness. Maybe she'll know what idiopathic pulmonary fibrosis is and if there's any way it could be connected to the treatment."

I'm too anxious to wait for his response. I continue down the hall until I get to Dr. Monroe's office, where I find a poster tacked to her door that wasn't there yesterday. I skim the poster while I wait for her to answer: *The American Society for Human Genetics* annual meeting next week at the Convention Center. I knock a second time.

"Screw it, she's not here," I say when still nobody answers. "Let's go."

It's impossible to compete with the "why" and "how" and "who" questions firing in my brain, so I don't say anything as we retrace our steps back through the genetics department. We've just passed the big lecture hall next to the stairs when the sound of Dr. Monroe's voice penetrates my mental disarray.

I stop walking and glance down the hall where I see her camouflaged in a forest of corduroy, tweed, and khaki.

"My tenure review meeting is in two weeks," I hear her tell the group.

"With these budget cuts anyone's lucky to get tenure anymore," one of the tweeds sighs.

"Adjunct professors are cheaper," a corduroy says.

The other tweed agrees. "They don't want to pay for tenure-track positions. All the classes in chemistry are being taught by TAs."

The lone blue jacket pitches in. "At the regents meeting last night they talked about the possibility of twenty positions being cut. Even tenured professors."

"You'll be fine, Kayla," the first tweed says, turning to Dr. Monroe, whose face has gone pale. "You have a good publishing record. RNA 120 speaks for itself. They can't completely gut the department, can they?"

"I don't know," Dr. Monroe answers. She is dressed in a tan skirt and brown blazer. "I'm not sure about the NIH grant. And Bickwell's lab is publishing a paper about their own antisense treatment. I just found out. An adjunct could cover my classes, and without money, who knows what will happen to my research." She looks up when she says this. Even though she totally sees me, she goes back to talking.

The group stands around contemplating their situation until one of the tweeds looks at her watch and says she has a class to go teach. The departure of one tweed causes a chain reaction, and soon the group breaks apart. Dr. Monroe lingers for a minute, as if unable to face whatever task comes next, then starts slowly down the hall in our direction. She stops when she reaches Jesse and me.

"Hi, Faith," she says in a voice that's polite, but not exactly welcoming. "If you're here to see me, I really don't have time."

"Please, this is important." I trail along next to her as she continues to her office. "You were right. There was an underlying illness. I just found out my mom had something called idiopathic pulmonary fibrosis. Have you heard of anyone else using your drug getting that disease?"

Dr. Monroe whirls around, fire flaming in her eyes. "I've told you, there is no indication that this treatment has side effects. Now if you don't mind." She opens the door to her lab and is about to shut it, but I stick out my hand.

"The medical examiner was covering it up," I blurt. "He knew she had the disease. Her toxicology report said there was no morphine in her blood. Someone was paying him to lie."

Dr. Monroe stares at me like I'm Swine Flu. "That's ridiculous. Why would you say such a thing?"

I glance at Jesse, who's too busy peering over Dr. Monroe's shoulder into her lab where the sequencing machine sits directly in his line of site to notice my plea for help. "I…heard him talking on the phone."

"Was your friend with you, too?" she says. There's accusation in her voice. "Did he hear the same thing?"

"No, but—"

"Well then don't you think it's possible that you heard wrong?"

The space behind my eyes starts to throb, but desperation eliminates any fear I might otherwise feel. I pull the autopsy folder from my bag and offer up my proof. "What about this?"

Dr. Monroe takes the folder and opens it without speaking. The air vent inside her lab makes a loud clanking sound, blowing dry, dusty air into the hall. I take off my jacket, but even in a t-shirt, my pits sweat. A class lets out as she looks through the pages. Students fill the halls with their backpacks, laptops, and post-lecture banter. Jesse tosses a comfortable "What's up" nod of his head at a guy while I stand there like a statue, my stomach swishing, as I wait for her to finish reading.

Dr. Monroe finally looks up. Her mouth is slack. Her fingers clamp around the folder. "Where did you get this?"

I twist my hands into a knot. I hadn't planned on showing her the file, and now that I have, I realize it would be crazy to tell her that the medical examiner, who I just said was being bribed to lie, gave it to me. I can't exactly tell her I stole it either.

"The medical examiner gave it to her," Jesse answers for me, apparently not caring how ridiculous the explanation sounds.

Dr. Monroe looks at Jesse with raised eyebrows. "Was that before or after Faith overheard him being bribed?"

"Before," he says, popping a mint into his mouth.

"Okay, look, Faith," she says, holding up her hands and the folder in surrender. "I don't know what game you're playing, and I'm sure you're under a great deal of stress, but there was a mistake on your mother's death certificate. A bureaucratic mess up. These things happen. I'm the wrong person to help you with whatever else you need. I'm sorry."

She hands me back the folder, but my feet won't move. There's something else. I reach into the envelope and take out the matchbox with the microscope slide. "Is this what I think it is?"

She opens the box and pulls out the slide. She studies it for a second, then puts it away with a nod. "It's a sample from your mother's autopsy. Cell tissue from her lungs. It's referenced in the report." She reaches out to give the sample back to me.

I stand there frozen, arms locked at my sides. Those cells aren't Mom. Mom was the music she sang, the words she spoke, the way she ran her fingers through my hair. She was the artist, the addict, the naturalist, and a hundred other contradictions and truths. But still, these cells, this sliver of her being, isn't that her, too? Isn't that what Mrs. Lopez taught us? That a bunch of molecules arranged in such a way form the code that builds us? What am I going to do with those molecules on that piece of glass? I can't just throw them in the trash. Discard her like everyone else has done.

"Keep it," I say. "You're a scientist. You'll know what to do with it. And you might as well keep this, too." I write my number on the folder and hand it back to her. "If you come up with anything else about the disease and your treatment, call me."

I turn and walk away before Dr. Monroe can protest. Any hope I had of finding an answer dies like a bird with a broken wing.

Jesse's bird, however, is alive and well and fluttering just fine. The second her door clicks shut he offers up his latest theory. "Maybe she's the one paying off the medical examiner. She knew her drug caused the disease and figured nobody would find out. And once Dr. Carlisle did, she wanted to cover it up."

We reach the elevator. Jesse punches the button, but I'm already opening the door to the stairwell. I have too much energy raging inside me to stand still. "Oh come on, that's ridiculous," I say, bounding down the steps two a time. "Your conspiracies can only go so far. A university professor buying off a medical examiner?"

We reach ground floor and cross the lobby. Jesse pushes through the front door and follows the path away from the building. "No way, man," he says, stopping beside the pigeon-shit statue. "There was this one scientist in Korea who said he'd cloned all these sheep and shit when he hadn't. And then there was the professor in Boston who got busted for faking data, and the guy at one of the Ivy Leagues who got canned for making up crap about some sleep study. These ass wipes will do anything to get their grants and tenure."

The emotions churning inside me swirl into a cyclone. I need a target to piss down on. I hit landfall with Jesse. "Oh, is that so? Well, how about this? Have you ever considered the possibility that you might just have the tiniest stick up your own ass about higher education, you know, with Doc and all? Maybe just a twig?"

Jesse points a finger at me, armed to poke me with another feature about ass wipes, but he stops himself and his hand flops to his side. "Maybe," he admits. "Man, I just want to keep it real."

"Real?" I ask as the clouds let loose and it starts to snow.

"Yeah, real. Like with Doc. Everything's about success. Get good grades to go to a good college to get a good job to get a good house to get a good life. When does it end? I mean what's the point? When do you get to live?" He pops a piece of gum into his mouth and works it in his jaw before continuing. "My mom was into all that, too. Big house. Expensive cars. Fancy schools. Pedigree. Career. All that bullshit. But it was too much. She cracked. It's the same with those professors. They're so scared of failing, they're willing to lie and manipulate their own research. Dr. Monroe, come on, what are her priorities? You heard them. They're cutting all these positions. You think the university gods are going to grant her tenure if they know her drug is killing people?"

I must look skeptical because he grabs my arm as if I'll decide he's crazy and make a break for it.

"Before Tia I had this girlfriend, Dawn. She couldn't do anything that wasn't for her college resume. She'd volunteer for the save the seals group or help the indigenous people of East Buttfuck, whatever. She didn't give a shit about who or what she was saving as long as it filled the volunteer experience on her college app. People are brainwashed, Faith. I'm telling you, the whole culture is brainwashed. That's why I like you."

I raise my eyebrows. "Because I'm brainwashed?"

"No, because you're not like everyone else. You're real."

I want to believe Jesse about the whole "real" thing. He sounds sincere. Acts sincere. Does that mean he is sincere? When push comes to shove which Jesse shows up, the one who lives by Doc's rules and can't stand up for himself, or the one who follows his dreams and carves his own path, a path where real is truly what matters?

I don't know what to say or what to believe, so I keep my mouth shut and start walking. Jesse walks next to me without talking. We pass a guy swaddled in blankets, his life possessions in a shopping cart next to him. I meet the guy's eye as we pass, the wounded, crazed look of someone messed up by life, war, drugs, who knows what. Staring into the guy's eyes, I shudder thinking how easy it would've been for Mom to end up in the same place, discarded and thrown to the streets. A junkie-addict-alcoholic-aren't-they-all-the-same homeless person that people go out of their way to avoid. I reach into my pocket and hand the guy a few bucks.

"God bless you, sister," he whispers, his eyes coming to life for a brief moment before the madness returns.

We keep walking until we reach a park with a pond surrounded by willows with arching branches that skim the water. A kid in a crocheted hat stands at the edge of the pond and throws in a penny, scaring away a bunch of ducks. We join the kid and Jesse reaches into his pocket and finds a penny. He tosses it into the water and watches it sink with all the other one-cent dreams.

"If I tell you something promise you won't laugh?" He digs into his pocket for more change, as if throwing in more money will increase the odds of the wish coming true.

"Depends on how funny it is."

"I want to go out west next year when I graduate," he says, tossing in a quarter. "Find some cabin to live in, or work on a ranch. Spend a few years taking pictures and shoveling horseshit for a living. And I mean the kind that comes out of a horse's ass, not the kind they feed you in college."

"Then do it."

"I don't know," he says. "It's complicated." He doesn't explain why it's complicated, though I have a pretty good idea what he means.

We stand side-by-side, listening to the chatter of two jays as they battle over a breadcrumb an old woman has tossed to them. The birds flap their wings and squawk at each other until one declares himself winner.

"What about you?" Jesse asks as the woman tosses a crumb to the loser.

"What *about* me?" I say, though I know exactly what he's getting at.

"What are you going to do with your life?"

I pull a pair of mittens from my pocket and take my time putting them on before answering. "I really like biology. I'm thinking about college…but…I don't know. It's kind of up in the air."

"Screw college," Jesse says with a convincing grin. "There's great biology in the west. Come with me and be my assistant."

I have no idea which Jesse is talking, so I make a joke. "Great. Just what I always wanted. To be a shit-shoveler's assistant."

Jesse opens his mouth and catches a snowflake on his tongue. I do the same. We stand there, enjoying snowflakes melting on our tongues until Jesse gets a sly look on his face. Before I have a chance to react, he scoops up a pile of snow and hurls it in my direction.

"Oh, is that right?" I pack a mean snowball and cock my arm. "Take this!" I holler, launching it at his chest.

"That's the best you got?" He pegs my right shoulder with a fastball. I dodge another attack and start to run. Jesse chases me around the pond. My feet slide around on the slippery ground. I can hardly stay upright I'm laughing so hard. Jesse's laughing too, howling like a wild thing, all the while lobbing snowballs at my back. We circle the pond until neither of us can move, and we're doubled over in laughter, trying to catch our breath.

That's when it all comes back to me with a gale that makes my knees weak—death reports, diseases, side effects, drug dealers, lies, bribery. I drop onto the nearest bench and surrender to the weight of worry.

Jesse sits down next to me and drapes an arm around my shoulder. "Reality's overrated. How about we ignore it a little longer and catch a movie?"

"That's the best idea I've heard all day."

A half hour later we're at the eleven-plex theater on south Columbus. I have no idea what's playing, and I don't care. Sitting in the dark with Jesse and losing myself to Hollywood is all that matters. Jesse picks some action flick about terrorists and conspiracy and a bunch of guys who blow stuff up. We buy tickets and then stand in line for the mandatory popcorn, soda, and candy combo.

"They say never eat anything that comes in a bucket," Jesse says as he hands me a tray holding a bucket of popcorn, an extra large soda, and a jumbo bag of candy.

I reach for the popcorn. "Words to live by."

We exit the movie theater some three hours later and step outside into the early winter night, a different kind of night than any other season. The sky is darker, lonelier. I look up to find the stars, but the city lights mask their presence. The dark of the street blends into the dark of the sky like a big, black curtain has been draped over the heavens. I feel lost without the guidance of the stars, without their burning reminder that we're just a speck in time. Orion, Pegasus, Ursa Major and Minor. Names Mom taught me. Looking out the window some nights, good nights when she was straight, she'd teach me about the order of the universe, even when I was too little to understand. Everything that is born dies. The entire universe is made of the same atoms. Planets revolve around the sun. Unbreakable truths. In the chaos or our lives, she told me, the laws of nature always remain the same.

Here in the starless city night the buildings are their own stars, burning bright lights coaxing you in off the street, into that fake security that if you build enough walls and buy enough stuff you can insulate yourself from the natural order of things. But no matter how much you own, how many walls you put up—the laws of nature always win. Ashes to ashes, dust to dust. Everything that is born dies.

Or gets killed.

Fifteen

Anj is the first to call the next morning with the news. "What did'ya do, kill the guy?" she says when I pick up.

I wipe sleep from my eyes, wondering if it's possible I'm still dreaming. "Kill who?" I yawn.

"Dr. Carlisle, the medical examiner. I mean it's a good thing you talked to the guy yesterday. Now that he's dead and all."

"What?" I blurt, awake now.

"Yeah, it's on the front page of the paper. I saw my dad reading about it and totally flipped. Hold on." I hear her shouting something at Chrissy about nail polish and the dog. " 'Kay, I'm back. It says his car went off a bridge into the Schuylkill."

Off a bridge? Into the Schuylkill? Dr. Carlisle dead? That can't be. People don't just drive off bridges. I hold the phone to my ear, a million thoughts racing through my mind, all of them trapped.

"Uh…hello," Anj says. "You still there?"

"Still here," I manage to get out.

"Gosh, sorry. I didn't mean to be the bearer of bad news. I just thought you'd want to know since you met the guy and everything. You were probably the last one to see him alive. From the way his car swerved, they think his brakes might've failed. Anyway, gotta run. My sister's trying to put nail polish on the dog's claws again. See you at school."

I say good-bye and rush out of my room and into the kitchen, still wearing underwear and a tank. Aunt T's at the table, already dressed, drinking coffee with the newspaper spread in front of her. If I weren't in such a panic, I might stop and enjoy the smell of coffee. I might even sit at the table with Aunt T and feel the warmth of morning sun streaming in through the lace curtains. I am in a panic, though, and a clumsy one at that. I snatch the front page from the pile next to Aunt T and knock over her coffee mug in the process.

"Really, Faith," she sputters. She jumps to her feet and mops up the spill with the funny page. "What's gotten in to you this morning?"

"Nothing. Sorry. I just have to see something." I grip the greasy newsprint in my fingers and read the headlines: *Accident Leads To Medical Examiner's Death.* I try to read the rest of the article, but my hands are shaking so badly I can hardly hold the paper still. All I can make out are fragments. *Too early to state the cause of the accident…bystanders say he swerved to avoid a collision…happened sometime after five.…*

My stomach is suddenly violently ill. I flee the kitchen and run to the bathroom where I drop to my knees and heave into the toilet. My stomach buckles, and I heave again. Three times in all, until all that's left to throw up is water. I'm covered in sweat. My face. My hands. Even the bottoms of my feet are clammy. I sit on the floor and draw my knees to my chest.

Aunt T taps on the door and calls my name.

"Just a minute!" I drag myself to the sink, stick my head under a blast of water, giving myself a brain freeze, then perch on the edge of the tub and shiver. It's not the temperature prickling my flesh. It's a deeper cold rising from the sickening feeling that

Dr. Carlisle's death wasn't an accident. That it was connected to my mother, to the autopsy, to the secret he was keeping.

Aunt T opens the door and peeks in. "You okay, hon?"

"Greasy pizza," I stammer. "I ate too much last night with Jesse. Must've turned my stomach."

Aunt T studies my face. I can tell she doesn't believe me. I'd go for the too-much-beer barf-fest-hangover excuse, but Aunt T knows I don't party. She comes into the bathroom and leans against the wall. "Do you want to talk?"

Yes, I think. "No," I say.

"Faith, it's better if you—"

"Talk," I interrupt. "I know. But I have to go. I'll be late for school. I feel better now." I sound lame, even to myself. But what choice do I have? Aunt T warned me: *Your mother died of a heroin overdose. Don't go looking for problems when there aren't any.*

I make a halfhearted attempt at a smile and leave the bathroom before Aunt T can say anything else. The second I'm in my room, I check my phone. Two texts from Jesse. I'm about to respond when I get a call. This time it's Dr. Monroe.

"There's something I need to talk to you about," she says in place of hello. "It's important. Can you meet me today?"

Hearing Dr. Monroe's voice, Jesse's words stampede into my mind and crush every other thought in their path: *For all we know she's the one paying off the medical examiner. Maybe she knew her drug caused the disease and figured nobody would find out.*

What if he's right? I think with a rising feeling of dread. What if Dr. Monroe *is* behind this, and she had something to do with Dr. Carlisle's death? What if the meeting is a set up? Then again, what if Jesse's wrong? What if she knows something about my mom or has information about her drug?

"Faith? Are you still there?"

"Yeah, still here…sorry.…" The television goes on in Aunt T's room. Through the thin walls I hear an advertisement for winter boots. That's it. Shoes. We'll meet someplace public, someplace safe. The mall. "Okay. How about Footlocker? Springfield Mall at noon?"

Dr. Monroe agrees. Just as I say good-bye and hang up, I hear the front door open and the sound of Sam's voice. The TV goes off, and a minute later, Aunt T comes to my room.

"Sam's here," she says. "He's taking me to work. My car's vibrating again, but the garage can't work on it until tomorrow. We're supposed to go to some dealers this evening—car dealers," she says quickly in case I thought she meant she was going out for a score. "I don't have to go. I could call in sick. Are you sure you're okay?"

"I'm fine," I insist. "See?" I burst into a spontaneous set of jumping jacks, but the expression on Aunt T's face tells me the jumping jacks aren't enhancing my claim of miraculous recovery. They're just making me look like some kind of deranged athletic hopeful. "Seriously," I say, working up a smile now. "I'm okay. I'm leaving in a few minutes."

"O-ka-y." She hesitates and searches my face with her worried eyes. "But call me if you need anything. *Anything*," she emphasizes, and after one more worried glance in my direction, turns and leaves me alone.

The second she's gone I race to the kitchen and root around the drawers for her spare car key. If I drive I won't have to miss any classes. I can take the car to school, drive to the mall at lunch for the meeting, and get back for sixth period. It's only Thursday and I already have two half-days and one full-day unexcused absences this week. A fourth and Mrs. Stratberry, the school attendance officer who believes "thou shalt not miss school" is one of the original ten commandments, will be dragging my butt to the principal and putting in a call to Aunt T.

I don't care how badly the car vibrates, or that I don't have a license. I know how to drive—at least reasonably so. I'll have the car back before Aunt T's home. She'll never know I took it. I go outside and climb into the driver's seat, concentrating not on my meeting this afternoon with Dr. Monroe or on Dr. Carlisle's "accident" but on making the thing go without killing anyone.

I'm on Mill, blocks from school, when a car pulls into the next lane and starts cruising along beside me—probably some loser with a rude comment about what I'm doing later on tonight. My usual defense in situations like this is to ignore Homo erectus until he drives off to find some other fresh meat to drag into his cave. I'm in no mood today to be sexually harassed by a jerk with a hard-on who thinks he's hot shit. I glance at the driver, prepared to throw him the finger, but something about the way he rolls along beside me puts me on edge. I take a second look. This time the window rolls down, and the driver turns his head in my direction. The Rat Catcher's lips spread into a dark, crooked smile, and with a nod of the head, he gives me a look that says, "I'm watching."

I'm so busy worrying over what the Rat Catcher and his druggie mob want with me, that I blow through the four-way stop without thinking, forcing some girl in a Beemer to slam on her brakes to avoid a collision.

She rolls down her window and hollers, "Watch where you're going, bitch!"

I peel into the school parking lot and run to the back door where a group of girls dressed in matching school sweats and white tees stand clumped in a gossipy huddle. I feel my hair, which I hadn't brushed in the first place, sticking to my cheeks, my face hot and sweaty. My boots are heavy as tractors as I clump up each step. A girl I recognize from the school musical *Grease*, where she played Sandy, innocent virgin turned bad, whispers as I pass. The whisper is loud, meant for me to hear: *Check her out. She looks like a druggie. Did you hear the rumor about her mom?*

I think of marching back down those steps and taking a swing at the girl's pretty porcelain face. It wouldn't be the first time. I've been the cause of numerous bloody noses in my mom's defense, but I don't have time. I have to get inside and find Jesse.

The bell rings before I have a chance. I rush to my locker and grab the first books I see, which turn out to be entirely the wrong ones, and I show up in English class with my history textbook and lab manual. When Laz sees the lab manual on my desk he jokes that perhaps I'd rather dissect a cow's eye than read Steinbeck. A few people laugh. I don't care. I search the room for Jesse.

"You okay?" he mouths when our eyes meet.

I shake my head. I'm not okay. Not at all. I scribble a note and drop it on his desk on my way out on a bathroom pass: *Meet me out back after third period.*

Anj finds me in the hall after English. Her hair is wrapped in a colorful tie-dyed African turban, and she's wearing a matching sarong and shirt. Africa awareness day she tells me. "The cafeteria refused to go vegan, and we decided we didn't like the Happy Cows slogan, so we moved on from factory farming to world hunger. I'm supposed to look like I'm from Africa, but I think I look more like I'm from Macy's." She sighs. "Oh well. I try." She stops talking about her plight and focuses her attention on me. "How are you doing? That's so awful about Dr. Carlisle. You must be totally freaking out. What happened at your meeting yesterday?"

I start to tell her about the autopsy report and what I learned, but I don't get past the opening line. Tara and Sylvie Jackson, another member of the socially conscious gang-of-five, come rushing down the hall toward us. Tara races over to Anj and grabs her arm.

"Emergency," she pants. "Somebody stole the money we made this morning at the bake sale." She glares at Sylvie who's suddenly become busy studying the floor. "*Someone* was supposed to keep watch over the booth and not take off with their boyfriend and leave it unattended. Come on, we have to go talk to the principal." She whisks Anj away to Mr. Jennings' office before I can say anything else. Anj looks back over her shoulder as Tara pulls her down the hall and shouts, "Call me later!"

"Okay," I call after her, but suddenly I know I won't.

As I watch Anj walk away with her friends, something becomes clear to me: I can't drag Anj into this mess. Anj, who shops at Macy's and spends hundreds of dollars to dress up like she's from Africa, so she can raise awareness about famine and drought and all the horrible things happening in some other part of the world. She's not like me. I don't have to dress up.

What if by being my friend, something bad happens to Anj? What if she tries to help me and she gets hurt or worse? If someone really did kill Dr. Carlisle, what else are they willing to do to keep their secret safe? The best way to keep Anj out of this, to protect her from whatever danger I've gotten myself into, is to keep her away from me.

It's all I can do to make it through history and moron math. I check the clock every few minutes, as Mrs. Kempt, who has about the sense of humor of a dead fish, drones on about how changing the order of the addends doesn't change the sum.

Finally math agony ends, and I rush outside to meet Jesse.

"Dr. Carlisle's dead, Jesse," I say the second I see him. "Maybe whoever I overheard him talking to on the phone killed him because they wanted more money to lie to me." Fear pulses through my blood, causing words to tumble out before they can be screened for logic. "And I saw the Rat Catcher on the way to school this morning. Why the hell is he following me? Does he think I can pay off my mom's debt, or that I can trace the heroin back to him?"

I stop talking and wait for Jesse to offer his own theory. Instead, he takes me in his arms.

"I don't want you to get hurt," he murmurs.

His voice is a whisper in my ear as he pulls me hard against his body. I melt into his embrace. His lips find mine. I feel the tip of his tongue in my mouth and dissolve into the softness of the kiss. The world slips away as his hand slides up and over the curve of my hip. Before his hand can go any further, I jerk away.

"I care about you, Faith," Jesse says, pulling me back for another kiss.

This time I turn my head and his nose slams into my cheek.

Jesse doesn't belong in this mess any more than Anj does. I don't care that he's the first boy I've ever really liked, that Anj is the first friend I've ever really had. This isn't about Tia or about being real or about standing up to Doc. This is about getting killed. Murdered. Driven off a bridge.

If I want to protect my friends from whoever's willing to kill to keep their secret safe, I have no choice: From this moment on, Jesse and Anj get the Faith Flores friendship ax.

I try to run, but Jesse's got my arm.

"I don't care about you," I lie. "Not in this way."

I tear free from his grip and run away.

Sixteen

An hour after seeing Jesse, I'm pacing the aisles of Footlocker, waiting for Dr. Monroe, and looking over my shoulder a million times a second. Every time someone passes I feel like I'm going to leap out of my skin.

I'm lurking around a wall of sneakers with price tags worth half a month's rent, trying to play it cool and blend in with the shopping crowd, when Dr. Monroe shows up. In her khaki pants, black turtleneck, and blond hair sticking out from beneath a checkered beret, it's hard to imagine her a killer. She leads me to a bench at the far end of the store and wastes no time getting to the point.

"After you left my office yesterday, I realized it didn't matter how you got the autopsy file or if there was a mistake on your mother's death certificate," she says. "If your mother had IPF, then I have to be sure."

"Sure? About what?"

"Sure about what?"

"That there isn't some kind of biological vector that caused my treatment to target her lungs. What if my treatment *did* somehow make you mother sick? What if RNA 120 gave her IPF?" She stops talking and purses her lips as a girl in a belly shirt and pierced navel walks down the aisle in front of us.

If Dr. Monroe's trying to cover up her guilt, she's not doing a very good job I think as I watch the girl pick up a shiny, white basketball shoe and cart it away to find its mate. Why mention the connection between her drug and the disease if that's what she's trying to hide?

"I called Dr. Glass and Dr. Wydner to get their opinions," she continues. "Dr. Wydner was out on some kind of family emergency, so I left him a message. I did manage to talk to Dr. Glass. I told him about the IPF and the mistake in your mother's autopsy, and he told me that IPF, though a fairly rare disease, is not an uncommon effect of drug abuse, so it probably wasn't caused by my treatment." She pauses and looks around, then lowers her voice. "Still, I couldn't stop thinking about my vector theory and the possibility of my drug's connection to the illness, so I did a literature search to learn more about the epidemiology of IPF and heroin addicts. There was nothing in PubMed about IPF and heroin addicts in particular, and I didn't have time to search every database. I did, however, find something I think you might be interested in."

"Okay," I say, a sinking feeling that whatever this other thing I might be interested in is not good news.

"Here's the thing. I found out this disease doesn't manifest itself with the skin condition or the other symptoms your mother had." So then she didn't have the disease, I'm about to say, unsure if this news is a relief or a disappointment, but I can tell Dr. Monroe hasn't nailed the lid on the coffin. "Unless she had the genetic form of the disease," she finishes, sending the lid crashing down with a loud thud.

"What do you mean *the genetic form?*" I snort, studying her face for any clue that she's making up a genetic form of the disease as a way to deflect attention from the RNA 120/IPF connection. I'm not a human lie detector machine, though, and there aren't any obvious lying clues like shifty eyes or a nervous tick. What I see is pity. Pity is for stray dogs and orphaned babies. I ball my hands into fists and look away.

"There's the idiopathic form of this disease, which means nobody knows how you get it. The pathology isn't understood," she explains. "That's what's in the autopsy report. But there's also a dominant genetic mutation that causes the disease. That mutation also causes the skin condition like she had."

I've studied enough genetics to know that the word dominant and disease in the same sentence isn't a good thing. "So if it's dominant you only need one bad copy of the gene to be screwed," I say in a flat voice.

"Right. One bad copy and, as you put it, you're screwed. You get the disease."

At that moment, a smiling kid with a mullet, wearing a brown tie, matching vest, and a big circular badge that says, "My name's Kurt. I'm here to help" appears and asks if there are any shoes we'd like to try on. I'm trying to act normal, so I say yes and hand him the first thing I see and ask for size eight.

Smiling Kurt dashes off to find the shoes.

"We know the gene where the mutation for this disease occurs," Dr. Monroe says the second he's gone, "so to find out if your mother had the mutation, all we need to do is pull out a few hundred nucleotides on either side of the mutation position and then sequence. That sequence will tell us if the mutation is present or not. I have the tissue sample from her lungs, so it would be easy to do."

Mutation. Sequence. DNA. Nucleotides: Greetings, Earthling! Welcome to the planet Yurgon. I will be your host and genetic counselor.

An Asian woman with a screaming child who's waving the broken head of a doll stops beside the bench and reaches into her purse. The woman pulls out a lollipop and offers it to the girl. The deal is a good one, and the kid stops crying, grabbing for the lollipop and dropping the doll's head in the process.

I pick up the disembodied head once the kid and woman have moved on and stare into the big, blue unblinking eyes. "And what about Melinda?"

"What about her?"

"You think she and my mom both could've actually had the same mutation?"

"We don't even know Melinda had IPF."

"Well, she sure looked the same as my mother," I say, running my finger over the doll's tiny upturned nose, the white porcelain skin, the blond hair.

Dr. Monroe's expression doesn't change. She keeps the same detached look she's had since she first sat down, but there's a tension in her body, unnoticeable if you weren't looking for it, but I am looking. I see the flex of her wrists as she presses her ringless fingers down against her knees, the strain of her ankle as she arches her foot.

"Looking the same doesn't mean she had IPF, idiopathic or genetic," she explains, her crisp voice a veiled attempt to cover the tightness in her words. "They shared some symptoms that could've been caused by anything. I've told you, Faith, heroin use can cause a whole battery of health problems. Melinda could've had a skin rash. We have no reason to believe she had IPF."

"Fine," I say, turning back to the doll. "So say Mom did have some mutation, and her sickness didn't have anything to do with side effects from your drug. You said it's a dominant condition. That means I have a fifty-fifty chance of having inherited it from her. Those aren't exactly great odds. Is there any way to treat this disease?"

Dr. Monroe shakes her head as if to say you're-shit-out-of-luck, but she doesn't speak because what is there to say? That we could look into Mom's genes and find the cause of her death, which possibly means finding out I have the same fatal condition that has no cure? I stare at that broken doll head. Someone help me please! My head is no longer attached to my body. Call 911!!

I think back to the debate in science class that first time I met Jesse, exactly a week ago. I'd been so sure of myself then, so sure I'd want to know the secrets hidden in my genes, that I'd want to peek inside and know what was coming down the pike. But I never considered the idea of knowing you had some fatal genetic condition there was no treatment for. Having to live with the knowledge of your early death. It seemed like science fiction then, not reality. Once you've opened this Pandora's box there's no turning back.

I open my eyes and glance at Dr. Monroe, sitting with her hands folded in her lap, waiting patiently for me to return to planet Earth and say something.

"Look, Faith, if we found out your mother had the mutation there are a lot of facts for you to consider," she tells me when I don't speak. "You wouldn't have to decide anything for yourself right away. Maybe you'd want to know if you had the mutation and maybe you wouldn't. There's no right answer."

My thoughts are still too jumbled to respond. If what she says about the dominant mutation is true, I'm the fallout, the casualty. She's a professor, not a miracle worker. What could she do if I have the mutation, dig my grave? I feel around my pockets for candy or gum, even a cough drop, anything to take away the bitter taste on my tongue. Just lint.

"Okay," I say when I've found my voice again. "Imagine living every day knowing some morning I'm going to wake up and my skin's going to start peeling off my face and then as an added bonus I won't be able to breathe and I'll die."

"There's also the chance you wouldn't have the gene. Don't forget that. Fifty-fifty isn't a guarantee."

I feel like we're at a casino talking about our betting odds in a game of blackjack. "And while we're on the fact of the genes I've inherited from my mother, what about addiction genes? Am I going to find that out, too? That not only might I have some horrible mutation that's going to kill me, but maybe I got really lucky and inherited her addict genes as well? Great. Maybe I can be just like her, a junkie with a fatal lung condition."

Dr. Monroe jumps to her feet and steps in front of me, transforming into this she-beast professor. It's not hard to imagine her standing in front of a room full of hungover undergrads and commanding their attention.

"All right, let's slow down," she says. "One thing at a time. First of all, we're sequencing one tiny part of a gene, not your mother's entire genome, and even if we did sequence that, inheriting a dominant mutation for IPF is a lot different than this idea of some junkie gene. Addiction doesn't come from one gene, Faith, like you either have it or you don't. It comes from a lot of interacting genes and it's not just genes, either. There are environmental factors to consider."

"Great, like being raised by a heroin addict? Somehow that doesn't make me feel any better."

Smiling Kurt who's here to help arrives at just that minute with two shoeboxes in his arms. "We didn't have your size," he tells me. "I brought a seven and a nine instead."

I thank him for his help and pretend to show great interest in the shoes. He lingers for a second in case I require further assistance. I assure him I can tie the laces on my own. He smiles and darts off to help another customer.

"Okay, fine, so I might not be an addict like her," I concede. "But still, I might end up the same anyways, dead from some fatal lung thing. If I have the mutation, our destinies really won't be that different in the end."

"This is hard stuff, Faith, I know," Dr. Monroe says, sitting back down. "But right now I need your permission to look for the mutation in your mother's gene. If I find the mutation I'll know that she had the genetic form of the disease and that my drug in no way caused it."

For the first time since Mom died, I stop and ask myself what she would've done, because occasionally even my mother had common sense. She knew how to stay calm in emergencies, and she always zippered her coat and wore a hat when it was cold—she had the basics covered at least. Would she tell me to find out? No matter how hard I search, I can't find her answer.

"And what about Dr. Carlisle?" I say, remembering the other nightmare, the one where the medical examiner was just killed. "Say you find out my mother did have this mutation, then what? We still don't know who was bribing Dr. Carlisle to lie about her death or who killed him or what they were trying to cover up."

Dr. Monroe stares at me. "What makes you think someone killed him? It was an accident. They say there was a drunk driver, and Dr. Carlisle's brakes failed when he swerved."

"Oh, come on! You think it was an accident? The same day I overhear the phone call, his brakes just happen to fail and he just happens to drive off a bridge?"

Dr. Monroe protests and tries again to make me see the connection between my stress and my imagination, but I stop listening. The picture of Dr. Carlisle's car plummeting into the water—his bloated corpse being fished out of the river, the mutation, Mom, the Rat Catcher, the heroin—it's too much to take in. I'm no longer in my body. What sits on the bench is molecular Faith. The DNA, blood, and guts part of me. The soul part of me drifts, watches all this happening from someplace else, Hawaii, maybe. The moon.

"Fine," I hear molecular Faith says. "Do what you need to do. Sequence my mom's DNA. Get your proof. How long will it take?"

"Three days," Dr. Monroe says rising to her feet and grabbing her purse. "I'll have the primers by tomorrow, amplify the section, and then get on the sequencer. I'll call you when I get the results."

———

I wander out of the store and enter malltopia. It takes a second to adjust to the hip-hop music blaring from Hot Topic, the smell of pizza, fudge brownies, and corndogs emanating from the food court, the flashing neon lights advertising sales on useless crap. The whole thing is an exercise in attention deficit disorder, but slowly my soul reunites with my body. As I pass the sunglasses cart and ear piercing station, I start wishing I'd never heard any of this. I wish Melinda had just left me alone, and I'd taken Aunt T's advice: *Don't go looking for problems when there aren't any.* But it's too late to turn back now.

I stop for a piece of pizza, then sit on the bench next to the merry-go-round to watch the little kids on their wooden horses. Maybe if I sit here long enough, some of their happiness will diffuse into me. The longer I watch, though, the worse I feel. Nothing can penetrate the cell membrane of my anxiety.

As I nibble around the pockets of bubbling grease, my thoughts bounce around like a ball in a pinball machine.

PING! Genetic disease, lose ten points. PING! Murder and bribery, lose another ten. It's with Dr. Monroe that the ball sinks into the gutter. Is she making up this stuff about genetic IPF? Is she trying to hide something? What about Melinda and her symptoms? Did she just happen to have the same mutation?

I press my fingers against my eyelids and push the world into blackness until my thoughts settle. Then I toss my napkin into the trash and leave the mall to head back to school. The one place where life still resembles normal.

———

A layer of frost covers the windshield of Aunt T's car when I get to the parking lot. I start the engine and crank the defroster. I might as well wait for the glaciers to melt. If I want to make it back to school in this geologic era, I'll have to scrape. I manage to clear a notebook-size patch of glass before my fingers go numb. Good enough. I get into the car and start back to school.

I decide to take the back road. It's faster. Bio starts in ten minutes, and the threat of Mrs. Stratberry hangs over me. I'm a few blocks from campus when a squirrel darts into the road. Slamming on your brakes to avoid smooshing a small rodent is one of those no-no's they teach you in driver's ed, but what I know and what I do when the life of a small, fluffy creature is at stake are two different things. I hit the brakes.

The car doesn't stop. The wheels flatten the squirrel with a sickening thump. I brake again as I zoom toward the inter-section. Still nothing. I have the red, and the light's getting closer. I pump the brake, but the pedal is soft. It's then I see a car coming the other direction. I punch the horn and swerve hard to avoid a collision.

I don't know if it's minutes or seconds that I'm sprawled across the steering wheel, but when I blink open my eyes and find my view angled to the tops of the trees, I know something's wrong. For one concussion of a moment I think there's been a tectonic event, but then the truth hits me like my head must've hit the wheel: I crashed Aunt T's car. I don't have a license. I'm in a ditch.

I sit up, my head pounding, and turn the key, hoping by some cosmic miracle I can get out of the ditch as easily as I got into it. The wheels just spin with a helpless whir. As I rub my right shoulder, throbbing beneath the gray band of seatbelt, I see a dude in a denim jacket running from the top of the embankment and stumbling down the berm toward me. He reaches the car and jerks open the door. The smell of pot wafts off him. I cough and slowly sit up.

"Hey, man, you okay?" He's staring at the angle of Aunt T's car, and there's panic in his eyes. "Should I call for help?"

"No!" The strength of my response makes my head pound even more, and I slide back down into the seat. A picture of tow trucks, blinking lights, and cops runs through my mind, followed by the fact of having "borrowed" Aunt T's car and driven without a license. "I'm fine. Really." I open the door and wobble to my feet. The edges of me feel blurred. I reach to the hood for balance. "Don't call anyone."

"Hey, man, that's cool. If you say so." He looks relieved that I don't want to file an accident report or call the cops to the scene. I might've been the one who spun off the road, but driving while baked doesn't exactly endear yourself with the authorities. He's a polite stoner though, and adds, "Can I at least give you a ride?"

I agree to let him take me back to school. There's no blood, thank god. Internal injury, maybe, but no outer damage.

Nobody will know what happened. It's the kind of pain I'm used to hiding—on the inside.

I take one last look at Aunt T's car. There's already so many dents and dings on the thing, maybe she won't notice a few more. I'll get someone to pull it from the ditch later. I'll have the car home before Aunt T gets there.

One can always hope.

———

Five minutes later, I'm back at school. My legs are shaky and my right shoulder throbs like a mofo, but I down a few Advil, and head to the first-floor bathroom for a quick mirror check, so I don't enter bio looking like an extra from *The Night of the Living Dead*.

As I slap my face with cold water, the day replays in my head. The medical examiner's death. Dr. Monroe's call. Genetic IPF. My car accident. Car accident? All other thoughts screech to a halt as I hear Anj's voice: They think the medical examiner's brakes might have failed. Could my accident be connected to his? Did someone mess with the medical examiner's brakes and then mess with mine?

I slap more cold water on my cheeks. Or did the brakes just fail? Aunt T said the car was vibrating, but she never said anything about faulty brakes. Maybe I hit a patch of ice and skidded out. I close my eyes and recall the scene. I don't remember seeing anything but dry pavement.

My phone buzzes. I jump and pull it out from my bag to see a text from Jesse. *Where are you?*

I check the time. Shit. Class started fifteen minutes ago. I smooth my hair and head to bio doing my best impression of a normal girl.

Mrs. Lopez asks for a pass when I walk in fifteen minutes late. I tell her I don't have one, and she tells me to see her after class. I nod and go to my table. Anj's seat is empty. She must still be busy with Tara and Sylvie and the Hunger Days stuff, so when Mrs. Lopez says to find a partner for today's lab, I don't have to worry about making up an excuse to avoid her.

Jesse, on the other hand, charges over to my seat the second Mrs. Lopez finishes giving directions. Before he can reach me, I turn to Raven, an emo who hardly ever talks, and ask her to be my partner. She shrugs and grunts, something I interpret as yes. I open the lab manual and pretend to read the instructions. Jesse's not so easily cast off. He stands at my table, firing off questions about what happened and where I was during lunch and if I'm okay, until Mrs. Lopez orders him to choose a partner and get to work. I turn and swallow as he walks away. Thank god Raven's too into her own suffering and angst to notice mine.

I manage to get through lab without doing much of anything, and I'm attempting to sneak out at the end of the period and avoid my little after-class discussion with Mrs. Lopez when her voice stops me. She waits until all the other kids leave, then closes the door and tells me to sit. I drop my bag and take the seat closest to the front of the room. She leans against my table and folds her arms across her flowered blouse.

"You were late to class," she says, her brown eyes searching my face. I feel her watching me even when I look down.

"I know. I'm sorry. I—"

"Save it. I've heard every excuse possible. My favorite one was when Arnold Klint told me he was on the highest level of Angry Birds, and he had to finish the game before he could come to class." She sounds strict, but her voice hides a smile. For the first time today, I relax a little. It's strange to find a lecture about truancy relaxing, but after everything else that's happened, it's a relief to be in trouble for something so normal.

"I want to show you something," Mrs. Lopez says. "Come with me. You can leave your stuff, we'll be back."

I start to protest, but the look on Mrs. Lopez's face shuts me up. I leave my backpack on the floor and follow her out the door, through the empty halls, and upstairs to the art wing. The hall smells of clay, paint, and chemical fixatives. Combine that with the pizza, and my stomach is starting to turn. Mrs. Lopez stops in front of the current display of portraits without saying anything. I have no idea what we're doing here, and I don't care. I'm just going through the motions. If Mrs. Lopez wants to give me a course on art appreciation, I'll be her pupil.

Apparently anything goes in art class because some of the portraits on the wall are brightly colored cubist style, others are sketched with charcoal pencil, and still some are photographs. And then there's Duncan's piece. He's created an enormous digital collage, Andy Warhol style, of Anj, which, according to the explanation beneath, he made with some computer gizmo called a graphics tablet.

I'm vaguely scanning the rest of the art, when a kick of surprise nails me in the chest. At the far right corner, inconspicuous among the brighter colors and larger pieces, is the photo Jesse took of me with his phone. Below it, he's written one word: *Authentic.* There's a hundred ways I could interpret his meaning, but his intention hardly matters. The caption might as well be phony after what I said to him today.

I turn from Mrs. Lopez, so she won't see my face crumble, and wait for her to deliver the hidden reason for us being here. The message I guess is meant to be secret because all she says is, "These portraits take a lot of hard work, don't you think?" and leads me back down the hall. Soon we've come full circle and we're back to where we started. Mrs. Lopez stands outside her class and watches me like she's waiting for me to speak, but someone must've forgotten to give me the script. I have no idea what my lines are supposed to be.

"This could be yours," she finally says.

"A science classroom?"

"No. Science." She crosses the hall and comes to my side. "Think about it, Faith. You could get a degree in biology, a master's, a PhD. Commit yourself to something like those kids do with their art. You're smart. All your teachers say the same thing. But your grades, if you don't mind me saying so, are nothing to be proud of and neither, as I've been told, is your attendance record lately."

I lean against a locker and dig into my pocket for the lighter. "Thanks for the pep talk."

"Sorry. I don't do pep talks. This is a reality check."

"Well then how about a little fantasy for a change?" I smile, but the joke falls flat.

"I see how much you like science," Mrs. Lopez continues as the door to the chem room opens and Ms. Muller, the young new chemistry teacher with the hip clothes and trendy haircut, stomps into the hall.

"But there are no signs of rodents in my room," Ms. Muller snaps at someone still in the classroom. "I don't see why you need to lay all those traps."

"I apologize for the inconvenience, ma'am," says a voice that makes me stand up, stop digging around in my pockets, and listen. "But I'm the Rat Catcher. I'm contracted with the district to deal with pests, and someone reported a pest problem in the science wing."

"Well it certainly wasn't me."

The Rat Catcher steps into the hall. He looks directly at me, then he turns back to Ms. Mueller and shakes his head as if deeply concerned by this troubling prospect of pests.

He turns back to Ms. Muller and shakes his head as if deeply concerned by this troubling prospect of pests. "You can never be too careful though, can you? We have to keep the students safe. You know how many diseases rodents carry, and if a student got sick and you hadn't reported the problem, I'd hate to think of the lawsuit. I'll be back in a few days to check the traps."

The Rat Catcher tips his head at me, then strides off down the hall with the confidence of a king or a president or a drug dealer and thug moonlighting as a pest control guy. I stand there, jaw unhinged, heart beating in my ears until I hear Mrs. Lopez's voice coming to me from some distant region of the galaxy.

"Faith, are you listening to me...Faith?"

I turn slowly back to Mrs. Lopez. "Sorry, no. I mean yes. I'm listening."

"You might not turn in all the work, but your answers in class demonstrate your knowledge and interest. I know about your mother, and I know how hard this time must be for you, but I think you could get into college next year if you start really applying yourself now. I'd like you to see the school counselor. She can help you."

I know about your mother. Meaning what? That she was a junkie? That she's dead? I know Mrs. Lopez is trying to help, but rage shoots from my chest to my mouth, and I'm about to let it fly about how she knows nothing about my mother, nothing about me, but I stop myself and make my mouth stay shut. I still have the car to deal with. The last thing I need is to land my butt in the principal's office for mouthing off to a teacher.

Years of experience with teachers and their lectures has taught me one thing—if you want them to leave you alone, agree with their point and promise you'll do whatever they're asking.

"Thanks," I say. "I'll do that. I'll set up a meeting. I'd better get to class now. I don't want to be too late."

Mrs. Lopez sighs. I'm guessing she sees right through my promise as if my words are nothing more than a pane of glass. "Come in. I'll write you a pass."

When she opens the door to her classroom, Mr. Jennings and a cop are standing by her desk.

Seventeen

"Mr. Jennings, how can I help you?" Mrs. Lopez asks, keeping her eyes on the cop, a tall woman with a face that looks like it would crack if she smiled.

"I need to see Faith," the principal answers.

My first thought is relief. They know about the Rat Catcher. They're here to protect me. Quickly I see how stupid this line of reasoning is. To everyone but me the Rat Catcher's the pest control guy. He's here to keep the students safe and take care of rodents in the science labs.

Before I can say anything, Mrs. Lopez intervenes. "Why do you need to see Faith?"

"Probable suspicion of drugs." The cop's hand strays to the gun holstered at her hip like she's looking for a reason to use it. "We need to search her bag."

"Drugs!" I blurt. The idea is so absurd, I laugh.

Mr. Jennings, all six-six of him, steps toward me. "Well, if it's ridiculous, then you won't mind opening your bag and letting us search."

"And what makes you think Faith is carrying drugs?" Mrs. Lopez asks, matching Mr. Jennings if not in size in attitude.

Frau police officer eyes the principal and answers for him. "We received a tip."

"May I ask who that tip was from?" Mrs. Lopez steps in front of me and for one hopeful moment I think she's going to sort this all out, and my privacy won't be invaded. A science teacher, though, no matter how veteran, is no match for a principal and a cop.

Mr. Jennings presses his hands together and a smile that barely hides his impatience snakes across his lips. "That information is confidential. Now, if you don't mind, we can get started."

I turn to Mrs. Lopez. "Do I have to? Don't I have any rights?"

She shakes her head. "I'm afraid not. I'm sorry, Faith. If they believe there's probable cause, they have the right."

I stare at my purple backpack splayed on the floor like the lifeless body of the squirrel I just hit. Everyone's eyes are on me, waiting. I have no choice. "Fine, whatever," I say, picking up the bag and handing it to Mr. Jennings. "I don't have anything to hide."

Mr. Jennings lays the bag on a table and starts taking things out, one at a time. He studies each object with deliberate slowness as Frau watches. Sunglasses. Composition notebook. Social studies book. Phone.

"Hello, it's called a tampon!" I shout when he's gutted my backpack.

But apparently he's not done. Mr. Jennings pulls out one more thing and sets it on the table.

"Looks like you're coming with me," Fran says, holding up a plastic baggie packed with fat marijuana buds.

I try to protest, to insist the drugs aren't mine, but nobody's listening. Frau leads me to the door. I follow her down the hall, climb into the cop mobile, and sit in the gated back seat like a prisoner, my mind reeling. How did the pot get there? Who called in the tip?

And then I get it.

I'm such an idiot! I left my backpack unattended in Mrs. Lopez's room. The Rat Catcher must've called in the tip, then come into the classroom and planted the dope when I went into the hall with her. But why would he do that?

Frau drives me to the police station and walks me to a room behind the front desk that smells like armpits and cigarettes. She points to a chair and tells me to sit. I wait for her to offer me a dog biscuit and order me to roll over. She doesn't. I'm obedient, though, and I do as she says.

Frau leaves the room and a different officer comes in. This time it's a small, pear-shaped man with unfriendly eyes and a big nose. The officer's name tag says Varelli, but he doesn't bother introducing himself. He takes a seat behind his desk and opens a thick folder, which has far too much information to be about me. What's there to say? I was busted thirty minutes ago for having pot that wasn't mine. That doesn't exactly require an entire file.

"Your mother died of a heroin overdose," Varelli says. I want to jump up and throttle the guy. What does my mother's drug record have to do with anything? "She had two drug convictions. And you're how old?"

I narrow my eyes at the guy. "Sixteen."

"And you're here charged with possession of marijuana? That's a serious charge for someone like you."

"It isn't mine," I snap, the words *someone like you* ringing in my ears.

"Oh really?" He yawns, folds his fingers into his palms, and examines his fingernails.

"Yeah really," I say, wondering which class Varelli took first in police school, the one on rhetorical statements or the one on being a dick. "The Rat Catcher planted it there to make me look bad. He was at school. You can check. He's probably the one who called in the tip about me having the pot."

Varelli looks up from his fingernails, an amused twinkle in his eyes. "And would this Rat Catcher person be?"

"I don't know exactly." I try not to panic as I realize how ridiculous I sound. "Apparently he's the pest exterminator with the schools, but I think he's also a drug dealer."

"And he wants to make you look bad for what reason?" Varelli says, carefully enunciating each word as if I'm either retarded or in kindergarten or both.

I clench my hands into fists and press them against my eyes. "So you guys wouldn't believe me if I came in and told you my mom didn't die of a heroin overdose." I drop my hands when I say this and glare at Varelli. "There was something else going on before she died. The Rat Catcher's trying to cover it up. He wants her to death to look like an overdose."

Now Varelli is actually smiling. I want to strangle him. Kick those gleaming white teeth out of his stupid mouth. "I've heard a lot of stories," he says, "but I think this one might be the best. Come with me."

I follow Varelli out of the room to the front of the station where Aunt T and Sam are waiting. Seeing Sam, his Phillies baseball cap turned backward on his head, my shame jumps by a power of ten. I want to shout, *This isn't what it looks like! This isn't who I am!* Of course my aunt had to come, but why drag Sam into this? Then I remember—the car. Sam drove her to work today.

"Your niece has a pretty active imagination. She should be a writer," Varelli tells them, recounting my story. "Possession under an ounce is a minor misdemeanor. She'll receive a citation and a court date in the mail."

I sit on a hard, wooden bench with my elbows on my knees and my head in my hands while they talk. My mind is a black tunnel. There isn't even a light at the end. I wait while Aunt T finishes discussing whatever procedure there is for letting me out of here, though truthfully I'd rather be thrown in jail than have to face her.

When I've been adequately disgraced, I'm released to the custody of my aunt. Sam walks next to me and asks if I'm okay as we leave the station. Aunt T, on the other hand, strides out of the building, her head high, and her shoulders straight as if to say I have nothing to do with this place. Too many memories, I guess. Different station, different relative, but the scene is the same—busted for drugs and turning to Aunt T for help.

We cross the parking lot to Sam's truck. I climb into the cab and pull down the jump seat behind the driver. The commotion wakes Goldie from her snooze, and she sits up and explores me with her nose. After approving my scent and deciding she doesn't have to growl, she wags her tail, rests her head on my lap, and waits for me to scratch her ears.

I stroke her tawny fur and think of the bumper sticker, *Please Let Me Be The Person My Dog Thinks I Am.* What kind of person does Aunt T think I am? A druggie? A dealer? With all the time I spend alone in my room, I wouldn't blame her for whatever she thinks. Maybe I should just tell her the truth, get it all out, come clean, and face the consequences.

The theme tune from *All Things Considered* drifts into the cab from the front seat. I hear the ramblings of the NPR newscast, but the words don't register. The sound is nothing more than a disturbance of the air as I contemplate the risks of telling my aunt the truth.

I must've fallen asleep because the next thing I remember is Sam pulling into the driveway and Aunt T asking where her car is. I bolt up and close my hand around a clump of Goldie's fur. I've heard petting dogs is good for stress. I rub her sides like my life depends on it and brace myself for a bad situation about to get worse.

"I took the car," I say so softly I'm not sure anyone hears. Aunt T and Sam both turn to look at me.

"You took the car?" Aunt T repeats. "Is it at school?"

My hand moves harder and faster across Goldie's fur. Any more stress and she'll be bald. I swallow. "No. I crashed it."

Sam clears his throat and slaps his hands down onto his thighs. "Okay then, I think I'll leave you two ladies alone. If you need anything I'll be inside. Come on, Goldie."

Goldie knows where her loyalty lies. She's up and on her feet, shooting out of the car and across the lawn after Sam without a single glance back in my direction.

Without my furry Prozac, I start to panic. Here comes the inevitable, the fucked-up teenager gets the boot. I stare at the floor and await my sentence.

Aunt T remains motionless, her eyes fixed straight ahead on some unknown point. Finally, she turns to me and asks if I'm okay.

"Am I okay?" I repeat, not because I didn't comprehend the question, but because I don't know what to say.

What does Aunt T want to hear? That I'm injured and therefore she can't kick me out because sending an injured minor to the streets is probably against the law? Or does she want to know that I'm fine and therefore she can rinse her hands of me guilt free? And does she mean "okay" as in physically? If so, the answer is yes. Or does she mean "okay" as in mentally? If that's the case, the answer is no. Not even close.

"Look, Faith. I don't care about the car," she says when I don't respond. "It's the drugs that worry me, and not just the drugs. I got a call from your school today. They told me you've been skipping most of the week. Then there's this crazy story you told Officer Varelli about some person called the Rat Catcher. Was that true?"

The light of understanding in Aunt T's eyes dims and disappointment moves in to take its place. I can't stand being the cause of that in her. I can't stand knowing how she sees me—exhausted, dirty, dishonest. How many times did I see Mom like that and look at her with a mix of disgust and pain, love and hate so deep, I thought the feelings would tear my chest in two?

She's given me an opening, a chance to come clean. The big confession where I open up, purge all my wrongdoings, and my sins are forgiven. I can't do it. I can't tell her the truth and let her down even more. I look out the window to the neighbor's yard where a little boy investigates a snowman that's been deformed by the afternoon sun.

"No, it's not true. I made it up," I say, still looking out the window as the boy starts to cry, and his mother rushes from the house to comfort him. "I bought the pot off a kid at school. I was messed up when I was driving, then I crashed and I was scared about what would happen if the police knew I was driving stoned without a license, so I left the car and figured I'd get it when I wasn't high." The lies make me feel dirty inside, ashamed. "I knew you'd be mad, and I didn't want to call you. Then the police found the pot and I guess I was still high when they were questioning me. I panicked and made up the story."

Aunt T sighs and closes her eyes as if weighing which version to believe, which one she *wants* to believe. The one where I'm lying and going against her wishes and playing detective in a world of heroin and dealers and murder, or the one where I'm buying drugs and getting high and wrecking cars. Some choice.

I try to be patient while I wait for her response, but I can't sit still. My arms itch. My back. My legs. My whole body prickles. I drag my fingernails across my flesh, but I don't get any relief. It's like my own skin isn't right. Like I'm like a snake, and I need to shed into something new.

"I took you in so I could help you, Faith," Aunt T finally says. The disappointment in her voice hurts more than anything else. "And this is what happens?"

"I don't need your help," I retort, aiming my arrow at her heart.

"Oh, really?" She opens the glove compartment, slaps around the maps and registration papers, and finds a loose tissue. "Why's that?" she asks, loudly blowing her nose. "Because you were doing so well with your mother? Living without enough food half the time. Picking up, moving to some new flea-infested dump every time your mother lost her job? How many schools have you been to since ninth grade, Faith? Answer me that. How many?" I don't say anything, and she fills in the blank. "Four. You've been to four schools. You are still a child. You are not an adult. I'm not going to just let you go out and live on the streets somewhere. I didn't abandon her, and I won't abandon you." She reaches back and grips my arm. "Our family has had enough secrets and lies for a lifetime. Is there anything you want to tell me?"

There is. I want to tell her thanks for taking me in, thanks for always being there to clean up Mom's messes. I want to say I care about you, maybe even love you if I understood what love meant. But as usual, when it comes to crawling out of my emotional fortress and risking a bullet, I stay bunkered down where I'm safe. "No. Nothing," I say. "I'm sorry about skipping school and about the car and about getting high. I'll pay for everything. It won't happen again. You can trust me. It'll be different now." I stop talking because if I say any more the tears will come, and I'm afraid they'll never stop.

Aunt T clucks her tongue. "Different? Do you know how many times I've heard that?"

She doesn't have to finish this thought. I can read between the lines. I'm just like my mother. Another mess to clean up.

She gets out of the truck and goes into the house.

My phone rings and breaks the silence. I check to see who's calling: Jesse. I don't answer. I don't want to talk to him. I don't listen to any of his voicemails, or the ones from Anj either. I turn off the phone and climb out of the truck, too dejected even to wave at Mrs. Dunnings who's outside checking her mail.

I slog across patches of snow and grass and go into Aunt T's to serve out my self-imposed solitary confinement.

———

At school Friday morning, the story of my drug bust has already become legend, the tale having spread through the gossip mill of texts, tweets, and emails. Depending on the crowd, the story has either confirmed people's suspicions about me—a junkie mother with a druggie daughter—or else I'm being inducted into the stoner hall of fame. Either way there is no truth. Both sides hijack my story and tweak the details to validate whatever it is about me they want to believe.

I spend the morning ignoring the stares, the whispers, the high fives, good jobs and front-page news my life has temporarily become. *Ice Caps Melting! Unemployment Reaches Record High! Faith Flores Gets Busted For Dope!*

Jesse tries to corner me at my locker, but I'm the star of my own reality show and my adoring fans seek my autograph, so

I don't have to talk to him, thank god. I can't face him now. I can't face Anj. I don't want to explain anything. I don't want a lecture, or a sympathetic smile and a shoulder to cry on. I don't want to be asked how I am. I just want to be left alone, which turns out to be easy since afternoon classes are cancelled and the entire student body is called to the gym for a pep rally. The place is one big anonymous blob of bodies. Locating anyone would be impossible even if I wanted to.

I sit on the bleachers squished between two girls I've never seen before and listen to Mr. Jennings dazzle us with his thrilling reminder that the varsity boys' football team will be playing tonight for the right to compete in the state championships, and we should therefore all sacrifice an afternoon of learning in their honor. Who cares about chemistry? There's a football game! He's even hired some one-hit wonder band from the eighties to play their hit song for us, which is the worst part of the whole thing, since I love eighties music, and I can't even enjoy it.

There is one upshot to the event. My drug bust is already yesterday's news, forgotten in lieu of the big-hair wonders gyrating their stiff and aging hips on the stage. It's almost worth sticking around for, but without Jesse to sing along with, what's the point? I push through the bleachers and ditch the extravaganza right as the disco ball comes down.

I'm alone in the hall when I have a close call with human contact as Mrs. Lopez, who despite the state championship, apparently believes biology is more important than football, comes out of her classroom. I dodge into the library.

I'm hanging out in the H row, looking for more Heming-way, when I hear laughter, Jesse's laughter. I guess he bailed, too. I tiptoe to the end of the row and see him, back to me, sitting at a table with a well-dressed, well-toned woman with perfectly highlighted hair swept up in a clip. She's the kind of woman who doesn't sweat. Who lives on a diet of low fat lettuce and Diet Coke. Who drives a Jag and never loses her cool. Then I remember. The alumni interview. Today in the library. She's the Harvard lawyer.

This ought to cheer me up. I slip to the end of the aisle to hear what Mr. Cynical has to say to Moneybags. Without Doc there to keep him in check, I expect a discourse in sublime absurdity.

"So, what would you say is your favorite literary work?" Moneybags asks in the kind of put-on voice filled with practiced pretense.

Come on, Jesse, tell her *Harry Potter*. Or *Twilight*. Tell her you like vampires.

"I know it's not one of the more conventional choices," Jesse says in a pompous voice to rival any ass-kissing Harvard wannabe. "But I'd have to say although Hemingway's always been my favorite author, *Slaughterhouse Five* by Vonnegut is my current favorite piece. I like the nonlinear narrative."

Moneybags brushes a strand of streaky blond hair from her eye, showing off the big rock on her ring finger in the process. "Really? What an interesting choice. I never cared much for Vonnegut. I always found him somehow inaccessible. I prefer the romantics, Bronte, Keats."

This is the part where Jesse nails Moneybags on her pompous *Wuthering Heights* bullshit and pseudointellectualism. I poke my head out from the bookshelves, so I can see her face when he drops the bomb on his real opinion of going to the Ivy League.

"I know the Harvard department of English offers a well rounded program of all the classics, so I'm sure if I'm accepted I'll broaden my perspective," he says instead.

Somebody bring me a barf bag, please.

Moneybags goes on to ask Jesse about his interests, and he recites perfectly from his brag sheet. Music, of course, being interest number one, but not in the punk-rock-wailing-guitar-freak kind of way, more like the rock-critic-with-an-up-and-coming-career-at-Rolling-Stone-magazine kind of way.

They laugh so easily. The two of them. All this drivel about postmodernism and the global influence on American music and collective consciousness. He's doing a splendid job of playing the part of eager high school senior trying to make an impression, so good, in fact, I'm not sure he's playing a part.

"Well, it was lovely to meet you," Moneybags says, reaching out to shake his hand. "I'll be sure to put in an excellent recommendation for you when the time comes."

I'm out of there before I can hear Jesse's response.

With mostly everyone in the gym, the halls are deserted and the school feels like a ghost town. It's just the fliers taped to walls and posted on classroom doors that hint at an actual student body: Join the yearbook. Tickets on sale for Romeo and Juliet. Help the homeless. Glee club. Spanish club. Fencing team. Lesbian, gay, bisexual, and transgender student alliance. If you like to mow grass there's probably a club for it.

In all this fitting in and belonging, I've never felt so alone.

Eighteen

Anj and Jesse call and text me a total of eleven times before noon on Saturday. I listen to and read each message and then delete them all. Dr. Carlisle's death made one thing clear: If I don't want my friends ending up in body bags, they need to keep away from me because I'm not giving up. My mind doesn't idle. It revs.

Saturday morning Aunt T uses Sam's truck (her car now being ditch free and safely in the shop where it belongs) to drive him to the airport for a weekend visit to his family in Miami. The second she leaves, I wrap myself in a blanket, grab a jumbo-size box of Captain Crunch, and get on the computer for some research.

I start with genetic IPF to confirm that the disease is real and Dr. Monroe's telling the truth. I discover that the disease, though rare, does exist. I move on to the Rat Catcher, hoping to find out something about him. I Google the words "rat catcher" and then "pest control," but unless I want termites exterminated, or I have a roach problem I'm out of luck. I Google "Philly's most wanted," "Philly drug dealers," "rat control services," "vermin," "the plague"—all a dead end. What am I supposed to look up next, thugs for hire?

I sit on the couch with the laptop, rotting my teeth with Captain Crunch, reruns of *Friends* playing in the background, and move on from the Rat Catcher to Dr. Wydner, then to Dr. Monroe. The information I get on them is what I already know, so I Google Dr. Glass. The name alone gets about a million hits, but when I cross-reference his name with PluraGen I hit the jackpot.

On the PluraGen homepage is a tab that says researchers. I click the tab and there, nestled between Dr. Girard and Dr. Gupta, is the name I'm looking for: Dr. Steven Glass. I click and read his bio. *Johns Hopkins…Harvard…board certified pulmonologist…board certified clinical geneticist…specialist in idiopathic pulmonary fibrosis.*

The handful of Captain Crunch I'd been about to stuff in my mouth slips through my fingers. I stare at the words *idiopathic pulmonary fibrosis* and it's not until I feel Goldie at my feet, vacuuming up the Scooby snack, that I let out a breath.

Idiopathic pulmonary fibrosis. IPF. The man running the RNA 120 clinical trial is a specialist in the disease that killed my mother. What does that mean? Is it just a coincidence, like Dr. Monroe saying Mom and Melinda had the same symptoms? I don't believe that for a second. Mom and Melinda's symptoms weren't a coincidence, and neither is this. I don't know what it means, but I think of Officer Asshole again, then Mom and her smile, telling me she'd be okay, and I pledge to find out.

———

Sunday at eleven, I'm camped out in bed, depressed and exhausted from my dead-end search into the Glass/IPF/RNA 120 connection, when I'm startled by a knock on my door. Aunt T and I have hardly spoken since Thursday, so I have no idea why she'd be knocking now.

I roll over to face the wall, hoping if I ignore her she'll go away. She knocks again and this time calls my name. The least I can do is not be a total a-hole. I sit up and tell her to come in.

She pushes open the door and holds out a box. "I have something for you."

"What is it?"

"Open it and see."

I reach for the box, pull off the lid, and stare at a pair of shiny new running shoes glinting up at me like bad dream.

"I got us each a pair," she says. "Get up. A little exercise will do us both some good."

I groan and pull the blanket over my head. "Please tell me you're kidding."

Aunt T doesn't say anything. I peel back my covers and peek out. She's in my room now, standing by the door in a neon-blue windbreaker, black Spandex tights, and white running shoes to match mine.

I groan again. "You aren't kidding."

Aunt T smiles. "Nope. I'm not kidding. Coming?"

The shoes and the offer are a form of peace making, so despite the fact I've never jogged a day in my life, I say yes. We've hardly spoken since the car accident/drug bust. I figure if we're sucking air we won't have to make small talk. Suffering in each other's presence will be bonding enough.

I pull out a pair of gray sweats and a matching West Philly High Girls' Soccer sweatshirt from my dresser. Having never once in sixteen years kicked a ball on purpose, I have no reason for owning these clothes, except for the fact I found them in the school's lost and found last January on the coldest day of the year. I was so grateful for something warm to wear around the apartment when the heat got turned off that I never tried to find the real owner.

As I get dressed I remember all Aunt T's attempts to get mom into fitness, as if exercise would do what methadone couldn't and cure her of her heroin habit. One time she actually got Mom to go to a step aerobics class. Mom suited up in a sweatband and Spandex, and the two of them set out for Nicolla's Body Sculpting Fitness Center across town in a strip mall. I'd seen the ads on TV, Nicolla being a Botox blond with a boob job and a voice like she'd been huffing helium.

Four hours later, Aunt T brought Mom home from the emergency room, her ankle in a splint. The three of us sat around that night hysterically laughing each time Mom recounted the way she'd toppled off the step platform, taking out Nicolla in the process.

Aunt T and I make it around the neighborhood three times before collapsing on the front porch in near cardiac arrest. It's not until she leans back against the top step, folds her arms behind her head, and tells me there's something we have to talk about, I realize there's a second part to this mission, an ulterior motive that has nothing to do with good health habits and getting into shape.

"Great. I'm free tomorrow," I say jumping to my feet and taking the stairs two at a time. We've been doing fine with surface banter. Why ruin a good thing with serious conversation?

"It's about your mother's ashes," I hear her say as I reach the door. "You said you wanted to spread them. Maybe it's time."

I picture the blue urn in the armoire outside the kitchen, the residue of Mom's being—her skin and bone burned into a box of ash, and my throat tightens. I can't let her go. Not yet. Not like this when I still don't know what happened.

"Faith," Aunt T begins again.

"No," I say. "Please. I'm sorry. I'm not ready."

I go inside without waiting for her response.

Monday morning, I drag my sorry ass to school. Literally drag. After my brief encounter with exercise, not only can I hardly walk, but the muscles in my butt—muscles I never knew existed—are so tight I can hardly sit either.

I'm at my locker getting books for first period when Jesse approaches me.

"Hello works," he says to my back when I don't greet him.

"Hey," I say into my locker.

He stands there, I guess waiting for me to say more. "I'm fine thanks," he says when I don't. "How are you?"

I don't answer.

I feel his eyes on me, but I don't turn. I bend down and dig through the detritus that's collected on the floor of my locker, thinking if I act busy enough, Jesse will get bored and leave me alone.

As if.

Jesse plops down next to me, leans against the currently unoccupied neighboring locker, and shoves his phone in my face. "This is called a phone," he tells me. "The first one was invented in the 1870's by Alexander Graham Bell. It's quite easy to use. Would you like me to show you how? Because I left you eight messages this weekend, so I'm assuming you forgot."

"Jesse, please," I say, but I stop speaking before I can finish my thought. Please what? Please go away? Please don't go away? I feel pressure building behind my eyes. Tears. No way. Not now. I stand up and slam my locker without even taking out any books. I'm about to march off when Anj shows up.

"I've been calling you all weekend," she says, extending her hand to Jesse and yanking him to his feet.

From there her words flow like blood from an open wound. Before I can even figure out the blood type or the source of the wound, Jesse joins in the hemorrhage.

*Work to do…What happened…Don't return my call…What's going on…*Etc., etc. They form a flawless duet. Their accusing voices harmonize in perfect unison.

Anj breaks from the choir for a solo. "And we need to meet today in the library after school. I have to talk to you. Can you do that?"

At that moment there's an announcement over the intercom followed by a burst of cheering from some classroom. In the commotion, Anj loses her train of thought and nods as if I've agreed to meet her. I don't bother making the correction.

I sit through the rest of my classes, but it's just my body the teachers have. My mind is busy alternating between being depressed about Jesse and Anj and worrying about Dr. Monroe. She said three days. That means today she should have the results from Mom's DNA. I wait all day for her call, but it's not until school ends that she sends a text: *I have the results. Come see me.*

I know Anj will be waiting for me in the library, but I slip out the back door. Whatever she wants will have to wait.

I don't want to risk a kink in the current jogging-induced peace with Aunt T, and if I truck off to the university without telling her, she'll freak. I call her at work and ask if she minds if I go into Philly for some research. I tell her Mrs. Lopez put me in touch with a genetics professor who's offered to speak to me for a biology assignment. Aunt T doesn't mind, and not only that, she's picking up Sam this evening at the airport and she'll be out anyway, so she can give me a ride home. I give her directions, and we agree to meet at six.

Before I set out to catch the downtown bus, I consider going for the incognito movie star thing and wrapping my hair in a scarf and wearing Aunt T's fashion sunglasses, but I decide against it. Something tells me that if the Rat Catcher is following me, he'll see through the disguise; that if he wants to find me, he will. The best defense I have is vigilance and crowds. No back streets. No short cuts. Vigilance, however, slows me down. It's hard to move quickly when you're checking out every person as if they might be some al-Qaeda sleeper and it's not until almost five thirty that I finally make it to the genetics department.

I hurry up the steps to Dr. Monroe's office and knock. No answer. Finally, after a third knock, she opens the door.

"Sorry, I didn't hear you," she says. "Have you been standing out here for long?"

I'm too shocked to answer.

If I'd thought Jesse's clothes looked slept in the morning we went to Denny's, they were no match for Dr. Monroe's. She's wearing the same khaki pants and turtleneck I saw her in four days ago. Her eyes are bloodshot, and her hair hangs limp and greasy around her shoulders.

"Um…are you okay?" I ask, standing by the door and wondering if I should come back later.

"Fine. Just busy. The genetics conference is in a few days. I have another grant due, one of my top students was accused of plagiarism, and well…" Her voice trails off. "Anyway," she says, shaking her head, as if shaking herself from a dream. "I'm glad you came. Come in."

I follow her through her lab and into her office. Books, papers, and journals litter the counters and tables. A fresh round of fast food take out boxes clutter her desk and the windowsill. The atmospheric turmoil escalates my nervous turmoil, and suddenly I'm unsure if I'm ready to hear what she found out about my mom.

"Did you know Dr. Glass studies idiopathic pulmonary fibrosis?" I ask, putting off the question of Mom's mutation and the possible implication for my own life.

"Of course," Dr. Monroe answers as she picks up a pile of books and stands on her tiptoes to put them on a shelf.

"Don't you think it's a little strange that the person running the clinical trial also happens to be an expert on the disease that killed my mother?" Dr. Monroe doesn't answer. I don't know if I should take the silence as agreement or not, but I feel my boldness slipping and my voice faltering as I add, "Maybe he has something to do with this."

"To do with what?" she asks, turning from the shelf and looking at me. There's something in her eyes that makes me take a small step back.

"With my mother's death. Maybe he knew about the side effects and—"

"Stop right there, Faith! You can't just go around accusing people of what, hiding results? Tampering with data?" She runs her hand over her face then presses a thumb and finger to her closed eyes. "The university licensed RNA 120 to PluraGen, and PluraGen put Dr. Glass in charge of the clinical trial because he's a respected scientist. He's been in the field for a long time. Whatever conspiracy you're imagining, you're wrong. There are no side effects."

"How do you know?" I ask, taking another step back. This one leaves me pinned to the wall like a dartboard. I wait for Dr. Monroe to shoot the first dart.

Her eyes flutter open. "Because the drug doesn't cause the disease. Your mother had the mutation. She had genetic IPF. I'm sorry."

Bull's-eye! The words shoot straight into my heart. The best I can do is nod. Finally I have the answer about Mom I've been waiting for, the real cause of her death, and it comes with a possible price tag of my life.

"Your mother was sick for a long time," Dr. Monroe continues in a tone like a funeral director might use when asking what kind of casket you prefer. "There wasn't anything you or anyone could've done to help her. People with genetic IPF are born with it. They first get sick in their twenties. It's when their skin first starts to peel and blister. As you get older, the condition gets worse and you start to deteriorate. It gets harder to breathe, to climb stairs, things like that."

"But she didn't have any problems with her skin when I was a kid," I say, finding my voice and peeling myself off of the wall.

"The condition was always there, you just didn't notice."

"Didn't notice?" I snort. "How could I have not noticed that? You don't just overlook someone who looks like they've had acid thrown on their face."

Dr. Monroe steps toward me with open arms as if for an embrace. What does she want me to do? Rejoice at the brilliance of her discovery? Get out the tambourines and patchouli and sing Kumbaya?

When I don't move, she drops her arms and sighs. "Your mother had a lot of other problems. Heroin makes a person sick. It would've been easy to overlook a skin condition with all the side effects from the drugs. You were a child. You can't blame yourself."

It might be an answer I could accept so I could let go and start moving forward like everyone keeps telling me to do, but I don't want another lie being told about her. Another fact about Mom someone thinks they're the expert on.

"I'm not blaming myself," I say, squeezing the lighter. "Her skin was fine until just before she died. If her skin being fine all those years means she didn't have the mutation then I'm telling you, she didn't have it."

"I sequenced the gene, Faith," Dr. Monroe insists. She goes to her desk, pulls open a drawer, and takes out a piece of paper. "She had the mutation. The results are right here." She hands me a paper covered with rows of A, G, C, and T's, letter upon letter, like the genetic sequence she showed me that first day we met. One letter is circled in red pen.

"What's that?" I demand, pointing at the circled letter.

"The mutation. This should have been a T and it's a G instead. A single base change caused the disease. I'm sorry. This must be scary for you."

"I'm not scared," I snap, heat rising to my face. "That's not what's going on. She didn't have the mutation. I'm telling you."

"Faith, you're in denial. You have to realize—"

"Will you please stop telling me what I'm feeling because I'm not scared, and I'm not in denial. My mother didn't have this condition. I'm telling you. She never even had a zit until the end."

Dr. Monroe steps out from behind her desk. She puts a hand on my back and tries to lead me to a chair. "Faith, come on, sit down. The paper is proof."

I shake off her hand and shove the paper in her face. "Well you know what? I don't care about your proof. Everyone has proof! They had proof that she died of an overdose, too, and look what happened to that. It was a lie. Everyone thinks they know what happened. But you're wrong. Sometimes people make mistakes. Even in science. People can make mistakes."

"I can help you, Faith," Dr. Monroe says. "We can sequence your gene and—"

"No!" I shout, backing away. "I don't want that kind of help. I don't have the mutation because she didn't have it. You're just like everyone else. You don't listen. You think because I'm sixteen I don't know what I'm talking about, that I'm not old enough to figure things out for myself. Well I am, and I'm telling you, you're wrong!"

Dr. Monroe lays her darling paper, her proof of Mom's mutation and her trouble-free drug, on the table and gazes out the window. I look out, too, at all those picture-perfect university buildings. Screw it. Screw them. All their high-priced knowledge and learning and theories are filled with loopholes and mistakes.

"Why should I believe you anyway?" I say, turning from the window. "That paper could belong to anyone."

Dr. Monroe sighs. "Okay, look. You've been through a lot. You've been told all sorts of things about her that weren't true. I understand. I'll do one thing for you. I'll sequence something else. If proof of the mutation is what you need to let go and move forward, I can give that to you."

"How?"

"I'll run the test again. I'll replicate the results and rule out error." She walks to her god, her sequencer, and lays her hand on the machine. "I'll repeat this test if that's what you need. I'll sequence the same position from a different DNA sample from your mom, just to make absolutely sure. I can have the results by Thursday. But you have to promise me one thing."

"What?"

"If we get the same results, which we will, you have to face this and you have to move forward."

It's an easy promise to make because Dr. Monroe's wrong. I know she is. "I promise."

"Okay, good, then bring me something from your mother that would still have her DNA. Something from a while back, before she was in the clinical trial, say five years ago, when she was younger."

"What kind of thing?"

"A postage stamp, or a strand of hair from a comb. Maybe an old toothbrush. The mutation will be in all her cells, so it doesn't really matter what sample we use. Do you have anything like that?"

"I don't know. Maybe," I say, thinking of the box in the spare room at Aunt T's—the random scraps of Mom's every day existence that for one reason or another we couldn't get rid of.

"See what you can find and bring it to me. It can be old. The DNA lasts for years. We'll sequence something from your mother when she was younger and you'll see. The mutation will be the same, and it's up to you to accept this and move forward from there."

It's dark by the time my meeting is over. I say good-bye and head to the loading dock on the west side of the building by the parking lot to wait for Aunt T and Sam. I stand under a floodlight between a basement stairwell and a dumpster where a raccoon is working over scraps of cafeteria foods.

"Hey, buddy," I say to the animal. He hisses and dives down into the trash.

Pretty soon the beam of headlights breaks through the dark and a truck pulls up in front of me. Sam hops out and opens the door so I can squeeze in.

"How was your trip?" I ask as I slide into the jump seat.

"Too many relatives and good to be back." He smiles at me, then leans over and kisses my aunt.

I'm off the hook for conversation making after that, thank god, because after a few days apart Aunt T and Sam only have eyes for each other. They make it look so easy. The laughter. The kisses. The way he rests his hand on her thigh as she drives. They adore each other. It's obvious and right. Aunt T deserves love. She deserves a man like Sam who tolerates opera and doesn't mind country antique stores, a man who loves to cook up big, exotic dinners, then crawl into bed, lock the door, and "go to sleep early."

Their loving banter and closeness should come with a warning: Possible side effects include severe loneliness and risk of depression. I stare out the window at the suffocating sameness limping by—black road, black sky, black night—then slouch down into the seat, close my fist around the lighter, and start thinking of Jesse. Of Anj. Of Mom. Even of Dr. Monroe. Of how many ways there are to push people away—fear, drugs, work. Different paths to the same isolation. I close my eyes, turn on my iPod, and try to lose myself to the mellow guitar and keyboards of Snow Patrol.

Distract and check out. The best drug of all.

When we get home, I hide out in my room and wait for Aunt T and Sam to go to bed. Once the house is quiet, I creep across the hall to the spare room and flip on the light. There, before me, lies the sum total of Mom's existence—one lonely cardboard box pushed up against a white wall.

I take a breath and cross the room. I pause for a minute at the box, then reach in and grab the first thing I touch—the black and white photo strip of Mom and I taken at a photo booth in the mall this past September. I glance at the grainy image. She was healthy that day. There were no scabs. No genetic disease. The photo is proof.

I reach in again. This time I pull out the clay pot I made for her in second grade, followed by her high school yearbook, then a small journal covered in blue fabric. I open the journal to the first page where a postage stamp with a picture of a kangaroo has been pressed to the paper. Mom's foreign stamp collection. I sink to the floor, the journal in my hands, and glance through the pages—the Matterhorn, some colorful tropical bird, a yak, someone playing bagpipes. The Eiffel Tower.

"Someday we're going to see the world," Mom would tell me when she was in one of her I'm-going-to-get-better-and-anything's-possible phases. Then we'd walk, or take a taxi if we had money, to the Philly Coin and Stamp Company on Chestnut where Mom would spend hours searching for just the right stamp. When we got home, she'd lick the small token of her dream and stick it in the book, turning the stamps into a scrapbook of possibility. At which point came the inevitable melancholy. She'd pore through the pages of her book like she knew a postage stamp was the closest she'd ever get to any foreign country. Then the drinking would begin, the drugs.

I turn to the Eiffel Tower again, the last stamp she bought before she died. This time she meant it. This time she believed her dreams really might come true. Dr. Monroe said a postage stamp would have the DNA she needed. I rip out the page with the kangaroo stamp from two years ago when Mom was in her Australia phase and slip the paper into my pocket, but I don't leave. Now that I'm here, I want to know what else is in that box.

I dig in again. This time I pull out a Neil Young concert t-shirt. I bury my nose in the blue fabric, and it's memory by molecule, each scent a story. A hint of clove cigarette and Mom and I are at the Wachovia Center for a Rolling Stones concert with some dealer friend who managed to score us not drugs, but tickets. A trace of patchouli and she's burning incense to rid the place of something gone bad in the fridge. A touch of lavender and Mom's slathering on hand cream, doing battle with the dry skin between her fingers.

But it's the visual reminder that leads me straight to the kitchen table where we're sitting the last time she wore this shirt. The day we saw the white bird. I start thinking about faith, about angels, and science, and the laws of the universe. Most of all I think of her.

She's become a piece of scientific curiosity. A gene. A mutation. A disease.

I want her back before she was all that.

I know just what to do. I put down the shirt and paw through the rest of her stuff, searching for the bird feeder, the one thing I know for sure I kept. I grab the splintering wooden feeder from the bottom of the box and head straight to the kitchen to paw through Aunt T's culinary collection for something birds will eat. I settle on a mix of sunflower seeds and peanuts, then creep outside into the cold, starless night and go straight to the oak outside my window to hang the feeder.

Maybe Mom's angel will return.

Nineteen

Tuesday morning, I put on my running shoes and tell Aunt T I'm going jogging before school. Instead of a brisk early morning sprint, I slog to the Bank of America parking lot where Dr. Monroe's agreed to meet me so I can avoid another trip to the city. She's waiting in a red car by the ATM machine when I get there. I check around for the Rat Catcher, then slip her a plastic baggie with the kangaroo stamp. She promises to be in touch as soon as she gets the results, and drives off.

My mind starts churning the second she's gone. I don't know what to do with myself, how to stop my brain from boiling over, so I start to run. I choke down the fumes on Eagle, then turn left and cut through a neighborhood lined with postcard-quaint colonials and old trees with massive trunks and gnarled limbs.

Cold air scorches my lungs. Words and images pound my mind as my feet pound the pavement. Genetic IPF. Cover up. Autopsy report. Dr. Glass. Dr. Monroe. Dr. Wydner. The Rat Catcher. Side effects. Mutation. Heroin. Overdose. Over and over again the words sing in my head like a mantra. I break into a sprint, hoping to outrun my thoughts, but the faster I run, the faster the images come until I have to stop. I can't run. Not from this.

I double over on the sidewalk to catch my breath. A committee of crows argues in the trees above me. Gray clouds hang low in the turbulent sky. I lick salt from my lips, and for a few seconds it's just those birds and me. A moment of still before the thoughts start to churn again.

Ten minutes later I arrive at school exhausted and sweaty. First period is a blur, and by the time I get to social studies I'm so out of it, it's not until I'm at my desk that I realize something's wrong. Not a single butt crack is showing. Not a single pair of boxers, and there definitely isn't any cleavage.

Then there's me.

My face is flushed. My hair is tangled. I'm wearing a gray sweat suit, which is about as attractive as being dressed in a garbage bag, and I'm painfully aware that I didn't shower yesterday *or* this morning. I'm so out of here. I'm creeping across the room when Anj catches my eye. Her stony look stops me in my tracks. Then I remember. Presentations are today—*our* presentation. That's why she wanted to meet in the library yesterday, to work on our project.

Before I can say anything, Anj turns and marches to her seat. I stare at the back of her head, at the neat bun and pearl drop earrings, and remember how I judged her when we met, how I assumed she'd be stuck up and wouldn't give me the time of day. I was wrong. She was the one who reached out to me. I swallow hard and put my head on my desk as the first presentation begins.

"…the economic transition to a market economy during colonial times…" I hear Logan Axleman say.

I drift in and out of attention through Logan's presentation and as the others drone on: "…political ideology…witch hunts…early democracy…Faith Flores."

Faith Flores?

I sit up to see Mr. Robertson looking at me. Anj is already at the front of the room. I straggle up the aisle and take center stage beside her as she carefully arranges moccasins and stone tools on a table. I pick up a whittled stone for inspection. These aren't toy store trinkets, I think with growing despair. These are museum quality artifacts.

Anj finishes her display, turns to the class without a single glance in my direction, and begins. "On his first trip to the New World, Columbus encountered the native Arawak people. Instead of appreciating this new culture, Columbus saw the people as a commodity." She clicks on the first slide of an indigenous child, peers at her notes, then looks up at the class in perfect public speaking fashion. "Columbus' mission was to go back home to Spain with gold and spices. But he quickly realized that the real treasure in this new land was not gold. It was not spices. It was the Arawaks. Instead of returning the welcomes of these people, Columbus brought them back to Spain as slaves." I stand there like a tick, parasitizing her hard work and efforts as she goes through each carefully crafted slide and delivers her flawless talk. "Unfortunately, we all know that history has repeated such brutal, such outright horrible crimes against humanity many times. We can only hope that we've learned a lesson and such treatment of indigenous people will end! And don't forget to donate to our Africa awareness campaign. We will be collecting donations outside the cafeteria before homeroom."

"You go, Sistah!" Marissa, a hippy chick who spends wads of cash to dress like she didn't spend a cent, shouts.

Beside Marissa and Duncan—who stands up and calls, "Right on, Lass!"—Anj's conclusion is met with silence. The status quo tipped to the liberal left is not the way things go around here. The winners write the history books and that's who we're taught about, but soon Mr. Robertson, with his gray comb-over and red sweater vest, starts to clap and the rest of the class takes the lead and follows.

When the bell rings, I slink out of the room, the word "asshole" attached to me like a kick-me sign. I've just managed to slip through the door when Duncan stops me and smiles.

"What?" I snot off. I don't mean to sound so harsh, but seriously, what reason does he have to be smiling at me after I just blew off his girlfriend?

"Nothing," he says, putting up his hands. "I'm just happy."

"Well good. I'm glad for you."

I'm about to walk my bad mood to a bathroom stall, the one speck of privacy in this place, when Anj bursts out of the classroom. She throws her arms around Duncan and nails his face with kisses. I'm thinking um, sure the presentation was good, but it wasn't that good, was it?

"Mr. Robertson is recommending me for the independent study in Scotland next semester!" she squeals. "It's going to happen. My parents agreed and my grandmother already said she'd give me the money!"

Scotland? Independent study? Anj is leaving? Is that why this assignment meant so much to her? So Mr. Robertson would write her a recommendation? I should be relieved. If Anj goes to Scotland, she'll be nowhere near me. The Atlantic Ocean ought to be enough distance to keep her safe. Still, my stomach plummets to my feet, and my heart isn't far behind.

Duncan's freckled face goes blotchy. He springs Anj off her feet and spins her in a circle. "Bloody awesome! You'll meet my mum and dad and stay with us in Glasgow. I'll show you where Bruce and Wallace slaughtered the English at Bannockburn and Hamden Park where we've been slaughtering each other in football ever since, and I'll take you out on the

North Sea, and I'll teach you how to drive British style and…
On second thought that's a scary idea." He laughs so hard he
has to put Anj down.

When he finally stops laughing, he elbows Anj in the ribs
and they both glance in my direction. Duncan gives Anj a
purposeful look, pecks her on the cheek, and takes off just as
the bell for fourth period rings. Everyone darts off to class, but
my former best friend and I don't move. We stand on opposite
sides of the hall, our backs to the lockers like we're about to
draw pistols and duel.

"You're going to Scotland?" I snap, channeling all my anger,
sadness, and guilt into a fight. "You could've told me."

"Sor-ry," she snaps back, glaring. "It's not like you asked
about my life. Besides, I did try and tell you. That day at the
methadone clinic, but you were so preoccupied with whatever
was going on with your mother, I didn't have the chance."

It's my turn to drag out my syllables with pissed-off righ-
teousness. "Well ex-cuse me for not asking. I've had a few
things on my mind if you didn't notice."

I expect her to throw a match on my gasoline, so our friendship can really go out with a bang. Instead she drops her eyes
and lowers her voice. "I didn't want to hurt you, you know? Be
another person who leaves? I tried to tell you again last week,
but you wouldn't return my calls, and you didn't show up in
the library after school, and then I figured you just didn't care."
She pauses and looks up at me. "I'm going to finish junior year
abroad. Duncan's family agreed to host me."

Words like "sorry" and "you're right" are on the tip of my
tongue, waiting to be formed, but Anj isn't safe in Scotland
yet, so instead of building a bridge, I go for dynamite and blow
it up. "That's cool. Whatever. Doesn't matter to me. I've gotta
go. Later." I turn and start heading for my locker.

"You know what your problem is?" she calls after me.

I stop.

"You're too scared to get close to anyone. I guess I thought eventually you'd open up or at least trust me. I wanted to be your friend, but you would never really let me be. I mean I get it. You took me to that place in West Philly where you used to live."

My whole body tenses. How did she know I lived there? I never told her.

"I figured it out, Faith," she says, answering to my body language and inner thoughts. "You didn't have to tell me. And I see how hard it must've been for you. But the whole world isn't shit just because you had a rough time." She pauses and sighs, but I will myself not to turn. "All the times I've invited you over, you never said yes. It's not even about the project and doing all the work myself this weekend. Because I did it, and I feel really good about that. It's just that you didn't return my calls. You didn't even give me an explanation about what was going on. You just turned your back and for no apparent reason blew me off. It's as if our friendship is a joke."

I hear the click of her clogs on the tile as she walks away, but I don't turn. I don't tell her that our friendship's not a joke. Never has been. Never will be.

<hr/>

For the next two days I wait for Dr. Monroe's results and try to concentrate on school. I've pissed off Anj enough to make her totally ignore me and possibly hate me. (Big sarcastic pat on the back for that). Jesse, on the other hand, doesn't ignore me, but rather turns up wherever I go. Need a sip of water? There's Jesse at the drinking fountain. Bathroom? Jesse's gotta go, too. Every time I see him, he breaks into conversation, monologue actually, since I don't answer.

A few times I almost crack a smile, like when he tells me about his new organic hemp boxers (standard rise, roomy cut), but alas, smiling will only egg him on, so I remind myself of Dr. Carlisle's "accident," put in earbuds, and tune him out.

I haven't seen the Rat Catcher since my drug bust, so I'm thankful for that at least, that and the fact Aunt T and I have made a full, superficial recovery. I don't care how superficial it is. At least there's *someone* to talk to, even if it *is* about the weather.

Dr. Monroe's text comes Thursday during a biology lab on cell division where we're supposed to be peeling onions and making microscope slides. I grab a pass with the excuse of too much onion burning my eyes and escape to the bathroom to check the message. *Call me* is all it says. I stand by a dripping faucet and punch her number. She picks up on the first ring.

"We have to talk."

"Okay, when? Can you meet somewhere? I don't know if—"

"Now."

"Now? Uh, okay." I slip into a stall and perch on the edge of the toilet. Someone's doused the place with air freshener. The stench, that has nothing to do with flowers and everything to do with chemistry, makes my eyes water. "I'm listening."

"When was that sample from you brought me?"

"About two years ago," I say, feeling defensive, though I don't know what about.

"This doesn't make sense," Dr. Monroe mumbles.

"What doesn't make sense?"

"I sequenced the DNA on the stamp."

"And?"

"And the mutation wasn't there. Two years ago your mother didn't have the mutation, and before she died she did. *That's* what doesn't make sense. I thought maybe there was a mistake and the samples were from two different people," Dr. Monroe goes on, "so I did a genetic profile and sure enough both samples are from your mother." I try to cut in with a question, but she doesn't let me. "I've spent the day researching this, Faith. Every known case of genetic IPF is something you're born with. The mutation has never been known to happen spontaneously. Never."

I feel like I've been trapped in some surreal Salvador Dali painting. *Attack of the double helix! Revenge of the death spiral!* "Then how did she get it, unless someone gave it to her?"

Dr. Monroe doesn't answer.

"Hello? Are you still there?" I lower my voice as the bathroom door opens. A tall, skinny Goth chick with black lipstick and bone-white skin crosses the room, cracks the window, and lights a cigarette.

"Still here. I'm thinking."

"About what?" I say, closing and locking the stall door.

"About what you said."

"What I said about what?"

"About someone giving her the mutation. It's not impossible, but why would someone do that?"

"Not impossible!" Screw whispering. I don't care what Goth Chick hears or thinks. I'm the junkie's daughter. The druggie who got busted for dope. Now I'll be the crazy girl in the bathroom stall ranting into the phone. "That's insane! You're saying my mother had some mutation when she died that she didn't have two years ago, and the only way she could've gotten it is by someone giving it to her? How the hell would someone do that?" I don't actually expect an answer. I expect Dr. Monroe to laugh and tell me I'm on some candid camera reality show.

"They could've used a gene therapy vector that targets the lung, something like a modified adenovirus," she says instead.

Either I'm losing my mind or Dr. Monroe's losing hers. Is this a trick? Some way of trying to confuse me and throw me off the track of what really happened? Like the genetic IPF is a scam and it's all about the side effects? A curl of smoke rises above the stall. The odor seeps into my nose and makes me cough. Then again what if it's not a trick? What if what Dr. Monroe says is true? Why would she lie?

"Okay, fine, say you're right. How could I find out more about that adenovirus thing?"

"Well, there's the GenBank database," she says after what seems like forever. "It might be possible to look for adenovirus vectors and see if there's a specific modification to the virus that's used for gene therapy, but—" She stops suddenly. I can practically hear the thoughts whirring around inside her head. I don't need words to know what's coming next. "Look Faith, this is way out of my league. I have no idea what happened to your mother, and frankly right now investigating this is beyond my capability. Maybe it *was* a spontaneous mutation. Just because it's not in the literature doesn't mean it doesn't happen. Diseases mutate and change. Or maybe there's some other explanation. I don't know, but right now this is more of a scientific problem than I can handle. We can get together after my tenure review and the conference, but until then, I just don't have the time."

"Well who does have the time then?"

She sighs. "I don't know. Maybe Dr. Glass at PluraGen. He knows more about IPF than I do. I'm sorry, Faith. Really, I am."

"Okay," I say, and thank Dr. Monroe for all she's done to help me. She apologizes again for not being able to do more, promises to call when she gets through her tenure review, and we say good-bye.

Goth Chick takes off, and I have the bathroom to myself. I don't waste any time digging Glass' card from the trashcan of my bag and dialing his number. The secretary answers and gee, what a surprise, a high-up dude like Glass is busy and unavailable to talk to a peon like me. She puts me through to his voice mail and tells me to leave a message.

"Hi, Dr. Glass," I say to the machine. "This is Faith Flores. I met you the other day." I jog his memory about my mother, and then say, "So, it turns out my mom had a genetic form of idiopathic pulmonary fibrosis. There are a few things I don't understand, though, and since you're an expert in the disease, I was hoping I could ask you a few questions." I leave my phone number and hang up, but I don't leave the stall, my safe haven from the watchful eyes and burning ears minding the halls and trolling for gossip.

There's one more person to talk to. I'm not sure what he'd know about the disease, but he is a doctor and he's been part of this, so I figure it's worth a try. I punch the number for the meth clinic. When Veronica answers, I tell her I'd like to speak to Dr. Wydner.

"You and about a hundred other people," she says. "But ya'll can't 'cause he's out on family leave."

"Family leave? Is it about his daughter?"

"Normally that sort of information's confidential, but the doc asked us to let people know since it'll be a while before he's back." There's a brief silence, and then she says, "She died." Another silence, and then, "I can take a message."

I rest my head against the plastic sidewall of the stall and remember the father-daughter routine in Dr. Wydner's office. "Just tell him Faith Flores called," I say. "He'll know who I am."

"I will," Veronica promises, and after taking my phone number she hangs up.

For some reason, more than anything that's happened in the past few days, Dr. Wydner and his loss bring all the pain I've been keeping down rushing to the surface. At first it's one tear, but then another falls, and another and before I know it, I'm doubled over, clutching my stomach, hardly able to catch my breath. My chest heaves and snot drips onto my chin, but this time I don't try and hold it in or hide from my grief. I open the floodgates and let the feelings gush, a full-on emotional deluge.

The tears leave me eroded, a battered landscape, and soon I can't cry anymore. I stumble out of the bathroom in a wobbly daze and walk straight into Jesse.

"Ahh, crap. Geez, Jesse," I say, wiping my nose with my sleeve. "Can't you give a girl some space?"

"No. Not when you disappear for half a class, or should I say for a whole week. You don't return my calls. You won't look at me. You've been avoiding me and—" He stops himself when he notices how I look, which I'm guessing from his expression isn't so hot. "What's wrong? Are you sick? Did something happen?"

I steel myself not to answer. At that moment Chip Walker strolls by and calls out to me.

"Hey, Stoner!" He winks and lifts his hand to give me the high five. The hand and wink are meant as compliments, an invitation to some sort of insiders club, but I shoot him a fierce look that says "eat shit and die." I'm not one of them. I'm not one of anybody.

"Bitch," he mutters and keeps walking.

Before I can react, Jesse's on Chip's back with his arms locked around Chip's gorilla neck. Jesse's half Chip's size, but he has the element of surprise in his favor and for a moment he hangs off Chip like a lion hanging off a wildebeest. Chip grunts and with a strong shake of his shoulders, drops Jesse to the ground.

"Faggot," Chip mumbles under his breath and struts off to find someone else to harass.

Jesse leaps to his feet ready for more action, but I grab his arm. "Ignore him. The guy's got an IQ of like three. Give it a rest."

Chip rounds the corner. Jesse breaks free of my grip. For a second I think he's going to go after Chip, but he just kicks a locker and lets out a string of creative expletives starting with the word *mother*.

I fiddle with the bathroom pass, unsure what to say. "Are… you okay?" I finally stammer, fully aware of the lameness of the question. "You didn't have to do that for me."

"You're welcome." He flashes me a dark look and slaps dust off his butt. "You can pay me back. Come."

He drags me down the hall and down a flight of steps to the first-floor auditorium where the stage is set for the production of *Romeo and Juliet,* the tale of star-crossed lovers. The auditorium is empty. Dress rehearsal isn't until the evening, so we have the place to ourselves. I sink into a front row seat. Jesse hops up onto the stage.

"I'm Romeo. You're Juliet," he says, looking up to the balcony of his beloved with his hand over his heart. It's meant as a joke, some way to blow off steam, but I think of Moneybags, of Tia, of Doc, and I don't laugh. Jesse and I aren't from rival families, but still, our worlds are totally different. We might as well belong to feuding clans.

After a few minutes of messing with the set and spewing various incomplete lines of Shakespeare, Jesse hops off the stage and plops onto the piano bench. I feel him watching me.

"Tell me what's going on," he says.

"Nothing," I mumble, keeping my eyes trained on a piece of neon-pink bubble gum stuck to the floor.

"You're lying. You're up to something, and you're not telling me."

"What, like you tell me everything?"

"What's that supposed to mean?"

I look up and in a snide, mocking voice say, "I know the Harvard department of English offers a well-rounded program of all the classics, so I'm sure if I'm accepted I'll broaden my perspective."

For a second Jesse looks confused, but then his lips tighten and the usual warmth in his eyes disappears. "You were spying on me?"

"No. Well, yes actually."

Jesse runs a hand across his mouth. He stares at me like I'm a stranger, and it's this look more than anything that kills me.

"Why didn't you come over?" His voice is soft, tender even. I wish he'd yell at me. Anger is easier. I know how to put up a good fight and pretend not to care. "I would've wanted to see you. I would've wanted you there."

More than anything I want to believe this is true, but believing requires hope, and I've been burned by hope far too many times to get high on that drug again. Hope is worse than heroin. Instead I go for mean.

"You were doing such a nice job of ass kissing and being a two-faced hypocrite, I didn't want to get in the way. You have to make a good impression you know."

"Come on, Faith. That's not fair. You don't understand. I—"

"That's the thing. I do understand, Jesse," I say, cutting him off. "Face it. Your life is totally different than mine. You have the Doc MD, PhD gene. I have the junkie one. You have

Harvard. I have the community college. It's only a matter of time before real gets dull."

Jesse doesn't say anything. He just starts tinkering with the piano keys, punching out a one-fingered rendition of "Twinkle Twinkle Little Star." "Doc made me start taking lessons when I was six," he says, running through the do-re-mi scale. "I hated it. My sister, Stacy, she's really good. She can sing, too." He plays a few notes that sound like the opening to something boring and classical and then, without warning, his fist comes crashing down on the keys in a loud, discordant sound that makes me jump. "When I'm with you I feel…" He stops and searches for the right word. "Confident," he finally says, "like I know who I am and what I want. But when I'm at home it all goes to shit. I guess I'm just tired of fighting."

"Then stop fighting. Be yourself and stop trying to impress people. It's boring."

"I'm working on it," he says and slumps over the keyboard.

I'm figuring out the wording for a speech, which starts with something eloquent like, "You're never going to get what you want if you don't stop being such a lame-ass wuss," when Jesse sits up and for the first time in days, our eyes really meet.

We don't speak, but we don't need to. The eye contact cuts through all the crap, leaving something deep and wordless hanging in the air between us. I know I have to stay away from Jesse to keep him out of danger, but I can't lie to myself anymore and pretend I don't care about him.

Jesse scoots the piano bench closer to me so our knees bump, and his fingertips graze mine. The touch is so soft it's barely more than an energy, a prickle of current, but the nerve endings in my fingers go crazy, and I think of the butterfly effect, how the smallest occurrence can change the course of the universe.

I close my eyes and let my universe be changed.

Jesse traces circles on my palm, tickling my skin with his feather-light touch. Just as our fingers lock, my phone rings. I should ignore the obnoxious marimba ring tone, but the reminder of the outside world has already broken the spell.

I pull back my hand and answer.

"Hi, Faith," a troubled voice says. "It's Dr. Wydner. I got your message. I need to talk to you."

"What about?"

"In person. The phone's too risky. They might be listening."

I turn from Jesse and press my cell to my ear. "What are you talking about? Who might be listening?"

"Meet me tonight. At the clinic. Seven o'clock." He doesn't wait for my answer. "Don't use the front door. Call me on this number when you get here. I'll tell you where to go."

The line goes dead before I can say anything else.

Jesse shoots to his feet. "Who was that?" he demands.

"Nobody," I mumble, staring at the red *Call Ended* words on the screen.

"Then why are you shaking?"

I look down. He's right. My hands are shaking. Bastards. Totally against my will they're giving me away. I jam my hands under my armpits and study my feet.

"It was my aunt," I lie, whatever soul-mate connection we were having a minute ago already light years away. "Something happened...to Felix."

"Felix?"

"Yeah. Her cat. He...ate chocolate and he's having some kind of seizure thing. She's freaking out. I've gotta go help her. She loves that cat. He's like...the child she never had. Well, I guess I'm like the child she never had, but...so is the cat." Stop rambling, Faith. Shut up and get going. "So, I have to go...to the vet. She needs me. So, yeah, I'll be going."

"Faith," Jesse says, reaching for my hand again. "I—"

"Forget it," I whisper, pulling back from his touch. "Please."

I push past Jesse and race up the aisle. He calls after me, but I don't hear what he says.

The door is already swinging shut behind me.

Twenty

At six that evening, I scribble a note to Aunt T telling her I've gone to the library to study, then take off to meet Dr. Wydner. By the time I reach the corner of Twenty-third and Jefferson, the smaller shops have been gated and put to rest for the night. The only light flickers from the distant skyscrapers that puncture the skyline. I'm not sure if it's my nerves projecting onto the environment or the environment messing with my nerves, but something tells me to turn back. I push away the thought and punch Dr. Wydner's number.

"Are you here?" he blurts before I can say hello.

"I'm out front."

"Did anyone follow you?"

"What? No...I don't think so." I shudder and look over my shoulder suddenly paranoid that someone is watching me from behind one of those blackened windows.

"Good. Come around the west side. By the parking lot. There's a back door in the alley. I'll meet you there."

I cross the empty parking lot and step into the alley. Steam rises from a vent, carrying with it a sour smell like bad breath. I cover my mouth and nose with my hand as I hurry toward the sliver of light where Dr. Wydner waits in the doorway. His appearance has taken a dive since I saw him a week ago. His perfectly coiffed hair has gone flat. Dark circles swell beneath his eyes, and there's a papery, washed out look to his weathered face. He seizes my wrist and pulls me into the clinic.

"This way," he grumbles. He hurries through a small room lined with shelves of medications, glass beakers, vials and syringes, then through a door leading to the nurse's station, and finally down a corridor, lit only by the glowing red of the exit sign at the opposite end.

When we reach his office, he lets go of my arm and scurries into the room. I stop at the door. The pictures of his daughter are gone. The drawers of his file cabinet are open. Papers litter his desk, and a big brown duffle bag sits on the floor.

"Are you going someplace?"

Instead of answering, he hands me a notebook-size yellow envelope. "Take this. It'll explain."

I reach for the envelope. "Explain what?"

"It was too risky to put in the mail," he says, evading my question again. "Don't tell anyone you have it. It isn't safe."

"What's—"

He silences me with a wave of his hand. "I don't have all the answers. There wasn't time. The doctor knows I'm suspicious and that I have information. I have to get out of here." I try to interrupt, but he keeps talking. "You can figure out the rest. Go home. Look at what's in there and then go to the police. I can't go to them after what I've done."

"What did you do?" I ask, my voice rising, a hard chill trembling down my spine. "You're not making sense. What doctor? What information? Why are you giving this to me?"

"You remind me of my daughter," he says, moving on to the next subject like a rambling mad man, and for a moment I think that's all this is, the delusions of a lunatic, and I've been snared in his web because something about me reminds him of his loss. "She had brown eyes, too, and you're smart like she was. I can tell." He dumps the contents from a drawer into his duffle bag and yanks open another with an erratic jerk of his hand. The light from his desk lamp slices his face into shadowy angles. "I knew something wasn't right when I took this job, but I was paid not to ask questions. I needed that treatment for Heather. But after you came to see me and the second patient died, I couldn't ignore it any longer."

"Ignore what?" I plead. "Is this about side effects?"

"I did it for my daughter," he repeats, deaf to my question. "But now she's dead, and I don't care about their drug or their money anymore." He stops talking and looks at me as if seeing me for the first time. "I'm sorry about your mother."

"What the hell is going on?" I explode in frustration. "You call me down here and mumble all this—"

"Shh!" He freezes like a mouse in the shadow of an owl and puts his finger to his lips. "Did you hear that?"

"No," I whisper, my gut knotting with fear. "I didn't hear anything."

"There it is again."

This time I do hear it. The clang of metal on metal. A door being forced open. Footsteps. Dr. Wydner turns off his lamp. We stand in the terrible pitch of night, waiting.

The sound of breaking glass shatters the silence.

In one swift move, Dr. Wydner lunges for me. He grabs my shoulders, throws me against a wall, and clamps his hand over my mouth before I can scream. My only thought is this was a trap and he's going to kill me. I beg with my eyes, even though I know he can't see me.

A second later he uncovers my mouth. I gasp for air.

"Stay here," he hisses. "Don't move."

"Wait!" I cry, but he's already gone.

I stand in the dark with my body pressed to the wall. When Dr. Wydner doesn't return, I clutch the envelope in one hand and feel my way through the dark with the other until I've crossed the room and reached the door. I peer out into the hallway and listen. I don't hear anything, so I slip out of the office into the eerie red glow and start inching down the hall.

I've taken about three steps when I hear murmurs.

"Dr. Wydner?" I call in a strangled voice.

No answer.

I try to call out again, but my voice sticks in my throat. My blood pounds in my ears. I scrape my palms along the rough textured wall and feel my way through the shadows. I'm half way to the waiting room when the murmurs turn to shouts. Something slams against a wall, and a second later Dr. Wydner runs out of the back room and races past the filing cabinets and computers toward me.

Faith!" he shouts. "Get—"

But before he can finish the thought, an explosion pierces the air. Shock waves ripple through my body. My eardrums split. It's not until I can hear again that I realize I'm screaming.

The white walls behind where Dr. Wydner stood are splattered red. Terror burns my lungs. I order my feet to move, but I've managed just one small step when a tall, lanky figure emerges from the back room and stops in the entrance to the nurses' station. The muted light from behind casts the form in silhouette. But even so, I know who it is.

The Rat Catcher raises a gun and points it at me.

I have just enough time to think how ironic it is for a junkie's daughter to get killed in a methadone clinic when the gun goes off. I fall to my knees, cocooned for the second time in temporary deafness.

As I grope my body, feeling for a bullet wound, I realize I'm not dead. I'm not even hurt. I'm not floating through a tunnel toward white light, and no deity intervened to save me—unless you consider Jesse a deity, because somehow he's come to be standing where the file cabinet had been. And somehow the file cabinet is on its side with all its drawers open. Plaster rains down around me from where the bullet hit the ceiling. The Rat Catcher is on the floor in front of the file cabinet, and behind him, in the doorway leading to the back room, Dr. Wydner's twisted body lies in a pool of blood.

My brain tries to catch up and connect the dots, but command central has a short circuit. My only thought is the gun. The Rat Catcher isn't holding it and neither is Jesse. As the Rat Catcher struggles to his feet, his burning eyes focused on me, one thing is perfectly clear: If he finds the gun, he won't miss his target a second time. The survival instinct every wild thing is born with kicks into action. I jump to my feet and do what millions of years of evolution have taught me: run.

The back room is the fastest way out, but the Rat Catcher is blocking the way.

"This way!" I shout, motioning Jesse to follow. It takes him about two seconds to reach my side.

We run down the hall and make it into the waiting room. I don't have to turn to know the Rat Catcher is behind us. His fingers claw the back of my head and grab my hair. I scream as he jerks me back toward him and locks a muscular arm around my neck. I struggle against the strength of him, biting, kicking, and thrashing any part of me that will move.

Jesse throws a punch, but his fists are nothing for the Rat Catcher. He drives his elbow into Jesse's stomach. Jesse goes down with a groan. The grip on my neck tightens and my mind goes dark, but for a tiny point of flickering light. I'm not sure if my eyes are open or closed, if I'm alive or dead, but the light gets brighter and I see my mother. *Keep fighting, Faith,* she tells me. *Don't give up.*

With sixteen years of hurt and anger fueling my muscles, I twist my shoulders as hard as I can. A scream like thunder rips out of me, and I yank free from the Rat Catcher's grip. In one fluid move, I raise my foot and blast the steel toe of my boot into his groin. The Rat Catcher's legs buckle and he drops without a sound.

I grab Jesse and pull him to his feet. We make it across the room before the Rat Catcher can get up and stop us. As we throw open the door, a deafening high pitch sound pierces the night. We've triggered the alarm. Any second the police will be here.

I glance over my shoulder as we flee, just in time to see the Rat Catcher rise and limp out of the clinic into the black night.

Twenty-one

People trickle into the street, but they're drawn to the methadone clinic, not to us, and nobody notices two shadowy figures racing through the dark, away from the crime.

"Holy shit!" Jesse cries when we reach his car and scramble inside. He turns the key, but the three-hundred-dollar beast just sputters and dies. "Fuck! Come on!" he shouts and turns the key again. This time the engine sparks to life. Jesse floors it and peels out onto Twenty-third.

My stomach roils as he blows through a yellow light and screeches around a corner. I roll down the window and heave painfully against my bruised throat, but nothing comes out.

Jesse glances from the rear view mirror to me. "You okay?"

I feel around my chest and neck, then take a few deep pulls of air to confirm, yes, I can breathe, and no, I'm not about to die. Breathing hurts, but the air goes in and out, and I seem to be able to swallow and do all the normal functions, so I nod. There doesn't seem to be anything wrong with me. No permanent physical damage anyway. Jesse, on the other hand, I'm not so sure about—he's sweating, his fingers tremble on the wheel, and his face has turned a shade of white that makes a vampire look tan.

He glances out the rear view mirror again. "I don't think he's following us."

"I don't think so either," I say, rolling up the window and locking the door. "But what the hell was the Rat Catcher doing at the clinic? He's a drug dealer. What does he have to do with Dr. Wydner?"

"I don't know," Jesse says, hands trembling. "But we have to go to the police."

"No way," I burst, remembering Officer Varelli's words: *someone like you.* "Not when I was at a methadone clinic after hours, and the only person who could be an alibi for why I was there is dead, so gee, I guess it looks like maybe I broke in and killed the guy."

"Then where should we go?"

"I don't know. I can't go home. The Rat Catcher knows where I live." The words have hardly escaped my lips when a new fear surges through me: *Aunt T.* I find my phone, still somehow buried in the recesses of my bag, and punch her number.

Come on, answer.

She picks up on the third ring.

"Hi, it's me," I blurt. "You have to listen. Where are you?"

"I'm home. What's wrong? Are you—"

"You're not safe. I'll tell you everything. I promise. But please, something really bad is going on. I'll explain later. Just get out of there."

"Faith, what are you talking about? What story are you making up this time?" I hear the eye rolling in her voice, the distrust.

"It's not a story. I promise. Just go someplace else." I'm begging now, groveling for her to leave before the Rat Catcher can find her and...I don't let myself finish the thought.

"Okay. Calm down." Aunt T doesn't sound scared. If anything she sounds annoyed. I picture her lounging on the leather couch, a glass of wine in hand, her stocking feet stretched on the coffee table. "You're acting crazy. Just tell me if you're okay."

"I'm fine," I insist as I pull down the visor and examine the purplish bruise starting to form above my collarbone. "Just go."

"Go where?"

"To Sam's. Anywhere. It doesn't matter."

"Faith, I just got home. I thought you were studying. What's this—"

"Listen to me!" I shout, cutting her off. "The stuff I told the police was all true. I can't explain now, but I will. I promise, but you have to leave."

"Okay, okay, I'll go to Sam's, but please, you're scaring me. Where are you?"

"I'm on the move. I'll call you later."

I hang up before she can say protest, then turn off my phone and press my palms to my eyelids. My mother's face flickers again into focus, but this time she's not so real. It's just the pixels of my imagination painting the picture of what I want to see. I swallow and the dots break apart and reconfigure. Now it's Dr. Wydner painted in my mind's eye. His broken body. His spilled blood. His eyes. His face. His words: *Take this. It'll explain…. It was too risky to put in the mail…. That's why you had to come here….*

My eyes jerk open. The envelope! I'd forgotten all about it. I reach into my bag. It's not there. I kick at the empty soda cans, books, and papers littering the floor. I turn my pockets inside out. Finally, I dump everything out of my bag.

"Oh my god, Jesse. Dr. Wydner gave me an envelope. He said it would explain everything. It's not here. We have to go back. I—"

"You mean this?" Jesse reaches into his coat and pulls out a yellow envelope tucked into the waistband of his jeans. He tosses it onto my lap with the rest of the clutter. "I saw you drop it. I grabbed it when the alarm went off. I thought the Rat Catcher was going to…" His voice chokes, and he doesn't finish the sentence.

In my mind I finish it for him: *Kill me.* Like they killed my mother. *Kill me.* Like they killed Melinda. *Kill me.* Like they killed Dr. Carisle and Dr. Wydner. I'm sure of it now. Their deaths were all murders.

The question isn't just why anymore, but who's next?

I touch my forehead to the cool of the glass and look out the window. Buildings warp and bend through my tears. Cars speed by like missiles, their headlights staining the night. We pass a sign that says *Thank you for visiting Philadelphia.*

"The city of brotherly love," I snort, then turn and slam my fist into the door. I'm about to take another swing, but Jesse reaches across the seat and grabs my arm.

"You're the bravest person I know," he says. "And the stupidest, too."

I drop a trembling hand into my lap. "Yeah? Well, I'm just glad there's someone stupider than me. How the hell did you find me?"

By some miraculous brain-to-brain osmosis, Jesse understands my clumsy attempt at gratitude for saving my life, and a trace of a smile passes across his lips. "When you took that phone call in the auditorium I knew it wasn't about the cat. You're a terrible liar. Like the child she never had? Give me a break. I knew something was wrong, so I followed you. The whole FBI could've been on your ass and you wouldn't have noticed." His smile disappears. The muscles in his forearm flex as he grips the wheel tighter. "I waited outside the clinic, behind a dumpster in the alley. Everything seemed okay at first. But when I saw the Rat Catcher go inside I got nervous. And then I heard the gun go off. I didn't think. The door was still open. There was glass everywhere. Someone was dead and…" He coughs and shakes his head. "They say you can lift a car if you have enough adrenaline. Compared to that, pushing a file cabinet onto a guy was easy." The explanation must spark his nervous system back into action because his fingers start to tremble again, and he's back to checking the rearview mirror. "What happened in there?"

I tell him about the call from Dr. Monroe earlier today, about genetic IPF and how my mom didn't have the mutation two years ago, but had it before she died. I tell him how I left messages for both Dr. Glass and Dr. Wydner to tell them what I'd found out, and how Dr. Wydner called me and told me to meet him at the clinic.

"He died to save me, Jesse," I whisper. "He was protecting me."

Jesse slows as he curves off the interstate. I hadn't been paying attention to where we were going, but the star-filled sky, unblemished by millions of lights, tells me we've left the city. I look out the window and see a fat bulldog dressed in a tartan sweater trot down the sidewalk and lift his leg on a hedge. His faithful owner, bundled against the weather, trails along behind. Station wagons and SUV's decorate the driveways of the big houses with the landscaped yards that even in winter look pretty. It's as if there's a protective membrane around this neighborhood that keeps outside shit at a distance, and we've just punctured that membrane and dragged in that outside shit with us like dog crap on the bottom of our shoes.

Jesse pulls up in front of a sprawling white house set back from the street. I've never been to this house, but I know exactly where we are: Hazel is parked in the driveway.

"No way," I say. "No friggin' way."

"Come, on, Faith. It'll be fine."

I slide down in my seat and pick at a crust of dried blood on my upper lip. "Even if Anj and I were talking, which by the way we're not, I'm not dragging her into this. And come to think of it, I'd rather not get you killed either, so why don't you just go home and drop me off at some motel or something until I figure out what's in this envelope."

Jesse doesn't flinch. He fixes me with his blue eyes and says, "Nice try, but you're not getting rid of me, so forget it."

"Well, it's not like she'd let me in, anyway," I mutter, pushing a limp strand of hair off my face.

"Wrong. You know what your problem is?"

"I'm too scared to get close to anyone?" I say, thinking back to my conversation with Anj the other day.

"No. You underestimate your friends."

Jesse rests his elbow on the steering wheel. From his very long pause I get the feeling I'm not going to like what's coming next. "Duncan told me what happened between you and Anj."

"And?"

"And I went to her after I saw you in the auditorium. We had a talk."

"A talk?"

"Yeah, I was worried, so I told her about the phone call and the cat and my suspicion that you were about to do something stupid and dangerous and that I was going to find you."

He opens the door and swings his feet to the ground before I can sock him in the face. Saving my life is one thing, interfering in my personal affairs another entirely.

"She told me to bring you to her house the second I found you. Where else are we going to go? You won't go the police. The Rat Catcher will never find us here, Faith."

I'm about to give Jesse a piece of my mind and tell him there is no "we" or "us" in this, but just then Anj comes barreling out of the house in slippers and pink flannel two-piece pajamas. She pushes Jesse out of the way, grabs my arm, and pulls me over the center console and out the driver's side door. At first I think she's going to beat the crap out of me and I try to protect my face with my arms, but then my nose is smashed against her chest, her arms are choking the life out of me, and I'm thinking the Rat Catcher couldn't kill me, but Anj's hug will.

"You're such a dumb ass," she blurts before I can say anything. "You look awful. Get inside right now. My parents are at Chrissy's basketball game, and I want you in my room and cleaned up by the time they get back. And then you can tell me why your lip is bleeding, your shirt is torn, and you look like someone just tried to kill you." She gasps when she says this, takes her hands off my shoulders, and covers her mouth. "Oh. My. God! Someone did try to kill you, didn't they?"

Anj leads us up the driveway. I must be too tired to protest because I follow her into the house, up the stairs, and down the hall to her bedroom. Her room is a page from the Pottery Barn catalogue, complete with a matching bedspread-pillow-curtain combo and a droopy-eared mutt lazing at the foot of her bed like he's been planted there for a photo shoot. I linger in the hall not wanting to stain such tidy perfection with my filth.

"Well, what are you waiting for? You're a mess." Anj yanks me into the room, then turns back to Jesse. "Wait there," she orders and slams the door on his face. The dog leaps off the bed and squeezes underneath Anj's desk. Anj scurries across the room and kneels beside him. "This is Zig," she tells me.

"Nice to meet you, Zig," I mutter, reaching out a hand for the dog to sniff. Zig just moves further back against the wall as if trying to disappear altogether. "You and me both, dude," I whisper.

"Don't feel bad. He's from the pound. You know how rescue dogs can be." She gets up and points to a door on the far end of the room. "Bathroom's in there. Use all the hot water you want."

"Look Anj," I say without moving.

"Don't 'Look Anj' me. You stink. Go get clean."

I sigh and follow her orders. No use arguing, and truth is I don't want to.

Anj must single handedly keep the local beauty and bath store in business. The rim of the tub is lined with about five hundred skincare products. I take my time under the hot water as I try to cleanse the evil from my naked body. When I've rubbed myself pink and raw, I step out of the shower and wrap myself in a fluffy monogrammed towel. Anj hands me a Haverford High track team sweat suit to wear, even though, like me, she's never been on an athletic team in her life. When I'm done dressing, she invites Jesse back into the room.

Jesse tumbles through the door and rushes over to me. "You okay?"

I nod. "You?"

"Like rock."

"Really?"

"No, but I can fake it until I feel it." He shoves his hands in his pockets and narrows his eyes as if daring me to contradict him.

Anj and Jesse stand there after that, watching me. I'm guessing it's an explanation they want, especially Anj who's still in the dark about what happened tonight. I'm about to give the details of what went down at the clinic, but I realize it's not an explanation I owe. It's an apology.

This part isn't destiny. There's no mutation that makes it impossible to say sorry.

"So," I say, biting my lip and digging my toes into the carpet. "I could go into the really long, really boring explanation about how my mom started slamming heroin when I was a kid, and how that left me pretty fucked up, but we don't have all night, so I'm going to cut to the chase." I take the breath Marta always nagged me about and let the oxygen carry the words to my lips. "I'm really sorry about ditching you guys. I'm sorry about not answering your calls and about lying and blowing you off."

I pop my knuckles, slowly and carefully, making sure each finger gets a proper crack as I search for the right words to explain my actions. "When Dr. Carlisle died I panicked," I finally say. "I didn't want you to get hurt. I thought you'd be better off without me."

I peek at Anj, at the look in her eyes I can't quite read, and brace myself for the possibility that my apology is too late.

Instead of slinging a comeback lecture about my behavior, she swallows and says, "I'm sorry, too."

"You? No way. Why?"

"Yes me. Totally. I should've been more understanding. I mean you've been going through a really hard time with your mom and all. I should've told you about Dunc and Scotland. I should've—"

Jesse clears his throat. "Okay ladies. You're both sorry. How's that? There's no such thing as true altruism. But the Rat Catcher's still out there, so maybe we should get the show on the road and move on. What's next?"

"This," I say, throwing my arms around both my friends. When I've sufficiently strangled them with my embrace, I cross the room to my bag, pull out the envelope Dr. Wydner gave me, and stare at the thing like it's Anthrax. "And this."

"An envelope?" Anj asks. She sounds disappointed, like she wishes I'd pulled out something more exciting than an envelope from my bag—a gun or a ransom note maybe. "Who's it from?"

I quickly explain about the envelope, Dr. Wydner, and what happened at the clinic, pretty sure the story of murder and cover-up will be enough of a reality check for Anj to put the wishing aside and order me and my envelope out of her house. But no.

"Well? What are you waiting for?" she says. "You're not going to know what's in there by standing around and staring at the thing."

"Okay, then. Here goes nothing."

I rip through the padding and pull out a paper with a web address clipped to a pile of what must be twenty pages of Dr. Wydner's hand-scrawled notes. Some of the papers are torn, others folded. I start smoothing the pages, laying each one on Anj's bed.

Anj hovers behind me and watches. "What the heck are those?"

"I don't know. Some sort of medical records I think. Jesse, check it out."

Jesse joins me beside the bed, but it's not one of the papers with the hand written notes he picks up—it's the one with the web address. He grabs Anj's laptop and starts clicking. Anj drags two pastel beanbags across the floor and slides onto the pink one. Jesse and I scrunch together on the baby blue one while his fingers fly across the keyboard.

The web address takes us to a site called *The Biotech Rumor Mill.* The home page opens to an archive of blogs, a bunch of news links, and a section called "Hot and Latest Rumors." Jesse and I exchange glances as we read through various headlines of rumors in the biotech world. *Pfizer. Roche Diagnostics. Executive compensation.* Fascinating stuff.

"Hang on," Anj says, snatching the computer off Jesse's lap. "Didn't Jesse say your mom had something called idiopathic pulmonary fibrosis?"

"Yeah, why?"

She drags the cursor to the drop down menu of recent headlines we'd just been browsing and points.

"'Funding for Idiopathic Pulmonary Fibrosis Treatment Threatened,'" I read. "Weird. Dr. Monroe said there wasn't a cure for the disease. Click on that."

Anj clicks, and a new page loads. She reads out loud. "'PluraGen Biopharmaceutical CEO, Brian Millman, is pulling funding for Alveolix, a new treatment for a rare condition known as idiopathic pulmonary fibrosis. With the patent on PluraGen's chief moneymaker, the depression drug, Fiboral, expiring, Millman is cutting research and development on smaller, less profitable drugs manufactured by the company and getting ready to cut hundreds of positions. 'Alveolix does not have a wide enough application,' Millman says, and therefore is not generating the revenue the company expected.'"

"Screw the sick people who need the drug," Jesse grunts when Anj finishes reading. "If it's not pulling a profit, they can eat shit and die. And while we're at it, screw affordable health care because who needs that, and screw…"

Jesse rattles on about things that should be screwed, but I ignore his anticapitalist rant and turn back to Anj. "What else does it say?"

Anj adjusts herself in the beanbag and props the computer against her thighs. "'Dr. Glass, lead researcher for Alveolix, declared bankruptcy after investing millions of dollars of his own and investors' money to develop the treatment.'" She closes the computer and looks from Jesse to me. "Who's Dr. Glass?"

I don't answer. Something dark and unsettling fights to make sense in my mind as I stare past Anj to a shelf of glass figurines above her desk. Dr. Glass. Head of the RNA 120 clinical trial. IPF researcher. He had a cure. I push myself out of the beanbag and dart across the room to the papers strewn across the bed.

I've just picked up the first one when I hear an engine and a car pulls into the driveway. A minute later the front door opens and muffled voices drift up from the first floor. Heeled shoes click the wooden staircase, followed by the clomping of elephant's feet.

"Hi, Hon," a woman calls. "We're home."

"We won!" Chrissy shouts.

Before I can scoop up the papers, someone's knocking. I try to catch Anj's eye, but she's already crossing the room. She flings open the door and a tall, thin woman with short, dark hair cut in a severe angle around her chin is standing there. A red-faced Chrissy, dressed in full basketball regalia, complete with an eighties' style sweatband, stands beaming at her side.

"Hi, Ma," Anj says, bumping me out of the way with her hip as I make a clumsy attempt to gather whatever belongings I can reach, so I can bail before her mother can invite me to leave. "This is my friend, Faith, and this is Jesse." While Jesse steps forward and offers his hand, I hover in the back of the room with Zig, the pound pup whose former life as a stray keeps him on guard against newcomers.

"I was just about to leave," I mumble.

"No, she wasn't." Anj shoots me a glance that says "shut-up-and-let-me-talk." "We have a biology assignment that's due tomorrow. I'm so lame. I totally forgot to tell you about it. Sorry, Ma. It's going to be a really late night. I invited Faith to sleep over. Jesse's helping out, too. He'll be leaving in like an hour." She snakes her arms around her mother's waist and gives her a girlish peck on the cheek. "How was the game?"

Chrissy pushes her mother out of the way and takes the spotlight. "We totally won. It was so rad! I scored fifteen points!"

Her mother smiles and pats Chrissy on the head. "She might not be tall, but she sure is aggressive." She squeezes her munchkin basketball pro and smiles at me. "Well, you three had better get to work. I don't want you to stay up all night. It's nice to meet you, Faith."

"Nice to meet you, too," I say as she shuts the door.

Anj locks the door and checks the clock the second her mother leaves. Before I can process the fact I'm staying, she picks up a notebook from her desk and kicks off her slippers. "Okey dokey. Let's figure this thing out."

I don't move. "Look, Anj, I really appreciate all you've done for me, but this is serious. Someone got killed tonight, okay? These aren't nice people. So I'll be going before the Rat Catcher finds me camped out in your family's home."

Anj races back to the door and puts her arms out. "Yeah? Well for your information, we have a burglar alarm and all the doors *and* windows are armed. And for your double infor-mation, who's going to think to look for you here?" She gives me the death stare and then adds, "So if you try to leave, just remember, I know Judo."

I sigh, but I can't help cracking a smile. "I knew there was a reason I liked you when we met."

"Good. Enough fluff. Now, let's get to work."

Twenty-two

We divide the papers into three piles, one for Jesse, one for Anj, one for me. No sooner do I sink onto the bed to study the first sheet than Jesse's voice stops me.

"There's something else in here," he says, reaching into the envelope and handing me a wallet-size black-and-white photo of the Rat Catcher.

"Victor Navarro," I say, turning over the picture and shuddering as I read the name written in red pen. "I wonder why Dr. Wydner has a picture of him?"

I don't have to say anything more. Mr. Search Engine's on it. Jesse sits at Anj's desk with the laptop and a few seconds later brings up an Internet article. "'Whatever happened to the beast?'" he reads. "It's from the Philly *Inquirer*, five years ago."

"The beast?" Anj asks. "I thought we were talking about the Rat Catcher."

I shrug, feeling as confused as Anj looks.

"'To many, Victor Navarro was known as the beast,'" Jesse begins reading, "'a talented NCAA Division I basketball player set to put his hometown of Pottstown on the map. But there was another side to this talented college athlete, a troubled teen, often at odds with the law, who struggled with a history of drug abuse and violence.' Blah, blah, blah—skip to the good part."

"The good part?" I say, getting up and punching Jesse in the arm. "No skipping."

Jesse doesn't acknowledge the punch or lift his eyes from the screen. "You ever hear of Cliff Notes? We don't have all night. Listen to this: 'Navarro stopped playing basketball and dropped out of school. So what went wrong?'"

"Seriously?" I ask. "What went wrong? That's the good part? He turned into a psychopathic drug dealer. That's what went wrong."

"Nah," Jesse says. "This is the good part: 'Two DWIs and a charge of assault led to Navarro's arrest. That's when Dr. Steven Glass, a renowned scientist and Navarro's uncle, came to his aid. 'I helped Victor get his life under control,' Dr. Glass explains. 'I paid his bail and found him a job as an apprentice with a pest control company. Victor did so well, he eventually started his own business. We're family. We stick together. We watch each other's backs.' Navarro claims he owes his life and everything he has to his uncle.'"

"So the Rat Catcher's working for Glass!" I utter as my brain cells go manic, and the connections start to fire. He must've messed with my car brakes. Then he came to school, planted the pot, and called in the tip. But it wasn't because he's a drug dealer. It was to scare me off the clinical trial. He's doing his uncle's dirty work."

"But why? What dirty work?" Anj asks.

"I don't know, but we have three piles of papers from Dr. Wydner, and I'm guessing the answer's in there somewhere." I dart to the bed, the chemical cocktail of my brain turning me into a Wonder Woman taskmaster, and grab my pile. "Let's get busy."

I've just turned over the first paper when Jesse interrupts me for the second time.

"I think you'd better check out this one yourself," he tells me.

I take the paper he hands me and angle it toward the light. There's a picture of my mother, her skin pockmarked and pale, her blue eyes bloodshot, clipped to a page that says *Patient #A1*.

"'Female. Caucasian,'" I read, my energetic supercharge slamming to a halt. "'Thirty-seven years of age. Extensive background of heroin abuse. Treatment history: August 1st RNA 120 first dose.'" I reach for the lighter, but of course it's not there.

"Is this what you're looking for?" Jesse asks, pulling the Zippo from my pile of clothes crumpled on the floor and bringing it to me.

I take the lighter and nod. I try to continue reading, but my voice cracks and I can't go on.

"Here, let me." Anj pries the paper from my hand. "'August 8th RNA 120 second treatment. August 15th RNA 120 third treatment.'" She reads a bunch of dates listing Mom's treatment history with RNA 120, and then says, "'September 12th PL44 first treatment.'"

"PL44? What's that?" I grab the paper again and scan the notes about Mom's vitals, her physical and mental condition at the time of each treatment—nowhere does it explain what PL44 is. "'September 19th PL44 second treatment,'" I read. "'Results of drug test indicate patient is no longer using heroin.'"

Tears prick my eyes. I see her smile, hear the words again: I'm clean. It's going to be okay. I clear my throat and continue. "'September 26th PL44 third treatment. October 3rd PL44 fourth treatment, appearance of facial scabs and lesions. Wheezing. Patient appears distressed. Complains of chest pains upon breathing.'"

I glance up at Jesse. He's stopped fidgeting with the other papers in his pile, and his eyes encourage me to keep reading. "'October 10th patient misses treatment. October 17th patient comes for treatment with a man identified as Victor Navarro. Patient appears agitated and frightened.'" I stop reading and drop the paper to my lap. "October seventeenth—that's the day Mom died. The day the Rat Catcher came to our apartment and we first saw each other. He told her she had a debt to pay.…I thought it was about money or drugs, but…" I don't finish the thought.

Jesse finishes it for me. "But maybe the debt had something to do with the clinical trial. Like maybe Glass wanted to make sure your mom didn't miss another treatment, so he had Mr. Douchebag bring her in himself."

"So why would Mr. Douchebag or the Rat Catcher or the beast or whatever you call him, do that?" Anj asks.

Jesse holds up another paper he's pulled from his pile. "Maybe it has to do with this."

I curl a pillow against my chest. "What is it?"

"Your mother's registration for the trial. Check it out."

I take the document and look at Mom's signature written at the bottom of the page in her bubbly cursive. "Okay, and?"

"Read the last line."

I skim the rows of small print details, details you'd need about five years to understand, and read the last clause. "'Patient agrees not to miss any appointments in their course of treatment.'"

Anj looks at Jesse. "So you think the debt he was talking about was because Faith's mother missed a treatment?"

"Could be, right?" Jesse says, lifting his eyebrows. "I mean it makes sense. The notes say she skipped a week."

"But what difference would that make?" Anj asks, looking from Jesse to me.

"Dr. Monroe said RNA 120 had to be given weekly to work," I say, remembering my first conversation with the professor. "Glass probably wanted to make sure everyone followed the right protocol, so he didn't mess up his data." Even as I say this I feel certain it's not the truth. Dr. Wydner's notes say Mom appeared agitated and frightened the day she died. She didn't want to get the treatment. Navarro made her go. She knew something; like that the drug was making her sick—or worse.

"Let's see what else Doc gave you," Jesse says. "Maybe there's something about Melinda."

We search our stacks until Jesse holds up a picture of Melinda clipped to another page of notes. "Bingo! 'Patient #A2. Female. Hispanic. Twenty-six years of age. August 1st RNA 120, first treatment.'" He skips the descriptive details about her condition and focuses on the treatment history. "'August 8th RNA 120, second treatment.' It's the same as your mother's," he says, peering at me. "Whatever that PL44 thing is, Melinda was getting it, too, but she didn't start getting it until November."

Top-forty sing-along pop drifts in from down the hall, but I don't mind the boy band's auto-tuned crooning about true love. The music is a floatation vest. It keeps me from drowning in the murky waters of clinical trials, hired thugs, and my mother's death.

"Check this out," Jesse goes on, ignoring the music while Anj scowls at the door. "It says Melinda missed a treatment on November 28th, and on November 30th, a Saturday, Glass called Wydner into the clinic and ordered him to give Melinda her treatment. Victor Navarro accompanied her. 'Patient seemed agitated and at first refused treatment. After a conversation with Navarro, patient consented.'" Jesse puts down the paper and we look at each other.

"November 30th," I say. "That's almost two weeks ago. The day we saw him at Melinda's."

"Yep, looks like Melinda had a treatment debt to pay, too."

I pick up the grainy, black-and-white shot of Navarro again. As the song ends and a new one that sounds mostly the same begins, I drift back to the day Mom died.

"The night when I found Mom dead, I ran out for help," I say, battling a new round of tears. "Navarro must've been hanging around waiting for his chance. He must've seen the paramedics leave, slipped into our apartment, and planted the heroin to cover Glass' tracks. Glass counted on the police to see the heroin, and see her, and let their stereotypical little minds do the rest. Well, it worked. The case was closed before it was ever opened."

The story fuels my rage. I jump to my feet and start to pace, stomp is more like it, although it's hard to actually stomp on a carpet that feels like a pillow.

"Wait a minute," Anj says as I stomp past her. "Didn't you say there was a fund for dependents?"

"Yeah, so?"

"Then I don't get it. I mean at first the clinical trial people didn't think your mom had a kid, but before you said the Rat Catcher found out about you the day your mom died. He would've told Glass about you. So why didn't Glass tell you about the money then?"

"Because there is no money," I say, stopping in front of the bay window and turning to the bed where Anj is propped against a set of pink pillows. "There is no fund. They made that up to buy me off. Don't you see? Glass is covering up something about the drug. The day you and I went to the clinic, Glass was coming into Dr. Wydner's office when I left. Wydner must've told Glass who I was, so Glass got his thug-drop-out-loser nephew to get me to stop asking questions. But just in case Navarro couldn't intimidate me, Glass invented this bullshit fund to buy me off and get me to shut up."

"But how do you know the fund was bullshit?" Anj insists. "Maybe it was real."

"There's one way to find out." Jesse's back on the computer in half a second. He links again to the PluraGen website and brings up a section called Compensation to Human Research Subjects in Clinical Trials.

We read every clause, every situation that could possibly involve compensation: Medical Care for Physical Illness or Injury, Out-of-Pocket Expenses, Compensation for Time and Effort. Nowhere does the website mention a compensation fund for dependents.

Jesse gives a long, slow whistle and a look of amazement crosses his face. "Looks like Faith's right. The compensation fund for dependents is a scam. We'll give you money if you keep your mouth shut. Man, the Kennedy assassination conspiracy doesn't have anything on this."

I go to the bed and grab another paper with a new patient's treatment history. This one has something called PL45 listed in the notes. "Okay, look, there's still a ton to figure out. We have to go through all this stuff if we're going to understand what's going on. And we can't read through every single page together. That'll take too long. We have to sort through our own piles. Look for patterns and write them down. Can you guys handle it?" I glance at the silver wall clock hanging above Anj's desk. "It's pretty late. This could take a while."

"Hel-lo," Anj says. "It's called caffeine. I'll be right back." She slips off the bed and leaves her room, returning a few minutes later holding three cans of Spyke. "350 milligrams of good ol' caffeine for your all-night research pleasure. Ma's secret stash. My parents will totally kill me if they find out. I'm not supposed to touch this stuff."

I grab a can and pop the tab—caffeine and sugar, the legal drugs. It's the first thing I've tried to swallow since the clinic. It hurts, but I force down the liquid. In about a minute my head is zinging. "Here's the deal," I say as the magic potion bubbles through my veins. "Obviously, not everyone was getting the same treatment. So, we look at the treatments each person was getting and write down what happened to them. We'll compile everyone's notes when we're done."

Anj bounds to her desk and brings us each a spiral notebook and pen then sets off on another mission to the kitchen for snacks. For the next few hours, we munch on Cool Ranch Doritos and Lucky Charms as we pour over medical records and make our notes. It's midnight when finally we've gone through all the papers. Anj hands me her notes and collapses on the bed.

"Just closing my eyes for one teeny sec," she says, yawning.

Jesse slides next to me and plays secretary, handing me notes, but soon his eyes droop shut and he's crashed out, snoring next to Anj.

I sit with my back pressed against the wall, my feet stretched in front of me, the papers on my lap. The house is silent now. No music or television or voices drifting in from down the hall. Just me and the notes and a story to piece together. I study the notes, organizing the information into a table, so we can try to decipher what it all means. I've just finished the last column when Jesse opens his eyes and bolts up.

"Okay, man, I'm ready. Where do we start?"

"It's all done, Sleeping Beauty. Check it out."

I hand Jesse the papers and give Anj a gentle tap. She sits up, yawns, and looks over Jesse's shoulder. We huddle as we study the data.

Patient	RNA 120	PL44	PL45	Notes	Outcome
A1	8/1, 8/8, 8/15, 8/22, 8/29, 9/5, 9/12, 9/19, 9/26, 10/3, 10/17	9/12, 9/19, 9/26, 10/3, 10/17		8/21 Stopped using heroin, 10/3 Severe wheezing, skin lesions 10/10 Missed treatment 10/17 Accompanied by RC	Death
A2	8/1, 8/8, 8/15, 8/22, 8/29, 9/5, 9/12, 9/19, 9/26, 10/3, 10/10, 10/17, 10/24, 10/31, 11/7, 11/14, 11/21, 11/30	11/7, 11/14, 11/21, 11/30		8/21 Stopped using heroin 11/8 Wheezing, skin lesions 11/21 Missed treatment 11/30 Accompanied by RC	Death
A3	8/1, 8/8, 8/15, 8/22, 8/29, 9/5, 9/12, 9/19, 9/26, 10/3, 10/10, 10/17, 10/24, 10/31, 11/7, 11/14, 11/21, 11/28, 12/5	11/14, 11/21, 11/28, 12/5		9/4 Stopped using heroin, clean 11/30 Wheezing, skin lesions, less severe	
A4	8/1, 8/8, 8/15, 8/22, 8/29, 9/5, 9/12, 9/19, 9/26, 10/3, 10/10, 10/17, 10/24, 10/31, 11/7, 11/14, 11/21, 11/28, 12/5	10/24, 11/7, 11/21, 12/5		8/28 Stopped using heroin, clean 12/3 Wheezing and skin lesions	

Patient	RNA 120	PL44	PL45	Notes	Outcome
A5	8/1, 8/8, 8/15, 8/22, 8/29, 9/5, 9/12, 9/19, 9/26, 10/3, 10/10, 10/17, 10/24, 10/31, 11/7, 11/14, 11/21, 11/28, 12/5	10/3, 10/21, 11/14, 12/5		9/4 Stopped using heroin, 12/3 Wheezing and skin lesions	

"'Five people in group A,'" I say, reading out loud. "Each person started RNA 120 in August, then started PL44 in either October or November and received it in different time intervals, some got it every week, others got it every two or three weeks. The common denominator was that they got clean, then got wheezing and scabs."

I finish reading and turn to the next page where all the patients are in a B group.

Patient	RNA 120	PL44	PL45	Notes	Outcome
B1	8/1, 8/8, 8/15, 8/22, 8/29, 9/5, 9/12, 9/19, 9/26, 10/3, 10/10, 10/17, 10/24, 10/31, 11/7, 11/14, 11/21, 11/28, 12/5	10/3, 10/10, 10/17, 10/24, 10/31, 11/7, 11/14, 11/21, 11/28	10/24, 10/31, 11/7, 11/14, 11/21, 11/28	8/29 Stopped using heroin, clean 10/24 Wheezing, skin lesions, relapse of heroin 11/14-11/28 Less wheezing and scabs clearing, not using	Symptoms in remission

Patient	RNA 120	PL44	PL45	Notes	Outcome
B2	8/1, 8/8, 8/15, 8/22, 8/29, 9/5, 9/12, 9/19, 9/26, 10/3, 10/10, 10/17, 10/24, 10/31, 11/7, 11/14, 11/21, 11/28, 12/5	10/10, 10/17, 10/24, 10/31, 11/7. 11/14. 11/21, 11/28, 12/5	110/31, 11/7, 11/14, 11/21, 11/28, 12/5	9/5 Stopped using heroin 10/31 Wheezing, skin lesions, 11/21 Less wheezing, skin lesions still present, but starting to clear	Symptoms in remission
B3	8/1, 8/8, 8/15, 8/22, 8/29, 9/5, 9/12, 9/19, 9/26, 10/3, 10/10, 10/17, 10/24, 10/31, 11/7, 11/14, 11/21, 11/28, 12/5	10/17, 10/24, 10/31, 11/7, 11/14, 11/28, 12/5	11/7, 11/14, 11/21, 11/28	9/12 Stopped using heroin 11/7 Wheezing and skin lesions 12/5 No wheezing or skin lesions	Symptoms in remission
B4	8/1, 8/8, 8/15, 8/22, 8/29, 9/5, 9/12, 9/19, 9/26, 10/3, 10/10, 10/17, 10/24, 10/31, 11/7, 11/14, 11/21, 11/28, 12/5	10/24, 10/31, 11/7, 11/14, 11/21, 11/28, 12/5	11/14, 11/21, 11/28, 12/5	9/19 Stopped using heroin 11/14 First signs of wheezing and skin lesions 12/5 No more wheezing, skin lesions fading	Symptoms in remission
B5	8/1, 8/8, 8/15, 8/22, 8/29, 9/5, 9/12, 9/19, 9/26, 10/3, 10/10, 10/17, 10/24, 10/31, 11/7, 11/14, 11/21, 11/28, 12/5	10/31, 11/7, 11/14, 11/21, 11/28, 12/5	11/21, 11/28, 12/5	9/5 Stopped using heroin 11/21 Signs of skin lesions and wheezing	Too early to tell about remission

"Remission, every one of them but B5," Jesse says, running his finger down the Outcome column.

"And the wheezing and skin lesions went away when they started getting this PL45 thing," Anj says, glancing back and forth between the dates and the treatment, then turning to the C group on the third page.

Patient	PLRNA 120	PL44	PL45	Notes	Outcome
C1	8/1, 8/8, 8/15, 8/22, 8/29, 9/5, 9/12, 9/19, 9/26, 10/3, 10/10, 10/17, 10/24, 10/ 31, 11/7, 11/14, 11/21, 11/28, 12/5			8/29 Stopped using, clean	No symptoms
C2	8/1, 8/8, 8/15, 8/22, 8/29, 9/5, 9/12, 9/19, 9/26, 10/3, 10/10, 10/17, 10/24, 10/ 31, 11/7, 11/14, 11/21, 11/28, 12/5			9/12 Stopped using, clean	No symptoms
C3	8/1, 8/8, 8/15, 8/22, 8/29, 9/5, 9/12, 9/19, 9/26, 10/3, 10/10, 10/17, 10/24, 10/ 31, 11/7, 11/14, 11/21, 11/28, 12/5			9/12 Stopped using, clean	No symptoms
C4	8/1, 8/8, 8/15, 8/22, 8/29, 9/5, 9/12, 9/19, 9/26, 10/3, 10/10, 10/17, 10/24, 10/ 31, 11/7, 11/14, 11/21, 11/28, 12/5			9/19 Stopped using, clean	No symptoms

Patient	PLRNA 120	PL44	PL45	Notes	Outcome
C5	8/1, 8/8, 8/15, 8/22, 8/29, 9/5, 9/12, 9/19, 9/26, 10/3, 10/10, 10/17, 10/24, 10/31, 11/7, 11/14, 11/21, 11/28, 12/5			9/26 Stopped using, clean	No symptoms

"Nobody in the C group got treated with PL44 or PL45, and none of them ever got sick to begin with," Jesse says.

I flip back to the A and B groups and study the dates and notes. "People getting PL44 get sick unless they get PL45."

"And people who were only given RNA 120 never got sick to begin with." Jesse picks up a loose paper I'd clipped to the notes, but been too tired to read. "What's this?"

Anj grabs the paper and reads it out loud. "'Administer PL44 to patients in groups A and B. (Refer to addendum for specific time intervals.) Administer PL45 to patients in group B if skin lesions and respiratory problems develop.'"

She turns the page and shows it to us. At the bottom of the note is a signature: Dr. Steven Glass.

It's too awful to imagine, but I force the next words from my lips. "Glass is making people sick on purpose."

Anj drops the paper and stares at me, her blue eyes wide. "Why would he do that?"

I storm to the desk and wake up the computer where the biotech rumor mill site is still on the screen and read the IPF article again. "'The funding for his treatment's being pulled because it doesn't have a wide enough application, hundreds of positions are being cut, and Glass is bankrupt,'" I read more to myself than to anyone else. I don't have to say the next part, the horrible thing I finally understand. Jesse says it for me.

"The cocksucker's making people sick, so he can sell his treatment."

I stare at my mother's data, the scribbled notes about another dead junkie, a number, a test rat and nothing more. "I don't get it," I whisper, hardly able to speak. "So Glass sells his drug to a methadone clinic for a few people who think they're there for a heroin addiction treatment, and then what? He's not exactly going to get rich off that. There must be something more."

For the first time since I've met Jesse, he has nothing to say. He stares at me with a helpless expression, unable to dig up a conspiracy theory sick enough to answer the question.

"Okay, you guys," Anj says with a nervous laugh. "Time out. How would he make people sick?"

"If you can have a gene therapy to make people better, why not one to make them sick?" Jesse says without taking his eyes off me.

"That is totally crazy. If what you're saying is true I'm getting dressed and we're going straight to the police."

"We can't, Anj," I say.

She goes to the closet and yanks a blouse off a hanger. "Of course we can."

"Trust me. The police will just put us in some back room with some junior donut eater who rolls his eyes at us. They won't listen. It'll be a total waste of time. Believe me. Not to mention the fact I was at a methadone clinic during a murder and then took off. How's *that* going to look?" I swallow and take a deep breath. "Look, if what we think is true, PL45 is the treatment, right?"

"Right," Anj says, unbuttoning the blouse.

"And if you get PL44, whatever that is, without PL45 you die, right?"

She nods.

I go the bed, pick up the group A data table, and point at patients numbers three through five. "These are real people, Anj," I say, sick inside as I watch her face fall and her world, just moments ago a safe and ordered place, shatters. "For whatever reason not everyone's getting the treatment, those three people have been given PL44 and not PL45." I let the words sink in and then say, " If Glass is really doing what we think he is and those people don't get their treatment, while the police sit around and laugh at us, they're going to die."

"Fine," she says, without budging. "Then maybe your professor friend can help us."

I close my eyes and picture Dr. Monroe in her tenure-seeking frenzy, locked in her office, boxes of takeout food littering the tables, packs of students banging on her door. "Forget it. She can't help until her genetics conference is over and she's passed tenure review and…wait a minute…the genetics conference…it starts today."

"What genetics conference?" Anj asks as she goes to her dresser and pulls out a pair of socks.

I ignore her question and instead rush back to the computer and type in the name of the conference I remember seeing on the poster outside Dr. Monroe's office: *The American Society of Human Genetics*. I click on the link that says annual meeting and go to the schedule and look up the presenters. "Glass is the keynote speaker. He's presenting the RNA 120 clinical trial. He's on this morning at nine."

Jesse grabs a handful of Lucky Charms and falls back onto the bed. "Yeah, and…?"

"We have to go."

"Why?" Jesse and Anj blurt at the same time.

"What if we alter Glass' presentation?"

"What exactly do you mean by 'alter'?" Anj says, giving me a suspicious look.

"Alter it. As in change it. As in make our own slides with what we know and put them into his talk."

"Um, no offense, Faith," Anj says, stealing a very conspicuous glance at Jesse. "But I think the stress of yesterday and last night is starting to get to you."

"Not it's not. I'm serious. Think about it. You just made over a hundred PowerPoint slides for our Social Studies presentation, right? You're like a PowerPoint expert. How hard would it be to make a few graphs and copy a few photographs and turn them into a slide show?"

"Not very," she admits, "but how in the world would we get these new slides to replace Glass' old ones?"

"Duncan," I say, remembering Scottish Boy's brilliant performance in setting up the meeting with Dr. Carlisle and his mastery on the graphics tablet.

"Duncan? Seriously? That's your idea." Anj crawls back into bed and buries herself under the covers. "How about we just sleep on this and decide what to do in the morning."

"No! It is morning. We can't wait. I'm not kidding. Duncan can do all sorts of graphics. Why couldn't he make a fake badge and pretend he's part of the audiovisual crew and then sneak into the AV room and change the slides?"

"Why not? Well, let's see. To start with that would be illegal."

"Oh come on. People are being killed and you're going to worry about doing something illegal?"

Anj doesn't say anything. I explain the rest of my idea, doing my best to make it sound like a tangible plan and not an exhaustion-induced delusion. My friends stare at me as I speak, and finally, after reminding me that I'm crazy, acknowledge that they don't have any better ideas and agree to go along with my mine.

"But I can't go wearing that," I say, pointing to my clothes crumbled on the floor. As much as I hate sucking up to the conformist rules of societal fashion, I know one thing to be as true as the law of gravity: People judge a book by its cover. Always have. Always will. If I want to fit in, I need to look the part. I turn to Anj. "I need to look like you."

Anj laughs and stares at me like I've completely lost it. "Okay, how are you supposed to look like me? I'm like so white I'm blue, and you have skin like some kind of Mayan princess. Not to mention, ahem, the fact we're not quite built the same." Anj sticks out her chest when she says this to emphasize the difference in bra size, hers being on the larger end.

"It's not the twin thing I'm going for. It's subtler. Like I need to look, how do I say it, younger?"

"Younger? But we're both sixteen."

I glance around her room at the framed photographs, the art museum posters, the lace-trimmed window, and bulletin boards filled with high school memorabilia.

"Not like age, like innocence. Like someone who didn't grow up with a heroin addict mother and no father. Someone who has a nice room and who didn't know what a tie off and gear were when she was ten. Someone who wears ballet flats instead of combat boots, you know what I mean?"

A smile of understanding creeps across Anj's lips. "You've come to the right place." She makes an expansive sweep of her hands in front of her open closet. "My wardrobe at your service."

Jesse tosses more Lucky Charms into his mouth. "Great. What are we waiting for?"

I stare at him until he apparently feels my eyes boring a hole in his skull and looks up. "What?"

"I need your help, too."

"Totally," he says, swiping his mouth with the back of his hand. "I'm in, man. Hand me the computer and let's get this party started."

I don't move or drop my eyes.

He shrugs. "C'mon what's the hold up? Clock's ticking."

"Anj and I can handle the computer on our own."

Jesse flaunts an exaggerated look of hurt. "So it's not my brains you're after. It's just my good looks?"

"I need something else from you."

"Aye-aye captain," he says, saluting. "What do you need?"

"Your father."

Jesse sputters on the marshmallow piece he'd just stuffed into his mouth, then laughs. "Doc? Good one, Faith. I'm sure he has nothing better to do than join our little anarchist party and crash the convention center with us."

"I'm serious."

"So am I. No way. Leave Doc out of this."

"But he can help."

"Okay, humor me. Just say it wasn't one in the morning and Doc wasn't asleep and I was willing to ask for his help, what exactly is it you want?"

"He'll understand the data," I say, firing my attack.

"We already understand it," he counterattacks.

"Yeah, but we're kids. He's legit."

"Legit's overrated."

"I need you," I say softly. "I can't do this alone."

Jesse looks at me, *No Way* written on his face.

"Come on, Jesse. You told me before your dad knows everyone. He's the only one we know who might be able to get the data to a real journalist. Someone who will read it, and understand what it says, and might be willing to help us." Still no response, and I'm starting to get desperate. I make my final pitch. "We need a journalist that knows what's going on in advance and can take the lead tomorrow. Doc's the only one who can find someone on such short notice, someone who can get the word out to the scientific community and the press."

Jesse's tired eyes search my face. "You have no idea what Doc's like. What am I going to tell him?"

"How about the truth?"

Jesse gives a weak smile, then goes quiet. I glare at the clock as the minutes tick away and Jesse circles the room in his socked feet, wrestling with the demons of his father.

"Screw it," he finally says to nobody in particular. "What's the worst thing that can happen besides being disowned and maybe that wouldn't be so bad." He reaches into his pocket for his phone. "Hey Dad," he says a few seconds later. "Yeah, I know what time it is…. No, I'm not in bed. I'm at my friend's house."

I can't make out Doc's exact words, but what I can hear is a very loud voice on the other end. I look at Anj and raise my eyebrows.

"No, I'm not in jail….I'm not drunk, Dad." Jesse's voice rises, and for a second I think he's going to hang up, but he grips the phone harder and pushes on. "No, I haven't been partying…shit, why do you always assume I'm fucked up? I'm fine, okay?" He pinches his temples and drops his chin to his chest. "I need your help."

Jesse takes the phone into Anj's bathroom and closes the door. I sit on the bed and fool with the lighter, but the quiet of the room just magnifies the loudness of my brain. As the stars twinkle and the Earth spins and the world goes about its merry way, my stomach twists into knots.

I creep to the bathroom and press my ear to the door, but the whir of forced-air heat interferes with my listening space, and I can't make out what he's saying. I lean harder, so hard that when Jesse opens the door, I lose my balance and stumble forward. Jesse ignores the fact of my eavesdropping and marches past me.

"Well?" I demand as he drops onto the bed.

"He's pissed off and thinks I'm on drugs."

"Great."

"But he'll consider it. Doc doesn't do anything without seeing the data first. He won't wipe his butt without reading a consumer's review report on the toilet paper. I need to make copies of everything we have and bring it to him, and then he'll decide what he'll do."

It's not conclusive, but it's all we have. There's nothing else to do but get started and hope that Doc will help us and that my plan actually works.

Twenty-three

When Anj and I finally finish our PowerPoint and fall asleep, I dream of the white bird. It lands on a high branch of the oak outside my bedroom window. I climb the tree and reach out to touch the winged creature. Just as I'm close enough to stroke its silky body, the bird transforms into my mother. She's wearing her white bathrobe. Blood trickles from her mouth to her chin. I scream, and the bird vanishes into the moonless night.

I've hardly slept when the alarm goes off at five. Anj hits snooze and tries to go back to sleep, but I hit her with a pillow. "Come on sleepy," I yawn. "We have work to do."

Anj groans and drags herself out of bed. She stumbles to the closet with her puffy eyes and pillow-wrinkled skin and slides open the mirrored door to reveal a neat row of dresses, skirts, jeans, and blouses.

"Okay—you want to look like me, the first thing you need is an outfit. If I wanted to look younger, or maybe just stupid, I'd wear this." She hands me a velvet, flower-print dress with a round collar and buttons up the front, then sticks her finger in her mouth and makes a gagging noise. "My Aunt Martha gave it to me for Christmas last year. She thinks I'm still ten."

"Yeah, I see your point. It's um, not quite what I was looking for. I'm going for innocent, not dorky."

Anj laughs and pulls out outfit after outfit, throwing each article of clothing we decide is too dorky, too hip, or too cutesy on her bed. I sit in the beanbag as she terrorizes her closet.

"I like that," I say when Anj, having laid waste to her wardrobe, moves on to her dresser and pulls out a simple blue sweater with bright colored buttons sewn around the neck.

"Cashmere," she says, tossing the sweater to me. "Try it on."

I take off the sweatshirt I slept in and pull the sweater over my head. It's like slipping into a cloud. "Nice."

"And this goes with it." Anj hands me a silk scarf of muted blues and greens and ties it loosely around my neck. "And now, a skirt." She pulls out a straight knee-length black skirt with two big pockets in front, hands me a pair of black tights, and asks what size my feet are.

"Eight," I tell her, a bit defensively.

"Sorry, but if you're going for innocent, the whole combat boot look has to go. I'm seven and a half, but here, these are big." She hands me a pair of black clogs and waits for me to get dressed.

I pull on each layer of Anj's clothes, feeling less and less like myself with every new piece of clothing. When I'm dressed, Anj stands back and says, "You look like a dork."

"Gee, thanks." I instantly start to undress.

"No, I didn't mean it like that. I mean in a good way. It's just so not you. Check it out."

She slides the closet door shut. The second I see myself, I gasp. I mean, yes, it's me, but at the same time, not. My combat boots and thrift store dresses are my identity. Stripped of that and I'm someone else completely, which I guess right now is the point, so I should be happy.

"Now for the hair," Anj says, coming up behind me with a brush and guiding me to a chair. "Check you out girlfriend," she says a few minutes later.

For the second time I look in the mirror, and for the second time I hardly recognize myself. My tangles have been groomed to sleek perfection and tied into a graceful bun at the base of my neck.

"You really are beautiful, Faith," she tells me, "but the piercings have to go."

I take out all five of my earrings and Anj dabs me with lipstick and eye shadow. "We should start a TV reality show," she says when she's done. "We could call it American home makeover. We'll round up all the mall chicks with bad hair and bad outfits and turn them glam."

I'm too nervous to comment or even to smile. While Anj hunts down her own outfit, I stay glued to my makeover chair, mulling over what we're about to do and trying not to dwell on everything that could go wrong, the mile long list of *what if's*. I've come too far to turn back.

Once dressed, we go to the kitchen and Anj writes a note for her parents, explaining that we left early for school to put the finishing touches onto our biology project. "They won't be up for at least half an hour," she informs me as she places the note on the table. "They'll never know how early we left."

We're ready to go, but I linger and stare at the note, at the little heart Anj drew above the j of her name in place of a dot. The note says nothing except that we left early, but somehow every word is infused with love.

"What it is?" Anj says, jiggling her keys and heading toward the front door. "I thought we were in a major hurry."

"We are. Just hold on a minute. You can go start the car. I'll be there in a sec."

Anj stands by the door, her hand on the knob, eyes scrunched as if contemplating whether, say, I've lost my mind or chickened out. But then she shrugs, says okay, and goes outside. A second later I hear the engine start.

I pull my phone out of my pocket and punch Aunt T's number. She picks up on the first ring.

"Thank god. Where are you?" she says before I can say hello.

I sigh. "You're not going to like this, but I can't tell you. I'm okay though."

"Okay! That's it. You're okay? Christ, Faith. Sam and I have been up all night worrying."

"I know. I'm sorry. Seriously, I really am. It's just…there's something I have to do. I'm not going to stay on the phone long and I'm not going to tell you what it is, but I promise I'll call you when I'm done." The second the words leave my mouth, I realize there's a way to let Aunt T know what I'm doing, a simple way to give her direct access to the truth. "I'll have something to show you in a few hours. It will explain everything." Aunt T tries to talk, but I don't let her. "Before I go there's one more thing…. I wanted to say thank you for all you've done. I've been terrible. I know I have. This isn't going to make up for how I've acted, but…I just wanted to say that I love you."

I've never heard Aunt T cry, so I'm not sure if the sound I hear on the other end is a sob until her voice breaks and she says, "I love you, too."

Before I can take in the moment or hang up or decide what to say next, Sam's on the phone. "Faith, listen to me. We're here for you. If you're in trouble we can help. We can—"

"I know," I say. "Thank you. But this is something I have to do. Don't worry. I'm not alone. I'll be okay. I'll call you."

And then I hang up.

Anj attempts small talk once we're on the road, but pleasant chitchat proves impossible, so instead she puts on a CD to chase away the nervous silence. A Coldplay album later and we're on Arch Street, one block from the convention center, looking out over a backdrop of glossy buildings shiny as new credit cards. Anj doesn't even bother with the parallel parking routine this time. She goes straight for the convention center garage, and at eight o'clock we're positioned outside the Market Bakery at Reading Terminal to meet Jesse and Duncan as planned.

A minute after we arrive I spot Duncan and a clean-cut boy wearing a collared shirt and khaki pants heading our direction past Hershel's East Side Deli. It's not until they're upon us and I get a closer look that I realize who the boy is.

"You look like you belong at a yacht club," I snort.

"And you look like Martha Stewart," Jesse retorts, handing me a cup of coffee.

I thank Jesse for the coffee and turn to Duncan, who looks the same as always in his gray Edinburgh hoodie and jeans, and hand him our flash drive. "Did you make the badge?"

He pulls out a lanyard tucked into his hoodie and shows off the plastic sleeve holding a badge printed with the words *Randall Bell; Audiovisual Services* above a perfectly reproduced conference logo and grins. "All the credentials I need."

"And did you email CNN?"

"No worries. NBC, ABC, MSN, FOX, you name it, I sent them the information. 'You're about to learn of the biggest corporate conspiracy of the year,'" he says, trying to impersonate an American news anchor. "How's it sound?"

"The accent sucks, dude, but the tag line rocks," Jesse, captain of the sailing team, says.

It's my plan and now is hardly the time to doubt it, but nerves and exhaustion are messing with my confidence. "Do you think they'll buy it?"

Duncan opens his mouth to respond, but Jesse cuts him off. "Are you kidding? Those news agencies prowl for stories twenty-four seven. If one of them gets this feed and another misses out, someone's ass will be canned. They'll be all over it."

"And Doc?" I ask, worrying my fingers through Anj's scarf. "Did he agree to help?"

Jesse's eyes find the floor. "Not exactly," he mumbles. Before my stomach can drop all the way to my feet, he looks up and adds, "But my mom agreed for him."

"I thought your mom was sick and in bed."

"Yeah, well apparently she decided to get up. She was waiting for me when I got home." Jesse scratches at his neck like a dog with a new collar. "She must've overheard my little late night chat with Doc. Man did she kick butt. I haven't seen Mom in action in a long time. She made Doc promise to look at everything I gave him."

"That's good, right?" I say, hoping for affirmation. "I mean if Doc's looking at our data that means he'll get a reporter."

Jesse shrugs. "No idea. Doc's idea of taking action is locking the door to his study and thinking."

I rub my eyes with the heels of my hands, forgetting for a minute that I'm wearing makeup.

"Stop that!" Anj says, slapping my hand. "You'll make a mess of yourself and then what will we do? Now if you're going to sit here worrying over every little thing, we should've just stayed home." She checks her watch. "We don't have a lot of time. What's next?"

"Okay, you're right." I reach into my bag. "This is a map of the conference center. I downloaded the floor plan from the

Internet this morning." I unfold the paper and spread it on a table outside the bakery as the morning market comes to life. "Duncan, here's the audiovisual room where they project the talks for the presentations in the Terrace Ballroom. You have to get in and out as soon as possible. How much time do you need?"

"Ten minutes. It's simple. A little cut and paste, and I'm good to go."

"Good. Anj, you're running interference. You see anybody coming when Duncan's in there, get rid of them. Jesse, you're in the audience for Glass' presentation with me." I tap my fingers on the table and turn back to Duncan. "Everything you need is on the flash drive, you just have to—"

"Yeah, yeah," Duncan interrupts, covering my hand with his. "No problem. Trust us. We know what to do. Now stop your blethering, and let's go."

I fold up the map and put it back in my bag. "Okay," I say, taking in each of my friends and settling my gaze on Jesse. "I trust you."

We link arms like Dorothy and crew trundling off on their journey to the Land of Oz, and walk down our own yellow-brick road, past Kamal's Middle Eastern Specialties and The 12th Street Cantina, then across the glass-covered walkway over Arch Street, and finally into the convention center to bring down the wizard.

A young guy carting an easel over his shoulder directs us to the registration area in the Broad Street Atrium, a sun-filled corridor with a row of long tables. Anj pays our fees with her credit card, and I fill in the registration form with jittery fingers listing myself as Faye Fuentes, sophomore at Penn. The registrar, a gangly woman wearing a gray pantsuit the same color as her hair, takes my form and looks it over. I bite my lip, waiting for her to call my bluff, to see through my suburban-girl dress-up routine and uncover my real reason for being here. Instead, she hands me a badge, a tote bag, and a map of the conference center and turns her attention to the next person in line.

I breathe in a sigh of relief and follow a woman wearing a sari and a badge that says Panjab University through the exhibit hall and onto the escalator to the second floor. From there we wander down a corridor lined with easels announcing presenters and titles of talks: Dr. Petrosky, Micro RNA in Human Disease; Dr. Kambu-Chanelli, Genetic Factors for Human Type 1 Diabetes; Dr. Chow, Genetic Susceptibility to Human Obesity; Dr. Leonard, Genes in Estrogen Metabolism. Eventually we find the Terrace Ballroom.

"I have to pee," Anj moans the second we stop walking. "I'm sorry. I can't hold it any longer."

While Anj scurries off down the hall toward the restroom, Jesse and I worm our way into a group of people outside the ballroom, camouflaged by the sea of wool sweaters, blazers, and Polo shirts. Duncan lingers at the edge of the crowd, poised for duty. I give him the thumbs up and a nervous smile. He clears his throat, whips out his badge from inside his sweatshirt, and marches off toward the sign that says Audiovisual Services.

He's just reached the door when Jesse nudges me in the ribs. "Trouble," he mutters.

I follow his gaze and spot Starr Kelley, a gossipy exchange-student groupie from Duncan's AP bio class, heading down the corridor in his direction. A flicker of recognition crosses her face when she sees Duncan. She smiles and picks up her pace, weaving her way through the crowd toward her beloved pet foreigner.

I shoulder my way through students and academics, professors and doctors, no idea how I'm going to stop Starr before she blows Duncan's cover.

"Excuse me," I say, elbowing between two gray-haireds deep in conversation.

Starr waves her hands over her head to get Duncan's attention. Ten more steps and she'll be at his side. I call her name, hoping at least to throw her off course, but either she's ignoring me or she's gone deaf. She doesn't turn.

Duncan knocks on the door just as Starr calls his name.

I stop in my tracks and look down as angry tears fill my eyes. All this for nothing. Any second the door will open, Starr will be at his side, and Randall Bell, audio services tech, will transform back into Duncan Wallace, Haverford High exchange student. Our plan is shot.

Or not.

When I look up, there's Anj, barreling down the edge of the hall toward Starr. In the split second before Starr can reach Duncan, Anj intersects and throws her arms around Starr as if they're best friends.

"Hey, girl!" she coos, steering Starr away from Duncan. "It's so cool seeing you here!"

"Isn't that Duncan?" Starr asks, straining to look back over Anj's shoulder.

Anj gives Starr an earnest look. "Dunc? No way. He's home working on some art thing," she says just as the AV room door opens. I hear Duncan, oblivious to the near miss, say, "Hey, man. I have some last minute changes for the first presenter. Are his slides queued up and ready to go?"

I turn from Starr and Anj to see Duncan talking to the burly mohawked dude guarding the entrance to the audiovisual room. My heart, still hammering from the Starr episode, thumps against my ribs, as I wait to see how this drama will unfold.

Mohawk regards Duncan, eyeing his badge and then his face. "I just saw Dr. Glass ten minutes ago. He didn't say anything about changes."

"Yeah, I know mate." Duncan smiles and turns the Scottish-charm factor up a notch. "He stopped me in the hall and gave me his flash drive. Said it was critical these changes get made. It'll just take a few minutes."

Mohawk scowls at Duncan and doesn't budge. I check my watch. Five minutes until Glass is on.

"Randall Bell?" Mohawk says, consulting his Smart phone. "I don't have anyone on my crew with that name. Are you filling in for someone?"

I steal a glance at Jesse, who's on his tiptoes craning to see above the ridge of shoulders and necks. "Nigel Rogers," he mutters.

"What?"

"The guy at the door with the Mohawk. His name's Nigel Rogers—it says it on his badge."

Before I can ask another question, Jesse's striding through the crowd toward Duncan and Nigel.

"Nigel!" he shouts, causing Mohawk to look up. "Dude, total emergency. Major glitch in the system. Dr. Petrosky's talk is supposed to be broadcast to University of Lithuania, and the HD feed on the first floor's down."

"Dr. Petrosky?" Mohawk says, consulting his phone again as if the gadget might inform him who Dr. Petrosky is.

"Come on, dude, head of the whole human genome thing. Like the most prominent scientist in the world," Jesse says as if you'd have to be an idiot not to know this.

Nigel swipes a hand across his forehead. I see his mountainous shoulders brace beneath his black tee.

"I'm telling you, man," Jesse goes on, "It's your balls if this thing isn't fixed. I was told specifically to find you."

Nigel turns to Duncan. "A change, you said?"

Duncan jams his hands in his pocket and nods.

"Make it fast. Glass is on in five minutes. The talk's lined up on system one. Don't mess with audio," he snarls and then turns and follows Jesse down the hall.

The second they clear the corner, Duncan slips into the AV room to work his magic. I watch the door close and then head to the ballroom to grab a program and find a seat.

Twenty-four

It's not just the word *ballroom* that gives me the feeling that some guy in a tux is going to come around with a tray and offer me a glass of bubbly or a piece of cheese speared on a toothpick. It's the whole vibe of the place—the formal rows of black chairs lined up behind white-clothed tables, the domed ceiling and crystal lights, the stage with the podium set in front of three movie-theater-style screens. Instead of sequins and penguins, though, serious looking people with practical shoes and laptops primed for hardcore note taking occupy the chairs.

I take in the name tags and faces as I walk the aisles, searching out a place for Jesse and me to sit: Harvard, Penn, Cambridge, Beijing Genomics Institute, Universidad de Guadalajara, Institute for Systems Biology. The red carpet of the scientific community. But what about Doc? Is he here? Did he bring a reporter?

I'm starting to go woozy from the Saharan climate in the room and the lack of sleep when I spot him leaning against a side door, deep in conversation. I'd recognize the scowl anywhere. I ignore my churning stomach and march across the room.

"Excuse me, Dr. Schneider," I say, coming up next to him. "I'm Faith Flores. Jesse's friend."

Doc's eyebrows knit together over the bony ridge of his nose, and for a second I think he's going to snub me again. "Yes, I remember," he says, unsmiling, but at least this time he reaches out to shake my hand. "You look different. Where's Jesse?"

I ignore the comment about looking different and point to the door. "Out there somewhere." I try to remember how to breathe as I ask the next question. "So, Jesse gave you our data. Are you going to help us?"

"I'll tell you what I told Jesse," he says, his expression unreadable but his tone harsh. "You kids are sixteen. This idea that you can just march into a scientific conference and accuse the keynote speaker of murder is ridiculous." I'm still on the word ridiculous when he says, "But Jesse showed me the evidence, and I couldn't ignore it." He nods to the unshaven man with the wire-rimmed glasses and receding hairline standing next to him.

The man steps forward and shows me his press pass. "Tom Bradley," he says. "Lead investigative reporter for the *Philadelphia Inquirer*. Ryan showed me your data." I'm slow on the uptake, and it's just occurring to me that by Ryan he means Doc, when Tom shows me the stack of papers. "If what these indicate is true, we have something significant on our hands. I'd like to get the background on this. How…"

Before Tom can finish his question, a petite woman in tall boots and a knee-length skirt steps onto the podium, and the lights dim. Tom tells me we'll talk later, and he and Doc head to their seats in the front row. I slip into one of the only seats still available, halfway to the back of the room, and wait for the show to begin.

The woman taps the microphone, and the crowd goes quiet. "This year marks the sixtieth anniversary for the annual conference of the American Society of Human Genetics."

I peer anxiously over my shoulder toward the door for Jesse or Duncan. No sign of either.

"...and I'd like to thank the Philadelphia Convention Center for welcoming us..."

Where are they? They should be here by now. I fidget with a button on Anj's sweater, twisting the thing until the thread breaks and it pops off into my hand. Unless Mohawk figured out Jesse's scam and turned him over to some authority. Or he came back to the projection room and found Duncan tampering with Glass' presentation.

"...our distinguished speakers symposium will focus on the emerging field of genomic medicine..."

What about Anj? Did Starr get all best-friendish with her and ensnare her in some gossipy web of gal pal bonding? My fingers work my hair, tugging loose strands from Anj's masterpiece. What seemed like a great plan in last night's fury seems like foolish ignorance now.

"...exploring novel disease treatments, strategies made possible by the latest genetic technologies..."

Someone taps my shoulder. I whirl around and find Jesse sliding into the seat beside me.

"What happened?" I whisper.

He leans over and cups his hand around my ear. "Let's just say the emergency had been dealt with by the time we got to the first floor. Dr. Petrosky was nowhere to be found, and this AV-tech chick saved my ass when she blew a fuse to the sound system and Nigel was the only one there to deal with it."

"What about Duncan? Have you seen him?"

"Nope."

It's total I-might-hurl panic. I have no idea if Duncan downloaded the slides, and if he did, how Glass will react. What will the audience do? Will Tom lead an attack? What if

Duncan didn't download them? Just when I think my nervous system will blow, I spot Dr. Monroe in the third row. I'd been so focused on the details of the plan, I managed to push her from my mind. I don't dare guess what will happen when she sees the presentation. I'm about to speak, to try and offload some of my anxiety onto Jesse, when I see something even worse than Dr. Monroe.

"Oh my god, Jesse, look!"

He follows my pointing finger and stares at the Rat Catcher, standing by a side door. Instantly Jesse's on his feet. "We have to get out of here."

The woman with the bun sitting next to Jesse shoots us a dirty look and puts her finger to her lips.

"No way. We're safer here," I whisper, ignoring her, and shoving Jesse back down into his chair. "What can he do to us in front of all these people? Just try and stay cool and blend in. We have to hold him off until our slides come on." That is, if our slides come on.

"Our first speaker is Dr. Steven Glass," I hear the woman say. I point my phone at the stage and press record so I can video the show for Aunt T as proof of what I've been up to. "A graduate of Johns Hopkins Medical School and board certified in both pulmonology and clinical genetics, Dr. Glass currently works in research and development at PluraGen Biopharmaceutical, where he is directing a clinical trial for a novel opiate addiction treatment."

Dr. Glass walks onto the stage amidst a round of applause. He's just as I remember, slick as a pool of fresh blood in his charcoal suit and red tie, a smile Botoxed onto his face. He shakes the woman's hand and turns to the audience. The triplicate screens behind him open with the name of his talk: *Antisense RNA 120, A Genetic Hope for Addiction.*

"Heroin addiction is a chronic, complex disease with substantial genetic contribution," he begins. His booming voice fills the room with egotistical confidence as the second slide opens to a bunch of numbers and statistics.

I stare at the scatter points clustered on the graph like a cloud of black flies, then glance again at the Rat Catcher. His back is to the stage. He's not paying attention to the slides or the graph. He has no idea what's going on behind him. As if he's looking for us.

"Heroin addicts who fail with methadone treatment have been found to have more than a four-fold higher frequency of the A1 variant of the DRD2 gene." Dr. Glass lets this information sink in and then says, "Those abusers with a genetic predisposition toward addiction may be helped by innovative treatments."

I grab Jesse's hand as the next slide opens, hoping it's one of ours, but the slide isn't one of our creations. It's a bulleted list of current addiction treatments followed by statements of their limitations. Dr. Glass rambles on about the various therapies and drugs. I'm not listening. My attention is on the Rat Catcher. He's moving up the aisle, stopping at each row, forcing his soulless eyes on each audience member.

Three more rows and he'll reach us. Screw videoing. I drop my phone into the roomy front pocket of Anj's skirt and hold up the program of the talks to shield my face. Will he recognize me? Is Anj's makeover a good enough disguise? What about Jesse? I slink even lower into my seat, my heart thumping hard enough to vault right through my rib cage. Glass' words work their way back into my consciousness as I try to make Faith Flores invisible and morph into Faye Fuentes.

"Antisense RNA 120 is a genetically driven treatment offering great promise for opiate addiction." He clicks to the next slide, and continues to talk, but the collective gasp from the audience stops him. I pop up in my seat and cover my mouth.

It's not another self-congratulatory graph depicting the genetic promise to cure addiction filling the triplicate screens behind him, it's the first slide of our own presentation, *RNA 120—A Front to Kill: How Dr. Glass Got Away with Murder.*

Below our title is our table—a monument of murderous data as obvious as a row of A, T, C and G's from a sequencing machine. Beneath the data lie the handwritten instructions for administering PL44 and PL45 with Dr. Steven Glass, the executioner's signature, highlighted for us all to witness.

I can hardly breathe as Glass consults his monitor to see what all the murmuring is about. He's on his game. Quick as a snake in the grass. "Excuse me," he says, without faltering and clicks onto the next slide.

This time the title reads: *Dr. Glass Murdered These Two Women With His Experiments.* Two images share the screen, one of my mother, the other of Melinda. Their haunted eyes foreshadowing death stare at us like specters from the grave, the words MURDERED BY GLASS' VECTOR: PL44 printed in bold red letters above their scabby, ravaged faces.

People turn to each other. Confused muttering spreads through the room. I steal a glimpse at the Rat Catcher. He hasn't turned yet and seen what's happening on stage. He stops at the end of our row. I slide to the edge of my seat, ready to jump up and haul ass out of here.

Hurry up. Change the slide.

"I'm sorry, there seems to be a technical error," Glass says, scrambling to maintain his dominance at the top of the food chain. "If you'll bear with me, we'll have this figured out in just a moment."

He clicks the next slide. This time it's the Rat Catcher's face that fills the screens, the words HIRED TO KILL BY DR. GLASS bolded across his chest. The Rat Catcher smiles as he finally sees me.

Our eyes lock and he steps into our row.

"Look," I mouth, and point at the screen.

The Rat Catcher turns and glances at the stage. Before people can figure out what's going on, before they can connect the man in front of me with the man on the screen, he slips out of the row and disappears through the east side door.

Glass clicks again: The data table.

Click: Mom and Melinda.

Click: The Rat Catcher.

Click: Data table.

Click: Mom and Melinda.

Click: The Rat Catcher.

The woman who introduced Glass scurries onto the stage. She's flailing around in a futile attempt to correct the technical malfunction when a lone voice rises from the front row.

"Excuse me, but I have some questions if you don't mind."

I look to where the voice has come from and see Tom, Doc's journalist friend, rise to his feet. "Dr. Glass, can you comment on PL44 and PL45?"

The room has gone dead still, so quiet you can practically hear the beads of sweat dripping off Glass' forehead and spattering down onto the podium.

"I don't believe Dr. Glass will be taking questions at this moment," the woman anxiously informs Tom.

Glass ignores her. "I've never heard of it."

"But your signature appears to be on the paper giving directions to administer those things," Tom insists. Before Glass can respond, or his fashionable bodyguard can whisk him away,

Tom fires off another question. "I'm looking at data right now that indicates two women died in your clinical trial. The data also says that both of the women were clean, neither was using heroin at the time of death. Are those the women in the photo?"

"What data?" Dr. Glass snaps, his face hardening. "Where did you get that? You can't just—"

"Again, the data I have here from the clinical trial indicates that RNA 120 got patients off heroin," Tom interrupts, "but some patients were given a drug referred to here as PL44, and two of them receiving this drug died." Glass tries to interrupt, accusing Tom of slander, but Tom won't be silenced. "It looks like those patients who received PL44 died or got very sick, but those who received PL44 and another drug called PL45 got better. One might infer that you are giving some people in this clinical trial a drug to make them sick and then withholding the treatment!"

I can't believe I didn't see it before. The first row is swarming with press. Like ants at a picnic. They've come in droves and suddenly they're on their feet, vying for a piece of the action. They all start shouting at once, closing in on Glass with their voracious hunger for headline news.

Glass has sustained too much injury. Any second he'll leave the stage. I nod to Jesse. We slip out of our seats and position ourselves at the back of the room as Glass steps away from the podium and heads straight into the pack of salivating predators. He straggles up the aisle, elbowing past their cameras and questions. They shout. They paw at him. Questions fire from every direction. Big hitting words and insinuations. Murder... profit...greed...billion dollar company...conspiracy.

Finally Glass makes it to the exit and pushes through the door. Mohawk and the motley crew of security cops, who get paid to maintain straight lines and check badges and ensure that everyone plays nice, stand at the door doing their untrained best to hold back the onslaught of journalistic mayhem.

I have to get to Glass. While I still can.

I've just taken my first step when Mohawk looks in our direction. "Hey!" he shouts, bulldozing the less substantially sized beings out of his way and stomping toward us.

"Go," Jesse says, nudging me forward. "I'll deal with this."

I turn and race out of the ballroom without waiting to see what happens. The hall is crowded, but I spot Dr. Glass some twenty feet ahead of me, scurrying past the bathrooms.

"Dr. Glass!" I shout.

He keeps walking.

"Dr. Glass!" I shout again. When he still doesn't stop, I fling off Anj's clogs and start to run. I bump into a woman and knock a stack of papers from her hands as I weave through a web of people gathered outside one of the conference rooms.

"What the—" she calls after me, but I don't stop moving.

"Dr. Glass," I say a third time when I reach his side.

He whirls around and our eyes meet. There's a second of nonrecognition, and then his face pinches and his jaw sets into a hard, wolfish line. Before I can say or do anything, he pushes open a door and yanks me into a stale smelling, closet-sized room with a mop sticking out of a bucket of dirty water in the middle of the floor.

He closes the door behind him and shoots me a blazing look. "It was you, wasn't it?" he snarls. "You made those slides."

I reach into the deep front pocket of Anj's skirt for Mom's lighter. Of course it's not there. Faye Fuentes does not carry a lighter. Faye Fuentes does, however, carry a phone, and unless it's out of charge, the video is still on, and everything we say is being recoded.

"Yeah," I say, trying to keep my voice steady. "It was me, and you're so busted."

Glass takes a step toward me. I lift my right foot, aiming to maim, forgetting for a second that I'm shoeless and can do what—poke him with my toe? He stops, inches from my chest. His breath is hot and dangerous on my face.

"I don't have much time, so I'm going to keep this simple," he says, a vein in his forehead pulsing. "I'll make you a deal. You tell the journalists what you did was a stunt. That you were confused. That you wanted to blame someone for your mother's death. I publicly forgive you, and I make you a very rich young lady."

"You've got to be kidding," I snap, thinking I'd like to gouge his eyes out.

"Not at all. I know about you. You're smart, but you don't have a penny to your name. You'd like to go to college, but you can't afford the stamp for the application." He eyes dart wildly around the room, then land back on me. "How does a million sound?"

A stomach sick taste of bile and disgust burns my chest and rises in my throat. I want to tell him where he can shove his million, tell him that I wouldn't be bought off before and I won't be bought off now—but I run my fingers over my phone and play along.

"You're lying. You don't have that kind of money. No way one cash-strapped meth clinic can make that much."

"It's not just one clinic," he says. "RNA 120 is a front."

"A front for what?"

"To test my vector."

Everything inside me clenches. "PL44. Why did you need to test it?"

I hear footsteps outside the room. Voices. Some language I don't recognize. Glass glances at the door. White-knuckles the greasy doorknob. "Look, we don't have much time. I'm sorry about your mother, but she was a junkie. She would've died anyway."

I dig my fingernails into my palms until I can speak without screaming. "I said *why did you need to test it*? If you want me to cooperate, I need to know what I'm getting into."

"So I know how much people need in order to get sick, I give them IPF and they need the cure. My cure. It's that simple." His words spill out fast and breathless. "You have no idea how many ways I can make money from this vector. All the manufacturers I have access to. Drugs. Vaccines. A whole population of people with IPF needing treatment. The clinical trial was just the test phase. Now that I understand the dosing, the vector won't kill anyone else. It will just make them sick enough to need the medicine. It will be like getting the flu, only a little worse."

Drugs? Vaccines? A whole population of people with IPF? My stomach buckles, but I keep my game face on. "Sounds big."

"So do we have a deal?" he asks, sweating through every one of his Botoxed pores. When I don't say anything, he pulls a handkerchief from his pocket, wipes his forehead, and says, "Fine. Make it two million."

He reaches out to seal the deal.

I lift my hand out of my skirt pocket, but I don't go for a handshake. "As if, you asshole. I wouldn't make a deal with you for all the money in the world." I hold out my phone for him to see. "Did you know these things come with audio recording these days?"

"You little shit!" Glass yelps and lunges for the phone.

I jerk away my arm and he misses his target. He stumbles forward, kicking over the bucket. Dirty water slops around our feet. I step back as he regains balance and lunges again. The lunge is wild, off-center, desperate. I stick out my right hand. Using the force of his forward momentum against him, I drive my fist into his solar plexus. Not the most glamorous Judo move, but it works. Glass doubles over and collapses to the wet floor.

As he clutches his stomach and gasps for air, I look him in the eye one last time, and say, "And she wasn't a junkie. She was my mom." Then I open the door and release all my anger in one loud shout, yelling to the journalists crawling the halls that the scumbag Glass is in here.

A cop is the first to reach me. I'm too spent to be surprised or to ask questions. "Take this," I say, handing the officer my phone. "It'll make your job a lot easier."

I step into the hall just as Tom and the rest of the reporters arrive to pick the final scraps of meat from Glass' carcass.

I wander through the crowd, alone and disoriented, unsure what to do next. I search for my posse, for Jesse, Anj, and Duncan, but I don't see them anywhere. Did the Rat Catcher come back? Did Mohawk bust Jesse and Duncan?

I'm starting to unhinge when I hear someone call my name.

Jesse races across the floor and bear-hugs me the second we meet. "It's over," he says, nodding toward Glass, who's being mobbed by press as the officer escorts him out of the janitor's closet.

"But how did the cops know?"

"Tom helped me," he says. "We explained everything to Nigel, and he rallied the troops. It was rad. You should've seen Mohawk in action."

It's then I see the rest of them. And it's not just my friends—Dr. Monroe and Doc are there, too. I wind through the net of people until I reach them. Everyone starts talking at once: *daft numpty…clogs…are you okay?…what happened?…*I latch onto one voice first.

"I'm so sorry." Dr. Monroe puts a shaking hand on my shoulder. "You were right about Glass and the vector, and I didn't listen. You have some determination—I wouldn't want to be the person standing in your way. Most people would've given up, but not you. Where did you get the strength?"

I shrug and feel the world of tension rush out of me. "I had faith—in my mom."

A journalist calls my name, but I don't answer. I hook Jesse's hand with my right, Anj's, and by extension, Duncan's, with my left and turn away from everyone.

I'm not looking back anymore. Only forward.

"RNA 120: A Front"

December 14, 2013

By Tom Bradley
Philadelphia Inquirer

In response to documents and an audio recording provided by Faith Flores, an intrepid 16-year-old junior at Haverford High, the Federal Bureau of Investigations in Pennsylvania has opened a preliminary inquiry on Monday into allegations that Dr. Steven Glass, researcher at PluraGen Biopharmaceutical, was using a clinical trial for RNA 120, a drug to treat heroin addiction, as a front to test a biological vector known as PL44.

Medical records from the clinical trial indicate that PL44 causes a mutation leading to the genetic form of a rare disease known as Idiopathic Pulmonary Fibrosis (IPF). Currently, Alveolix, a drug developed by Glass and patented by PluraGen, is the only treatment for IPF.

According to reliable sources, funding for the drug is being pulled for financial reasons, and Glass' position is being cut.

Fifteen people were enlisted in the clinical trial, none of who were informed about PL44. Two of the participants died while undergoing treatment. Records from the trial confirm that at least one of the two women who died had been given the disease-causing vector. DNA testing is being conducted on autopsy specimens from the second woman.

In a statement released to the press, Brian Millman, PluraGen CEO, offered this: "We will cooperate with every aspect of this investigation, and we will be devoting two million dollars to a state-of-the-art drug treatment center dedicated to Augustina Flores and Melinda Rivera, the two women who died in the clinical trial. It is unfortunate that rogue doctors have damaged our company's reputation, but I can assure you that Dr. Glass was acting alone and that we are committed to stringent new oversight controls."

In a related incident, Victor Navarro, the nephew of Dr. Glass, was arrested and charged with the deaths of Dr. Raymond Carlisle, Pennsylvania State Medical Examiner, who is believed to be connected with the cover-up, and Dr. Joseph Wydner, the director of the Twenty-third Street Methadone Clinic where the RNA 120 clinical trial was being conducted.

Glass is being held without bail, pending further investigation, and declined to comment.

The clinical trial has been suspended.

Twenty-five

A week after Tom's article made the national news, I stroll along the spine of trees edging the Schuylkill River with Jesse at my side. Aunt T and Sam, Anj and Duncan, trail behind. I hold Jesse's hand and think about Mom as we walk. This little patch of nature butting up against the city was her sanctuary. *I don't need four walls and a preacher to find God,* she used to say as she held out a flower for me to inspect or pointed out the name of some bird trilling in a tree.

We step aside as a pack of joggers take over the trail, so they don't trample us with their aerobic enthusiasm. I feel Jesse's eyes on me as I watch the steely spandex thighs round a bend. Between meetings with cops, meetings with Tom, and more meetings with people who wanted to meet, it's the first time we've been alone since the convention center. There's so much to say, I hardly know where to being, but before I can find the first word, I'm in Jesse's arms, against his body, and my lips are too busy kissing to talk. I relax into the kiss and let it linger, forgetting for one soft moment why we're here, forgetting everything but his cool, soft lips and warm tongue, his taste like winter, and coffee and desire. And this time, I don't pull away.

"I told Doc I'm going out west this summer," Jesse tells me once the kiss runs its course. "He's not happy, but with a little help from my mom, he caved. He agreed I need a break before senior year. I'm going to get a job on a ranch someplace. I could really use some company."

It's an invitation, I know, but I don't answer. There's so many things to consider now, so many doors opening as old ones close. There's so much to do: Anj's going-away party before she leaves for Scotland and saying good-bye to Duncan and figuring out my future with Aunt T and Sam. And something else.

Aunt T comes up beside me and hands me the blue urn with Mom's ashes. "Ready?"

I look up at a stream of starlings dancing patterns in the cloudless sky, then hug my aunt. "Ready."

I walk to the water alone and let the frenzy of last week wash over me—reconciliation with Aunt T after her escape to Sam's, letting her hear the recording from my phone, our talk of legal guardianship, Glass' investigation, the Rat Catcher's arrest, head dude of PluraGen coming to our apartment with his entourage of press people to document his scripted apology. Then my thoughts turn again to Mom. Tears sting my eyes as images of her flow through my mind, but for the first time it's not despair I feel but hope.

I take in a long, sharp breath and fill my lungs with the air of this place she loved. I exhale and do it again. When my mind is clear, I open the tin, and plunge my hand into her ashes, feeling the grit of her bones and skin, hair and teeth between my fingers.

"You'll always be with me," I whisper as I scoop up a handful and cast her ashes to the earth.

I'm reaching in again, getting ready to scatter a second handful, when I spot a splash of white in the tree next to me. At first I think it's a white dove, but then I see the pink eyes. The bird looks at me for a split second before bursting into flight.

"Good-bye," I call, tossing the rest of her ashes to the wind.

It's not just what happened to my mom that I finally under-stand, it's something else. Genes aren't my destiny. They're just part of my story. It's the choices I make that will shape my future. I was given a starting place, the rest—what truths to reveal, what lies to tell, whether I give up and give in or stand up and fight back—that part is up to me.

I'm not angry anymore. No more blame. No more guilt. No more lies or hiding. I know the truth. Finally I can let her go.

I watch Mom's guardian angel disappear into the morn-ing sky.

Author's Note

Although everything in this book is scientifically plausible and I have strived to be scientifically accurate, addiction and its possible cures are treated fictitiously. I made up RNA 120 and the use of antisense RNA to treat heroin addiction. Alveolix is a product of my imagination. While the gene names I used are authentic, in reality the genetics of traits like addiction are truly complex, meaning a single variant is unlikely to make one an addict; these traits are the result of complex interactions among multiple genes and environmental factors. If you are interested in learning more about the genetics of addiction, please visit the Genetic Science Learning Center at learn. genetics.utah.edu.